THE GENOME OF THE ANCIENT CREATORS

"ABBA" EBEN!

By

VIE Loriot de Rouvray

ISBN: PAPERBACK 979-8-9897589-0-6
ISBN: HARDBACK 979-8-9897589-1-3
ISBN: E-BOOK   979-8-9897589-2-0

Printed in the United States of America

Independently Published by:
VIE Loriot DE Rouvray

"High Priest and Priestess Knew the secret of
higher consciousness."

Angels at Work; The God Duo

Let Light, Love, and Power Restore the Plan
on Earth

"Your sacred heart is your saving device."

THE QUEST
TO THE HUMAN PURPOSE...
"A GALACTIC CRUSADE"

"Let him who seeks desists until he finds.
When he finds he will be troubled; when he is
troubled, he will marvel, and he will reign over
the Universe."

"Whosoever finds the interpretation of these
saying shall never taste death" Jesus.

From the last Gospel of Thomas

"Always pray and never give up" - Luke 18:1

I dedicate this book to the Ambassadors of the
Council of Twelve

NOTE TO READERS

In writing this new book, I am conscious that my purpose, our mission, and our work as the God Duo might be criticized by unfaithful or unawakened beings. And it's OK. I am sure that they will still give them some reflection help them be opened, and awakened, and help them grow.

I am aware that it will take time to accept and internally receive. It will take some time to believe, as the long journey to earth has erased most of the memory, the knowing, the feeling when it is right in front of you but eventually, this will be your natural state of being.

As you go through your major life lessons, remember you decided to come here to Earth. Your job is simply to learn why you choose to come here., to know and fulfill your Soul Mission.

You may encounter obstacles as you step into your decisions of change. The life of following your calling is preparing you to go with the flow, but it is also one in which you stand up to challenges reach beyond your limits, and grow. Whether you are eighteen or eighty, why not choose now to be your true self and follow your dreams by listening to your heart?

It is fascinating that hardly anyone is wondering what we are doing on this planet, but accepting to go to work, eat, sleep, and entertainment as life without desire for a deeper understanding of our purpose in this universe!

You were born to grow and succeed, always reaching upward toward spiritual growth.

Your adventure is one of the separations from the source where you search for answers to the problems and limitations that you encounter. Your destiny is to grow, and to expand in consciousness, to find peace and prosperity. It is about gaining the freedom to be who you are, the freedom to do.

You have agreed to carry light and return light to this planet. As you begin to fill your body with light, your memory must be opened. You must evolve as DNA evolves, into a multidimensional version of yourself, spanning many layers of reality. You live in a web of invisible energy. The twelve strands of DNA serve as links to this web through the twelve chakras that act as energetic doorways into your body, connecting you to the vital force of existence. It is through the opening and activation of these portals of energy that you can know yourself.

World War III was a spiritual war.

No missiles are needed.

Fear is the only weapon.

The territory that is being fought over is your mind.

The Time has Come for you to Step into Your Divine Life Purpose!

Did you hear about the operation called "The Liberation of Mother Earth"?

All these experiences that we the God Duo, have had in our life did not happen for nothing. Even though we came here to do God's work we still had to make the choice. We have had so many ups and downs. We went down the path less traveled and we did not stop in our pursuit to help you. For you, we have been on a crazy roller coaster ride and did not settle for an average human life.

The moment you incarnate as a human you are just a human, and you have free will. Nobody is allowed to violate your free will. So regardless of who you are in other dimensions or if you are incarnated on earth with a divine purpose, you have the free choice to change your direction at any moment and you might choose to live a human life-unconscious, unaware, and in deep sleep. You have the right to freely choose to fulfill your mission within this incarnation or to live a human life and to forget or not even remember everything else.

You also know that human life can never satisfy you. Can you name one thing that other people do in the 3-D world that you're truly passionate about? When nice houses, cars, jewels, and not even lovers excite you then you know that there is only one thing left to do that sets your spirit on fire. So, choose wisely, and alter this system of frequency control. Assist the planetary ascension process. Build new earth and create change?

Humanity needs conscious businesses, teachers, readers, and healers that elevate this realm and contribute to the planet. I know that this thought excites your spirit because this is what your soul yearns for.

A new race is evolving. One that is not defined by color, religion, or politics but by their love, compassion, their conscious awareness, and by the peace they create.

You and your children are this new race of the people of the rainbow. The time to create a new earth is no longer in the distant future. It is nowhere. It is now here, and you must actively work now.

Love is an energetic glue connecting all things within the One. This reality has been ignored and disregarded through ignorance forming the basis of beliefs in separation. Many, through fear of being "different" continue to live concepts of separation long after attaining knowledge that only one "something" exists. This "Something" can be called God, Consciousness.

There is information coming through given to you very similar to ours but when the solar cycle 25 prediction will come you must be spiritually prepared and have been able to find your way among all the false prophets and cults. You must have found your way to the path of Oneness. Some of you have already split souls.

People must prepare themselves spiritually for this solar Cycle 25 coming, so that when they start seeing signs, like seeing storms becoming more energetic when volcanoes continue to get active all around the planet when more and more earthquakes begin to occur, they start seeing strange aurora borealis and plasma spheres shooting through the sky, it's when the solar cycle event is about to occur. These signs are prophesied when seen all over the planet. These ancient prophecies occurring, hopefully, it will be a wake-up call and you will all prepare yourself spiritually immediately. There is not much time left.

This is a note from Saint Germain "The Solar Flash that will help all of mankind reach deep down into themselves and realize, just as you have, who you are. Yes, certainly there will be those who will shine away from the Light, who and, are blinded by the Light. But even many of them will recognize that they are a part of the Light, just as much as all of you are. It is the Light that is your salvation. It is the Light that continues to pull you on.

It is the Light within every one of you that brings the creative force within you forward. To begin to use more and more your imagination, your imaging process, and your visualization skills, to create this new Age of Aquarius. And create it in any way that you want. It is your universe, both within you and outside of you. It is your creation.

Up until recently, the collective consciousness of man has believed that the creation process was outside of themselves, not within. Even though Yeshua told those that were gathered with him the kingdom of heaven is within. Many did not believe it or understand it. But those of you now are beginning to understand more and more fully what that meant, what he meant by that, the kingdom of heaven is within.

The creation source of your being is within. You have the power within you to create outside of yourself, create whatever it is that you want. For you have the power of thousands of suns within you if you would only come to believe and fully acknowledge that power within you.

I am Saint Germain, and I leave you now in peace and love, and the Violet Flame to burn and purge within each one of you

all of the old programming that still may be present within you, still may be held within your lower chakra centers."
Enjoy the journey. It is time for everyone to step together and make a new world, creating something very magical right here and now. I ask you to treat each other with respect and nurture one another.

"The devil's finest trick is to persuade you that he does not exist."

**Charles Baudelaire
and
"Since man has rejected God, he has "turned unto fables"
(2 Timothy, 4:4)**

Heaven exists and we came here to bring Home to earth. Earth is hell! Heaven is a real planet. Heavens have always been mysterious, fascinating, and so magnetically attractive to humans.

Why do you think Christians say only one way to God? John 1.6 Jesus answered: "I am the way and the truth and the life. No one comes to the Father except through me. If you know me, you will know my Father as well. From now on, you do know him and have seen him."

In the beginning, was and still is the eternal Light of the One that has always been aware of itself as One. The expression of that Oneness created a colony of forms where that One would interact with itself. A colony of enlightened society. And out of the eternal One I have come the universe. It began in a cluster of stars called the Pleiades and, in the Pleiades, comes a society of perfect expression of the One I am. The Pleiades is the first place any soul travels from source into form.

The love energy is part of the unfolding. Your heart is magnetic and the most powerful organ, and energy. Love heals. Love conquers all.

PREFACE

"This is part of a New Thrilling Adventure, of a series of books. A Journey to the Unknown and a Quest to Self-Mastery with an Angelic couple on an Earth Mission and called to teach and to guide you named CHADD & VIE. Known as the God Duo, sent by the highest Government of the Universe."

Every night as VIE gets dreams and, or visions she embarks on a new thrilling adventure to live with other people in another realm. When she astral travels and meets them, she receives crucial information and answers from star sisters or spiritual people from different realms.

It started when one day VIE's life changed drastically after the reunion with her blue flame, and she entered a world of conspiracy and lies. She is told that they are two angels at work sent by the highest government of the world on a Galactic mission. VIE is the door to the Divine.

CHADD is a baker act drugged upward of the state, kept on drugs, and holds the keys to the Divine wisdom. He is sent from one mental hospital to another by the corrupted justice system, and the drugs disable his brain's ability to filter information, blocking signals to his consciousness.

VIE as a metaphysical light & vibratory healer works with vibrational transformation energy. She is bringing knowledge and the hidden truth to the masses of people. It is the time when the elite will be overthrown. The elite are the dynasties, the families of wealth and privilege, and those in control since the dawn of civilization who worship Lucifer.

They are the God Duo, and they came back to guide and inform you with some important information. It is the time of awakening and remembering because people have been misguided by the institutions, religions, and churches and it is sad. But the world is living the last final battle between God and the governments, a world prison system by the government.

It's a system where law and money are integrated to bind the world population by and in that system. It's a world prison created to train that population to willingly consent to voluntarily bind themselves—to be essentially bonded servants to that system to become the mechanism by which the resources, the wealth of the world which comes from, all the natural resources, to be the mechanism to harvest, that reach the resources, to build out the global civilization that we live in today.

It is a modern adventure lived by the God Duo with tribulations through which Christianity is introduced to the world and demonstrates the path to Divine love.

The black mentalists are the same evil forces that destroyed Atlantis. When they found out that VIE was in the medieval city. They felt threatened. They made it all impossible for her to meet with one of the knights Templars she was supposed to. One designated black mentalist kept materializing and dematerializing following her on her trip to the Medieval City.

A man with a bag-pack and a woman were waiting for her inside the Gothic Cathedral and felt threatened by her, so poisoned her food twice. This was before the spiritual attack on the back of her neck with a big black wound, then the attack on the right side of the neck lymph. Then she was awakened in the middle of the night with horrible pain. They nailed the middle of her palms, her wrists, and every phalanx on both hands. VIE did not realize immediately what was happening to her, and when she called for protection to Saint Michael the Archangel it was too late.

The Gothic Cathedral in Carcassonne is dedicated to Archangel Michael and connected to the lineage of Mary Magdalene.

The Cathari is the link to the Catholic. The Cathari is all hidden power and becomes the Knight Templar forgotten by the Catholics. There are two elements to the Cathari, the Perfecti and the Believers. The perfecti are the ones that want to bring people to God. They helped defeat Hitler, protected women, and children, then disappeared into another time. While the Believers were the Nazis. The Gothic Cathedral is dedicated to Archangel Michael and connected to the lineage of Mary Magdalene.

The content of this book acts as a bridge between the mystical realms in the path of humans' awakening. As we can see the world is dramatically changing and the spiritual path is changing with it. Not only it will be a new world but also a new spiritual path that will be inclusive of your multidimensional energetic self fully integrated into the path of awakening that is rooted and based in the heart. With the focus being to remember the light that you are and the return to the love you have always been.

The Gregorian Calendar and the Gregorian Chant were created by Saint Gregory, Gregory the Great, and Gregory is still of the existing Templar. Knight Templars that are back on Earth.

Albassinian is connected to Avignon and the Knight Templar. "Les Cercles blancs" which are two circles that interconnect Albasinnian (that means white).

Now listen carefully, RA was the Ancient Builder Race. "The purpose of incarnate existence is an evolution of mind, body, and spirit" Ra, "Law of One."

Out there in the universe, humans are considered to be very dangerous, violent, unpredictable, and uncontrollable. Some alien extraterrestrials have been monitoring the Earth for that reason for some time. They are part of the Kuiper Belt group (also known as the Edgeworth– Kuiper belt) it is a region of the Solar System that exists beyond the eight major planets and has an agenda to remove the Deep State from this planet.

The Deep State and the hybrid reptilian race that seeks to occupy and control this planet and the human race, and then, incorporate it into a galactic universal inter-universal group, to continue our progression through our spiritual evolution. The Deep State, the Illuminati, they know that their days are numbered. Climate change is another Deep State-led ruse to establish the New World Order.

More and more experts discover evidence that shows a mixture of extraterrestrials in human evolution, and the church cannot do very much to cover it up and stop the quest to find the truth about humans' origins and history.

Spirituality and Technology were tied and connected at the beginning. Then technology was taken away from spirituality, and it became Science.

And somewhat in the truth path, man invented religion. Religions were primarily created for 3 basic reasons, fear, control, and greed. And it worked against spirituality.

You are co-creator and they do not hesitate to kill to clone you, and then make a transfer of your consciousness.

There is more to this reality that you are being told. And the old must give place to the new.

The further one goes with the mantle of power, manipulating and transcending realities, the further one can fall. To some extent, Earth has been turned into a magnetic vortex that attracts fallen energies.

For long periods of time, Earth has been pulling negative energies to herself. Beings associated with these energies have fallen from very idealized heights where they made decisions, perhaps wrong or inappropriate decisions, and lost the power to construct uplifting realities.

Yet, this was all part of the plan.

About CHADD & VIE.

Light is information; ignorance is darkness. We want you to be in the light, not in the dark. Where healing and realization meet.

The God Duo, CHADD, and VIE are here to assist, teach, and evolve as all go through this process together. Giving you a version of things only to bring you into a higher consciousness.

This whole teaching is designed with a great purpose in mind, and the stories that are narrated are set up to take you to a higher plane of consciousness. That is the intention.

The words that are chosen trigger codes that are stored deep inside of your body. Your bodies are waiting for the questions to be posed so that you can begin to resonate with the answers inside of yourself so that the cellular memories within your bodies can begin to remember what they already know. As You read, you will remember.

We would like to pride ourselves on being storytellers. There is a certain credibility and a certain sensationalism in the way we present data. However, a story that we tell you at one point is certainly not the only story; it is not the end, and it is never the only truth. It is only one fragmentation, one small portion of the bigger picture.

So, the story constantly evolves. Your task is to find your identity inside of the story, to find what you know not what you want to believe or what you have been told.

Trusting what you know is imperative, for knowing is your connection to the Prime Creator. Every one of you is going to have to know that your life is about something as you begin to remember your role. You chose to be here. You are on assignment to bring memory forward and to bring the value of human existence back to the forefront of creation.

The Karmic relationships of the God Duo have a romantic nature and happen between lovers who meet life after lifetime to solve the karma they once had, in another lifetime created together. When people who have a karmic relationship with each other meet they recognize themselves in each other and experience a sense of coming home to someone. And they understand each other.

True love is never difficult or painful. It is exactly the opposite. When two people are meant for each other like they are, it becomes easy, smooth, harmonious, peaceful, and happy.

Because their sexual bonding happened within several lifetimes the connection feels very deep and profound as recognition is established on a soul level. Sexual bonding is a spiritual bonding that lasts forever, throughout the circle of incarnation. Sexual intercourse intertwines the energies of both partners, and they might take on each other's traits and characteristics to a certain extent.

They are chosen in the ancient souls who come from the highest angelic realms and incarnate on earth as beings who can vibrate at the highest vibratory level within a human body. Their meeting ignited their flame and there won't be any separation between them.

Their connection within this lifetime is a divine plan. They come together for a higher purpose.

Synopsis

On a sunny summer morning, around 8:30 am, like every day of the week VIE is driving to her office when the phone rings, It's a woman with a strong accent. She talks about a man who went to a restaurant where she was, used the restroom, and was never found to pay his bill, though there was no exit, and no window inside the bathroom. Just his pair of glasses that are left in her car. This first made no sense to VIE.

Over fifteen years later with no doubt, it's an introduction about the mission of a couple, messengers, and warriors of God. The God Duo is on a galactic mission on Earth. When they are going through a series of traumatic events on a mystical and sacred journey. To bring you some hidden truth and show you that Love is the key to getting back home. In harmony, Joy, and peace. "Love was Jesus' teaching."

It started with VIE from her unexpected meeting with her blue flame CHADD to the thrilling culmination of a historical event interacting with the prophecies as of the day. It includes the ancient city of Antioch, fallen angels, ancient legends, and a secret religious sect created in the days of Jesus. It is built upon insight while times of political corruption and financial instability are growing, launching a spiritual adventure, blending the adventure to the real insight and visions that the characters, the God Duo warriors, encounter with a curse that has been put as obstacles to the couple.

VIE has been guided to deliver messages through stories she lived, as the archons which are reptilian bloodlines, have set some limitations in place because they do not like the idea of leaving Earth. They have called themselves the New World Order (NWO) or one global world. They are the controllers of the earth. Sometimes called the cabal, the Illuminati, the enlightened or dark forces.

The story begins with Henri the granddaddy married to Martha, and their son named Edward who was contacted by NSA to work for the government. Edward married Ethel and they had a son, CHADD. Edward divorced later and remarried Katherine.

At age five the government started to do testing on CHADD to understand his abilities. They found out that his DNA had been altered. CHADD was given multiple psychotropic drugs. He fell into a few months' coma after an overdose of prescription drugs and became blind, anemic, and incontinent due to the pharmaceutical drugs. He was placed in various state hospitals and became in custody of the state.

VIE found out that Katherine, CHADD's father's second wife, was an archon and reptilian bloodline when one day she saw her shapeshifting.

During CHADD's stay at the hospital, a group called the Guardians revealed themselves. They have existed throughout history. They were the Cathari. There were two groups: The Perfecti and the Believers. The Perfecti helped defeat Hitler and the Believers were the Nazis. They are serial killers and now want revenge against humanity. Extremely intelligent and hypnotizing at the same time, some of the Believers had guidance in genetic reproduction thousands of years ago, before and after the great flood, to create creatures seen as vampires, bigfoot, and reptilians. The Cathari were the descendants of the angels in the book of Enoch that mated with earthly women. The Perfecti took the virtues of love and kindness, and the Believers the love of money, power, pain, and destruction.

The Indian Thuggees re-materialized infiltrated and took control of state hospitals.

This time while CHADD is kept under the care of the harsh woman, Katherine, who works for the elite in power, he is forced to continue to ingest psychotropic drugs ordered by the court. And now VIE is viciously attacked.

VIE is attacked by the black mentalists and then by Katherine after visiting a thirteen-century Gothic Cathedral in France where she was guided to go. In the Gothic Cathedral VIE used her Vajra, spoke the language of the Light, and anchored and activated some frequency.

The words of the language of the Light contain vibrational frequencies to upgrade your energetic field to make the shift, and the integration through this process is much easier for you to maneuver.

(At the beginning was the word, and out of the divine mind proceeded the Light pictures, 2177 combined with the sacred geometry forms producing the spectrum of all forms coming out from 2178 the alphabet of creation. The Light language. It is the language of future mathematics. 2179 Light pictographs and ideographic cybernetics, coming out from the Light language 2180 spoken, serve the Father's will. The pictographs are energized image shapes symbolizing the 2181 meeting of ideas, which produce pictures and sounds in mental language. These pictographs of Light are 2182 essential for communication exchange between the human body and its overall body. Therefore, 2183 pictographs not only communicate higher spiritual wisdom to the brain but also provide us with a 2184 new circulatory system for linkage with our higher self. The transmission of pictograph cybernetics 2185 works through a holistic love process. 2186 Then the pictographic radiations reach the brain during a session that is ready to participate 2187 in an infinitely expanding scale of knowledge throughout its universe. What I call the holistic 2188 love process, is necessary.)

The ancient Testament already asserts that divine words play an imminent role in the creation.

It is a code source to remember who you are, and a tool for ascension. Because it is a higher vibrational frequency, the language of the Light will always break down anything manifested on the lower frequencies for transmutation or clearing. Tibetan monks who meditated on Empty Awareness for thirteen years were able to have every thought be a loving thought activated by their Rainbow Bodies.

Summary

The content of this book is taking you on a Galactic Quest to find the human Purpose on this planet, and to answer your questions.

We came before you, CHADD & VIE, to stand behind you and to tell you something that will help you grow and survive.

CHADD: Christopher ADD, VIE: Vibration Intuitive Energy.

Our bodies exist in a location in space and time called Oneness. However, our journey to bring this information has been fraught with many dangers. We were discredited and seriously attacked in various and many ways.

There is a plot of a few hundred of the richest reptilians that control the planets, with their bloodlines of archons- fallen angels mixed with human beings, that act as their minions. They are cold-blooded with no sympathy or compassion. Our world is indeed a very challenging one. One who has first seen the implications of hate, great fear, grief, and negativity. It's insane it does not recognize the virtues of love, peace, and joy, and so it does not collectively support the advancements of the Soul, which is unconditional love.

This odyssey began when VIE met CHADD in a wheelchair and felt a deep and strong connection, inexplicable. She got to know him better and became enveloped in a world of mysticism, government conspiracies, religions/cults, and upcoming prophesied events. Entered a world of lies deception, hope, and pain. Her spiritual journey began when she joined forces with her blue flame, CHADD, to bring the words of Jesus.

Henri was a professor who lived near an Indian tribal reservation and had a son, Edward, with his wife, Martha. Edward married Ethel, and they had a son CHADD, who was diagnosed with several behavior and mental problems after his dad took him to the government hospital that his father, Edward, used at the request of the NSA. At the age of five, they started to do testing on CHADD to understand his unique ability. Though he was never sick, CHADD was given multiple drugs at the age of five. Then Edward divorced, and during the time of Edward and Ethel's separation, he started dating a coworker named Katherine, an archon known as the harsh woman, or surnamed the Surrogate, working hand in hand with CHADD's half-brother, Paul. Katherine's son, Paul, was a sworn law enforcement officer at that time. Paul, Carlos, and Katherine were all involved with the corrupt government. The government would take the drugs from the drug dealers in the West, send them to Miami for sale in Florida, and generate money for the government's clandestine operations.

CHADD spent time in hospitals and medical centers, and during his stay in the hospital, a group called Guardians revealed themselves. They were the Cathari. There were two elements to them, the Perfecti and the Believers. The Perfecti were helpful and wanted to bring people closer to God. They defeated Hitler. The Believers were the Nazis and are the serial killers of today and the many world leaders that destroyed rather than created. Extremely intelligent and hypnotizing at the same time, some of the Believers had guidance in genetic reproduction thousands of years ago, before and after the great flood, to create creatures seen throughout history as vampires, werewolves, Bigfoot, and reptilians.

CHADD is a baker act drugged up ward of the state, holds the keys to the Divine wisdom, and with VIE brings humanity into the light of God just when it all seems lost. But all of this was a treat to the Anunnaki who wanted the Earth for themselves. So, they manipulated the story of Christ to be successful with the takeover of Earth...A never-ending battle of good and evil: the modern world is a literal and figurative warzone.

The straightest path to the truth is to expose all information that is officially forbidden.

The secret Government controls the population through false information Christ was a healer; He worked with the emotional body, and He resurrected from the dead. The Church stripped away the virility of Christ by hiding His true relationship with Marie-Madeleine, and the male was emasculated, and the female denied it.

Illuminati are in key places and all institutions are corrupted. Their agenda is to reduce the population and to manipulate humanity keeping them under their control through drugs, flu, antibiotic shots, implanted diseases, weather catastrophes, and wars.

The Thuggees medical doctors from India reincarnated and infiltrated every hospital in the state. They keep CHADD by court orders, in drugs, and in a foggy state between Mental Hospitals and asylums.

They shot him with dangerous drugs, brainwashed, programmed then manipulated him, in the land of freedom.... They sent an Asian couple to steal the Vajra from VIE after putting some drugs in her drink. She has been poisoned more than once, they invaded her body with alien parasites, crippled her hands and her feet, and much more. They were projecting to kill her by targeting her heart.

Jesus and Mary-Madeleine are returning to demonstrate the path of Oneness and Divine Love. To awaken new frequencies within One's being, defragment old programming that no longer serves so that humanity can embrace the Light and Sound of creation to expand consciousness.

Christ delivered His bloodline, and His star codes, through the Goddess (Marie-Madeleine) and He brought the ultimate

creativity that could transmute human violence: The Eucharist"
true Christ.

There is a powerful message brought to the world, and it is about the Matrix and the Ascension process to reach the Golden Age with warnings and future predictions that you may or may not want to hear but have to hear.

Once you'll remember your multidimensionality then Christ will awaken in you. And it is Time! The Golden Age is within reach.

CHADD & VIE have the knowledge that can be used to enlighten your world and help resolve the difference that separates you on Earth.

"Henri the Professor, and CHADD's grandfather has now passed away with Alzheimer's after being found lost in a hospital hallway. Edward, CHADD's father died after a long battle against diabetes II."

While CHADD is kept on drugs VIE is helped and guided by entities from other realms and Aliens. It's about an illegal program to experiment with mind control initiated by the CIA. How the moon influences life on Earth. The UN thought to eliminate all borders and genders to create an atheist human field human race since they realized that Christianity was based on the Essene teaching. The Roman Empire stepped in to eliminate the teachings from the Essene, the human ascension: the transformation of your body into a body of light or the rainbow body.

Other civilizations are back here to help the earth, just when the CIA & NSA target anyone, anywhere, anytime on Earth with mind control technology and program their victims en-training the brain to their remote neural monitoring system, while blaming the population for Global warming that they create.

Be Careful, there is no ascension without Spirituality or Divine Reconnection, and when you awaken and become a serious co-creator the cabal will have no more power to rule the world. But you have to make it. Watch out for Gurus, false prophets, and cults.

Christ will come down from revolving Light clouds with a multitude of Masters gathered around him. Many will be glad, and many will be sorrowful at the sight, for they did not recognize that their Masters were in the midst, walking among the Earth.

It is the ability to enrich the world through the journey of the mystics, the universal voyage. Everyone has to travel in their own time for it reveals the path of knowing and transcends time and space. This path reveals the higher truth of personal evolution that you are invited to find. The teaching of Jesus Christ is essential in respect to the awakening happening now. It is a teaching totally based on love and respect for each other. Non-believers in God are used for mind control or real demonic possession. The fallen angels, the Illuminati, have abused the physical creations. The archons are inorganic and artificial and make a bad copy of our original reality. The Illuminati want a one-world government, and they selected electronics to be brought to Planet Earth for that and to keep control of humans. The pineal gland is the key to ascension and to higher vibration, and the cabal does not want you to regenerate it. You must know about the new Klebsi plague "Klebsiella."

Once the regeneration process begins, they won't be able to stop it (there is no need for children 's transfusion of blood). People will no longer be susceptible to control human beings on the planet. What if the Library of Alexandria was the link to today's affliction of the world and the Cabal? The Templars fought the forces of Islam in Spain and on the sunbaked hills where Jesus lived and died. The knowledge that the Cabal has in sacred geometry forms to control and create a single government. But the new template is here. The New Tools for the New Earth.

The falling away of power and the manipulation that takes place stimulate life forms that are unevolved into finding something better. So, there is a great benefit in this whole process and nothing to be frightened of. Absolutely nothing. There is absolutely nothing to fear in these times that are coming. As you begin to honor yourself, you will draw to yourself opportunities beyond your conception.

There is power and importance in the colors, the light, the sound frequencies, and the vibration related to our health and why it has been hidden from you. What if there is a silent sound that they do not want you to know hidden in an ancient alphabet? You are the voice of the universe. You are the voice of all creation, and if any man has an ear, let him hear it.

Definitions

AJNA: The energy of Ajna allows us to access our inner guidance that comes from the depths of our being. It allows us to cut through illusions and to access deeper. The Ajna chakra is associated with light. As you work with Ajna, you may want to see the third eye as access to a cosmic vision.

VAJRA: Lightening, diamond-like. This means "hand of mighty me" The purpose of this emblem is to awaken human beings. Very Powerful.

ARCHON: Hybrid, Reptilian bloodline

CHADD: (tainted angel) Eagle blue ray on a wheelchair. Son of Edward and Martha. Under the care of the surrogate archon Katherine. CHADD: Christopher ADD

VIE: Door to the Divine. VIE: Vibrational Intuitive Energy.

GOD DUO: CHADD & VIE, Messengers and Warriors of God They have lived many lives together.

EBEN: Extraterrestrial Biological Entities

KATHERINE: Surrogate, voodoo woman, and archon. Get paid to let CHADD be involved in a brainwashed program under psychotropic drugs.

LUMITA: Gipsy woman

RON: VIE's friend's astrologist

HENRI: Professor and CHADD's grandfather. EDWARD: Henri's Son and CHADD's father. MARTHA: Edward" first wife and CHADD's mother ETHEL: Edward's second wife.

PAUL: CHADD's half-brother and Katherine's son CARLOS: Involved in government corruption.

Introduction

Writing this volume was another experience. It's somewhat fictitious, spiritual, and holistic to bring real and powerful messages. And it happened in a very difficult time in my life, but an important one.

You are about to embark on a quest to help you find your path and your destiny, that is now at hand. A quest to find answers to your questions. Why am I here? What is my purpose? Who am I? Is there another purpose for me on earth than to live to work, eat, go on vacation, and sleep?

This book will open many doors on many levels while reading this mystical and entertaining, though enlightening, journey. Bringing truths to spiritual seekers and others. It will awaken you and illuminate your soul. You will feel compelled to follow that mystical quest where physical reality intersects with spirit. It blends the best of the physical and spiritual worlds together in one story lived by the God Duo warriors.

I would like to say a word about the surrogate. A name and a word you will read many times here. A mother is not authorized to make a child bend to their will however, a mother has the authority to demand safety for this child no matter how old the child is. But this surrogate/mother was an evil one and an archon. A psychopath, with an inorganic body, a liar, hypnotizing everyone around the child for her purpose and imposing her will to deprive him of a normal life, any money, and real good friends that could have helped him regain his freedom and go on with his own life and purpose mission.

My name is VIE; I came back to guide you. I am a metaphysical light and transformation vibration healer. Many of you are beginning to awaken and search for the hidden truth. I have been initiated by Archangel Michael and chosen to be the door to the Divine. I work directly under the Father, for the Father, for the Infinite Creator.

In January 1987, I experienced a dramatic shift in consciousness resulting in a complete change of lifestyle. During my first contact experience, my spiritual galactic mission and purpose were activated. Today I have been granted many Gifts. My mission on this planet is somewhat (as it was not enough) holistic and spiritual at the same time. I am a leader, and Master conveyor of vibrational transformative energy.

My mission with my blue flame CHADD is to help you become your own master, reconnect you to your higher self, and raise your vibration. You will be guided on your path to your purpose and destiny. My alternative work is a gift for you. I have been chosen, and I am blessed with the Christ consciousness, I have been reconnected, following eighteen months of daily initiation and preparation from Archangel Michael. The gift clears and raises your vibration along with restoring your ultimate connection to the divine, from which you have been disconnected and more.

One day I attended an energy seminar, but something was missing. I was still looking for more. It did not feel complete or fulfilled. That's where my personal quest began.

I took a trip to Toronto for another seminar. I was looking for the Light. And a very specific one. Two weeks later Archangel Michael came to my help. He trained me every day for an eighteen- month period. Then I was told to offer my first seminar using the training I received and using my gifts to reconnect and raise the vibration of the attendees. A sort of test to graduate.

My entire star family was there supporting me, invisible of course to the human eyes, and it was a success. That is where I noticed how much the mind has been indoctrinated. When money is not involved it devalues your service. To their eyes. Not a thank you note, an e-mail, or a call. But, when you give you always receive, among the attendees I met someone who was going to be of great help later. He passed me during the seminar break and delivered me a message. I was going to meet my blue flame on May eight. He needed me.

Then I opened an office to be able to expand to a wider public. This was something else. The dark mentalist forces did not like it at all. One day I entered my office, and everything was trashed on the floor, all my files, and the furniture were gone. That was my first encounter with the unenlightened entities. I finally met, and reconnected, with my blue flame and co-worker. We both entered into a world of mysticism, government conspiracies, religions, and upcoming prophesied events. We entered a world of lies, deception, hope, and pain, full of unexpected twists and turns. And our work became not only invisible to the public but also discredited by jealousy and attacks.

And how can I explain to unprepared, unawakened people, to members of my family and friends that this is my calling? A mission I have been chosen to do, and an invisible battle: How can I explain the meeting a reunion of two angels with one common mission? Entering the world of mysticism, government conspiracies, religion, and upcoming prophesied events. With a life of constant challenges, and tests of spiritual faith that non-initiated can't understand.

As it was not enough our work has been discredited by greed and Jealousy, and attacks by an archon woman (a hybrid race), the surrogate cold-blooded with no sympathy or compassion, and her family. They took the opportunity of our spiritual mission and faith in God to lie, discredit, divide, and separate us (because that's what they do, they Lie and divide to reign better). Making me the liar, when I was simply going through some rough events linked to my humanitarian and Galactic mission with my co-worker. That was never understood and believed it was true. But I never meant to hurt anyone's feelings. Neither did my co-worker. By the end of this book her son, also an archon, will take over and continue to attack us in various ways. He will manipulate CHADD's phone and restrict my phone number while CHADD sleeps, warn him not to talk to me, and tell lies to my family about CHADD and my friendship and work. And he will continue to implant in my family and friends' minds a very bad image of CHADD.

Accomplishing our work has created a lot of attacks on my physical body in my life, and in my co-worker's life by the dark mentalist's forces.

Because of all the twists and turns, and trials since we met, I entered into connection with some Catholic Saints, an Archbishop, Priests, Monks, a knight Templar, and a Gallican priest, who are not of this world anymore, and many more that came into my help. And Mother Mary to whom I am very close. You'll see in the book that she appears many times in my life in different ways.

It is important for you to know and understand that Catholicism has been persecuted and the Vatican has a long history of tyranny. The Catholic Church was infiltrated by Freemasons and the Jesuits, dark energies, who actualized their agenda to subvert the Church by creating a New Church that looks Catholic but is not. Keep your faith and Jesus Christ in your heart. Our Christian God is the Holy Trinity. There is no Trinity in Islam and beware some Christians' community teaches that there is no Trinity!

The Catholic, Apostolic, and Gallican Church is the traditional Catholic Church that teaches since ancient times, the same faith in our Lord Jesus Christ without adding or omitting not like today. Gallican Priests are generally Romans, and after the council, Vatican II wanted to keep the church tradition and keep it sacred. There is no ambiguity, they are Catholic but do not depend on Rome's hierarchy, however, respect the primacy of honor of the Pope. The Gallican Church is the Church of France (Gallia, which is la Gaule, la France.) France is the cradle of Christianity. Which teaches the same faith that our Lord Jesus the CHRIST. Priests and Bishops can be married, Deacons are male and female, no mandatory confession, no excommunication, and the animals' world is taken into consideration.

(The Archon's way of existence is siphonic Souls and enslaving minds and bodies. They are not born of the Light. They are born of the dark possessing consciousness with no organic body to meet their lustful desires.)

Achieving my work has created for me again a lot of attacks on my physical body and in my life by the dark mentalist's forces. Like I mentioned previously I fortunately have received a lot of help from behind the veil. And received many visions and prophetic dreams that will give me even more availability to help you understand this world and the new one. Gifts to get you through pain, traumas, body unbalanced, and more. Like the opening of your third eye.

Be open to Oneness with all creatures, including those who the creator of everything, sent forth on his behalf.

You are co-creator and they do not hesitate to kill to clone you, and then make a transfer of your consciousness. You do not have much time to save your soul.

Other Books by VIE Loriot DE Rouvray.

Master Conveyor of Energy, Vibrational Transformation Energy Therapist, Energy Frequency Medicine Healer, Light and Sound Therapist, Chromo Therapist, Metaphysical Healer, Alternative & (W. Holistic Medicine- Body/Mind/Spirit)

Each volume of her books takes you on a trip for your growth and your well-being. It is opening your consciousness and expanding your mind to prepare you spiritually for the solar cycle coming. Guiding you back to the path of Oneness. Beware of the false prophets, Gurus, and cults. Gold, silver, copper, or lead will not help you ascend.

- 9.1.1. Complete Guide to Natural Healing
- Destiny of the Dog; Beware of the Almighty—Volume 1
- Time Is Ticking: The Fifth Amendment—Volume 2
- Karma through the Window of Time—Volume 3
- New Century, New Era, New Experiences—Volume 4
- Intonex—Volume 5

(These books should be read in chronological sequence steps)

Bio-music Frequency of Sound is a color vibrational balancing CD imprinted of the language of the Light and on a sonic base.

In Light and Love Always

Table of Contents

Chapters

CHAPTER 1
The Ancestors are Coming Back

Henri the Professor, and CHADD's grandfather passed away from "Alzheimer's after being found lost in a hospital hallway. Edward, CHADD's father died after a long battle against diabetes II. Katherine managed to have CHADD under her care and after a few months leaves him again with no money and nothing to eat. And now karma is catching her she is diabetic too.

Watch out for you reap what you sow.

And the Journey continues as I embark on this new adventure. I was busy window shopping on one of the most beautiful avenues of the world hoping to find an idea as a birthday present for my best friend Jackie when a man poorly dressed in a soft-looking face approached me. His brown pants were too short, and his shirt used, though very clean, and he was walking with a cane. "Do not fear me, I am just a messenger" he said.

I was given a task by the Galactic High Council of twelve.

And my mystic journey continues with the EBENS (Extraterrestrial Biological Entities) creators.

The Galactic Council said that our ancestors are coming back, and we have a lot of help. Without them we would not be able to have and use ATM cards, phones, computers, etc... There are a lot newer technologies available to make life easier, get and keep your body healthy, the air cleaner, etc. that you are not aware of. New technologies that have the capability to help get rid of heavy metals, and nano creatures, can give free energy and more.

The controllers of the planet, among many other things, like to spray the planet with chemtrails, and all that is coming out of these chemtrails are cleaned today with these new technologies.

We have been going to Mars for a long time with (ARV) Alien Reproductive Vehicle.

The controllers kill human beings to clone and then transfer consciousness.

At that point, I felt a strong connection. It was on a beautiful summer day late in the morning. I never, never normally experience any headache but I am feeling some pressure in my head. I am found by channeled entities. They said that they were the High Council of Twelve and asked me to release the information that they would give me about the genome of the ancient creators, and the Controllers of the planet. On the creators and the controllers, and about the altered genetics to create the human genome.

The timing is perfect, they said. We are monitoring the Earth. It is time everyone turns to love and service to others. The purpose of incarnation is the evolution of mind, body, and spirit.

Humans are violent, unpredictable, and uncontrollable. The deep state and the hybrid reptilians seek to occupy and control the planet.

Shifting my awareness, I looked up at the sky and something occurred. I began to recall all that happened since my meeting with my co-worker in a wheelchair for our common mission. The Vajra given to me by the Tibetan and stolen by an Asian couple, the Indian thuggees that keep many on psychotropic drugs in state hospitals, and all we went through. Also, my previous lives together. I saw the gifts that were passed to me from my ancestors. My gift of healing, and the powerful chevron that was passed to me by my ancestors.

And I witnessed the return of some Saints, the knights Templar and Catholic Gallican Priests exorcists, magnetizers, and mediums.

As it is the Earth's destiny to join the greater family of man and woman as a Galactic Civilization, unprecedented events are unfolding that have the potential to change the course and destiny of Humanity on Earth. It is an event in which my blue flame and I are doing our part, for now, we have been physically separated again, but not really because we live in a parallel universe at the same time and we are telepathically connected. The bad entities, the controllers fear the God Duo power when we are together.

The people of Earth are being offered a chance to join the rest of the universe in peace and participate in spiritual awakening with spiritual and advanced technology. Something that the controllers wouldn't like to see happening.

Chapter 2
A Private Message from the Pleiadean High Council of Seven was given to VIE

This first Sunday in July I received a message from the Pleiadean High Council of Seven.

"This is not the lifetime where you learn new things to achieve a mastery level of any kind. This is the lifetime when you remember that you already are an ascended Master and that exactly this is the reason why you have been chosen to incarnate and face the greatest challenge in the history of our entire universe.

Before you ever set foot on planet Earth for the very first time, you understood that this was a mission. You understood that Earth had a very special place in the galaxy and that you were embarking upon a very specific mission for all of consciousness.

While you knew that there would be some very dark times, quite a bit of pain, and a little too much suffering, you stepped right up to it and decided that this was the only place for you to be.

Now as you began your cycle of lifetimes on planet Earth, you also understood how far you would be able to expand. You understood that the reward for being on planet Earth was like no other in the galaxy. And so, you feel that the pain and suffering were worth it. You may not feel it now, from where you stand, but we guarantee you that you feel it on the level of your higher self and your oversoul.

And now your mission is about guiding humans to create and experience joy and unbridled, unconditional love.

This is the lifetime when you remember that you already are an ascended Master and that exactly this is the reason why you have been chosen to incarnate and face the greatest challenge in the history of our entire universe.

Do not let them get fooled by a corrupt system of manipulation and deceit, lies, and abuse of power. Those in control of planet Earth are not humans. They are monsters, occultists, Satanists, and evil worshipers. It does not matter if you believe in Satan, the only thing that matters is that they do.

They have infiltrated the light as they have infiltrated every area of existence on planet Earth. Do not let them be misled by those wearing a false torch of light. Those who picture themselves in light when all they have is darkness. Do not let them follow the false teachings that tell you things like to listen to music and dance and sing and everything is alright.

This is not how wars are won. And you are at war. You may call this the Third World War and in fact, this is a spiritual war. Good versus evil, truth facing lies, light against dark.

Today, we want you to empower by making you bring the fact that you already are an ascended Master into the forefront.

You have all the tools, the wisdom, the knowledge, and the inherent God-given powers to bust this system and change its frequency from one of fear to love.

The time is now. We love you. We are here with you. We are a family of light.

Chapter 3
A Fifth Dimensional Planet Called TARA

As I said earlier, I have been asked by the Counsel of twelve to inform you know about "ABBA EBEN"

You know indeed who you are and what you are. But what you "know" widely misses the mark. Your guide team is working steadily to help you acquaint yourself with you. We are helping you to learn the more outrageous facts that you'd never guessed about your own self.

This is the school of earth. and when you chose to come here, you left the greater part of yourself behind. This was done deliberately so that you would go on a quest. The nature of this quest? It is to find your own self, to uncover your own light.

The Council of Light were beings of love, highly evolved masters of creation. Although they were embodied in a physical form, they emanated and radiated light. To be in their presence was to feel love.

In a time known by the ancients as Zep Tepi, 'the first times', the Council of Light for this galaxy gathered on a star called Antares. The Galactic Council of Light assembled to discuss Earth (GAIA), a planet in one of the outer arms of the Milky Way Galaxy.

Their responsibility was to introduce life to those star systems that could support embodied physical life. They aligned with the Oneness, the creative force of the heavens, with the energy of God, so that they could create within these energy constructs, as God.

They met together on the star Antares in a cavern of crystal. Around the table on red satin chairs were seated many beings, members of the Galactic Federation from throughout the galaxy. And they had a discussion concerning Earthman and they should be given the capacity for both physical and soul evolution just as is given to other species within the lower-dimensional worlds. Which is a gift from God, the Creator-of-All.

They agreed that all beings in Population One Light Systems must be given the capacity for soul advancement. They knew that they could neither tell them what to do nor show them the way directly, for to do so would interfere with their free will and defeat the whole experiment in consciousness that they and the Elohim have been wanting to create on Earth. But they were wondering how they could be sure that Earth beings will make decisions based on love and peace. And were preoccupied with knowing that they might align with fear and with a possible misunderstanding or misperception.

Being aware that the Pleiadians have established a colony on the Earth. They were attempting to teach and demonstrate to the Earth beings the meaning of love and the tenets of peace.

They could not tell whether the beings of the Earth, being different from them, would respond to the teachings of love. Not having yet the same genetic capacity to reason and to show genuine concern for others. No, it was a risky business, not knowing what humans would do if they were to give them their gifts of new creation and bring them into a spiritual union with them.

Some were debating on who they were, to deny to the human beings their Lineage of Light, and some were saying you do not realize that you, yourself, by your own words, are not living by the truth of the Way. And somehow could suggest that humans be kept apart and not have an opportunity to rise above the other life forms on the Earth or one day join with us.

Finally, the beings on Earth were created by the Creator-of-All, just as they were. And now humans are confined to a world that, though beautiful, is a very challenging place to live. Planet

Earth. At that time, human beings did not have the technology, or the mental and spiritual capacity to advance. And it was up to them to help the Earth's beings evolve so that in some future time, the Earth might come of age and return to fifth-dimensional status as is the star Sirius.

Earth was once a fifth-dimensional planet called Tara. It is only because of their unwillingness to intercede with the free will of man that Earth fell in consciousness and vibration and became a third-dimensional planet and a place of illusion and challenge. So, they concluded that it is true that many of the Earth beings at this time are barbarians and do not vibrate with love. But others have earned the right to move forward by their merit and their actions that cannot be denied to these souls. They have the same right to soul advancement they enjoy.

The beings on Earth are part of the oneness of creation like they are and came to these lower heavenly worlds through the Stargate of Lyra. They have been trapped on Earth because of misinformation, fake news, and the malice of the fallen angels, but their souls still hold the purity and essence of their original creation. Humans' original genetic code has been corrupted and must be advanced for the Earth to be restored and redeemed. They knew that in the future Earth would come of age and be restored to fifth-dimensional status, and the Earth beings would need to be ready for this shift. They knew that after, and when each of four, 26,000 Earth years have come and gone, mankind would be ready. And the time has come 0010110.

There is a great division that is occurring now. And it is indeed the separation of the wheat from the chaff. But all of this must occur. In order to bring about order in your lives, to bring about complete and total freedom in your lives, there must be this awakening process to happen.

It is only those who succumb to the fear that allow for the immune system to fall. Those are the only ones that can get this COVID-19 virus and have the effects of it.

But it is not the virus itself that is what you need to be concerned about. It is all that accompanies the virus. The virus is just doing its thing. It is helping to bring about transformation and transition, here. It is a tool that is being used at this point, both by the dark ones and the Forces of Light to bring about this Great Awakening."

Chapter 4
The EBENS and the Human Genome

The dark forces deprived me momentarily of the use of my "AJNA", and forced me to work differently. The AJNA is what connects you behind the veil. My friend Ron, a very intuitive astrologist chose to help me, and will play a very important role. Until, in my sleep, a bad entity could for a split second create confusion in my mind, and I opened a box placed on the side of the road and picked a key with a number that I should not. A messenger was sent on a bicycle, but I doubted it instead of following him.

However, I still could access the information from a field of consciousness.

What is a Genome?

Genome is the entirety of an organism's hereditary information. It is encoded either in the DNA or, for many types of viruses, in RNA. The genome includes both the genes and the non-coding sequences of the DNA.

Human Genomes, human beings were intelligently designed with arithmetic patterns, and symbolic language encoded into human DNA. 97% of human DNA is genetic code from ancient life forms. All life on earth carries the genetic code of extraterrestrials and evolution is not what you think. The origin of human DNA is extraterrestrial. Humanity is engineered by sky people, who came to planet Earth to modify the beings that are here to work for them as slaves.

DNA absorbs and transports light. And it is through created viruses that they can change and disconnect the DNA. Your ancient history is stored within the scattered helices of your DNA.

In truth, humans are much older than what you have been taught. You have walked alongside dinosaurs...

Information is light, you need this light to rise above the frequency and the drama of the third-dimensional matrix system. The light body is created through the transmutation of our current physical body as it absorbs more light.

A multidimensional battle is taking place between two groups. There are negative Ets working through the group that is trying to do the depopulation control programs, bio-warfare, and everything else. Depriving some human population from a treatment that a professor has proven to be saving lives. And benevolent Ets are coming in now in huge waves and they are taking the negative ones out.

But beware of the Covid-19 "vaccination". It is not a vaccine, but an experiment guided by Satan's hands.

The Knights Templar are back to help with the teaching of Jesus and the great exorcism as exorcism has gotten darker these days.

One Et's group is to take out as many people as possible, the other group is trying to take us into a utopian society, where we have free energy, the cure for all diseases, and everything else. The good ones are the Kuiper belt. They have an agenda to remove the deep state from Gaia, and they have been monitoring the Deep state for that reason.

Ebens (Extraterrestrial Biological Entities) allegedly is from planet Serpo, a desert planet where skies are bright or dim, but never dark, that orbits one of the Zeta-Reticuli binary suns in a solar system 39 4 light-years from Earth.

One of the things that God impressed upon us is that there is only one I am that I am. Any other God is posing as God.

That is why ANU is only the supreme being of the Anunnaki gods, and Niburu has a story. Alien beings came to

Earth to mine gold and established bases on Earth, the moon, and Mars.

Running short of manpower, they decided to create a hybrid race and the formation of one world government under one leader between the North and the South of the planet. That was the beginning of the Anunnaki Kingship. It appears that at that time there was a breach in the planet's atmosphere which led them to decide to use gold to repair the hole.

The Extraterrestrial entities (Ebens) created different engineered entities.

There are some hostile and very dangerous alien visitors called TANTALOIDS or TONTROLOIDS. They can imitate humans, have strange materials, look blond and human, and have the ability to change their bodies. But they are not blond. They are ugly-looking insects that are one thousand years ahead of us in technology, and probably every other science. Their spaceships have a force field around them. But can be shot down. Their language is different from the Ebens, and they use a very high-band radio system. They are very dangerous and known as hostile alien visitors (HAVs) from the third planet in the Epsilon Eridani solar system, 10.5 light-years from Earth.

Ebens genetically created the "big-nose greys" that are cloned biological entities (CBEs) by rapid-cycle cloning. Ancient Greek archon word for "Ruler or Lord"

The Ebens placed their genetically created ARCHQUOIDS on planet Pontel, described as the 55th planet out and a little smaller than the Earth.

Ebens also genetically engineered some entities called QUALOIDS, with four fingers and toes. They placed these creatures on planet OTTO in the Zeta Reticuli binary solar system. They are lizard-like creatures.

Also, the EBENS created the HEPALOIDS from planet DAMCO, which is a planet that contains 11 planets, and

DAMCO is the 4th planet out of that sun. DAMCO is a little bit bigger than Earth."

Our ancestors are coming back to help with a lot of these new technologies that you are not aware of like the one that helps us get rid of heavy metals, nano creatures, and red blood cells. The controllers of the planet spray us with chemical trails, and all that is coming out of these chemtrails are cleaned with these technologies. And we have been going to Mars for a long time with ARV Alien Reproductive Vehicle..."

Space is a domain that matters, and cyber is an important domain, the threats are really urgent, and they are growing and important. People have really no idea about the intensity of the threat in space.

Because the adversaries know what they are doing. They know, some know what they are doing, but many have no idea. And if they knew and understood they would be alarmed.

CHAPTER 5
Incident in The Gothic Cathedral

As I started this new venture and, CHADD and I continued our mission, I recalled feeling excited and at the same time, particularly calm and relaxed. I had my eyes closed. Then I had a vision about the legacy of the Knights Templar that lives to this day. What is not very well-known is that these individuals were deeply spiritual, deeply mystical men who were responsible for the building of the Gothic Cathedrals in Europe.

Even though these imposing buildings are seen to be great bastions of the Catholic church, they were built on ancient energy sites (ley lines) well-known to the Druids and those who went before them, and they represented powerful tools for initiation and growth. This group is operating under the watchful eye and indeed the approval of the Catholic church and acted to preserve great secrets of the Light that the church itself.

Was hell-bent on destroying, just as it thought to destroy all evidence of the true history of the one known as Jesus, and initiated groups that followed his true teachings such as the Cathars.

The Cathari moved to France because of the constant persecution in Italy. Pope Eugene III began a policy to stop the progress of the Cathari. It culminated in the massacre on July 22, 1209. The doors of St Mary Magdalene were broken down and the refugees were dragged out and slaughtered.

When I landed at the airport in Toulouse, I immediately took a cab, dropped my suitcase at the hotel, and went straight to the Gothic Cathedral in Carcassonne. A Gothic Cathedral located on the Voltaire. It is the seat of the Roman Catholic

Bishop of Carcassonne and Narbonne. The building was built in the 13th century as a parish church, dedicated to Saint Michael. This Cathedral is also connected with the lineage of Mary Magdalene and their descendants.

I entered the Cathedral and was emotionally overwhelmed by the sacredness of the place. A man with a backpack was standing there looking at me intensely and he attracted my attention right away. Next to him was a short woman with short white hair. I walked straight to the front where on the right side was a huge statue of the Holy Mother Mary and some seats in front of it. I sat there in silence and communion for a few minutes then took off my VAJRA from around my neck and began to use it in a circular motion quicker and quicker to raise up the energy. I continued by adding the language of the Light, followed by singing out loud.

The VAJRA I was wearing helps change one's karma to be more harmless and self-centered. The double Dorje and its four points radiate out elementally like a compass. North, South, East, and West, which aligns to the earth's geomancy as a square. They align to the Schumann wave and the telepathy found in the earth and heightened at sacred sites. Telepathy is increased via the earth as the earth contains psychic forces that raise human psychic ability. Energy ley lines converge at sacred sites, like this thirteen-century Cathedral dedicated to Saint Michael, which increases telepathy and spiritual thinking rather than the common concrete mind. This facilitates higher thoughts that are Dharmic in nature to flow through the mind.

The man standing there with his disrespectful backpack to this holy place began to walk towards me trying to understand what I was saying with a weird look in his eyes. A look I did not like. When he was close enough, I felt kind of unease and stopped him from coming closer with a few light language words. He passed by me and went back to stand next to the white-haired woman. Then I decided to have a bite in a bistro and the black mentalist found a way to poison my food for the first time on this trip. The second time I was poisoned was on the plane.

We are now in neo-Atlantis and reaching the same technology we had. These black mentalists are the same evil forces in modern times that destroyed Atlantis. I was a scientist back then and invented an artificial skin to heal the burner. CHADD was working with me, and he was a high Priest. They then blocked me from my scientific work and imprisoned us. And today they are ready to try to block my work again and the release of this seventh book.

The Christ cross represents the manifestation of the Cosmic Christ in a physical body on earth. These evil forces would not like human beings to hear, or learn about the Cosmic Christ and the blessing of Christ's sacrifice for humanity to help them sustain their soul and their Cosmic nature. As the teacher who teaches Solar principles, Christ in incarnation is the doorway, or the provider of cosmic light on earth. Christ's consciousness is a protective reality where one is virtuous, one receives sanctuary, refuge, and regeneration.

Letisha, a great and very advanced being and Russian incarnation ancestry appeared to me. She says that she is aware of me and is still in incarnation in Atlantis. She is telling me that I am not left alone with my work.

Touch is still the truest medium of expression, she said. When two people shake hands, they connect a myriad of chakras printed on their palms. I looked at my hands and realized they were severely attacked. But everything always happens for a reason. It will help me later to get in contact with the knight Templar I came to meet. To reconnect with the Catholic and Apostolic Gallican Healing when Christ Jesus, son of Father God gave the power to all Apostles to crush under their feet the serpents and scorpions.

Following the poison put in my food twice and my energy lowered my hands are crippled, my feet swollen, and my left knee has a trap energy that makes it difficult and painful for me to walk and unable me to pray on my knees.

But Letisha is telling me that I am not alone and had great help sent to me from another realm when I was attacked again. Attacked again that time by a spiritual attack on the back right head and on the side of my neck a few days later. That time it's on the lymphatic system.

She is also telling me that the poisoned cookies given to CHADD by the harsh woman on a visit during its last forced admission in Chateau Ushi (a state psychiatric Hospital) have done a little bit more damage to CHADD's body. Over a year after surgery, he can't swallow bread or drink water with his meals.

"But all this is about to come to an end now. You will get the dream soon of all that is about to take place now," she said.

CHAPTER 6
"The Cabal are the Controllers"

CHADD and I are separated I am alone and on my way to the medieval city of Carcassonne, I let all passengers disembark the airport's bus and board the plane before me, when a mysterious man, with dark hair, appeared and made a gesture saying, "after you, please". Climbing the stairs to the plane the man showed me the title of the book in his hand. It was about "laying hands an ancient healing" and he added "and numbers also are important". Who was this man? He did not seem to be dangerous or to have some bad intentions.

He was talking about the attack on my hands and announcing that I would receive a lot of messages through numbers. As you'll see.

I entered a trance state of mind and felt the adjustment made in my mind and I telepathically received this.

"It's a Galactic update. The big battle for the 7 dimensions was won by the light where millions of light forces won against billions of dark. The forces of light won the battle outside of our atmosphere to allow us to move on a better timeline and skip calamities and other events. It's huge news the light has won.

The Cabal are the controllers guided by Lucifer, whom they worship in many ways. Cults, ceremonies of black magic, voodoo, or what other islanders call, boucan. They are killers, Rappers, and eating the flesh. Some Asian countries are selling their dead people in tins to Africa as corn beef in tin. At Christmas, they all eat babies.

But the religion will return to what it is supposed to be. It will all return as Jesus Christ set it up. The religion will not return by control anymore, but it will be teaching about healing and love like Jesus did.

It will come back with the return of Jesus and Mary Magdalene.

It's a wondrous place that this world is coming to, and as you experience the differences in your mind and awakening, you are seeing what maybe you in the new world of this loving energy that you are carrying to all of life, and living the Love that you know can bring about the miracles that you have dreamt of and experienced in your awakening to the new day. Take the newness of your thinking and allow it to become the day of your dreams, and the life of your awakening."

CHAPTER 7
About Mary Magdalene and the Secret of the Cross

Mary Magdalene is the Bible's Key witness to one of the most important events in history. The resurrection of Jesus. Without her Christianity might not exist, and yet almost nothing about her is really known. Except that the early church called her a whore.

In fact, Mary Magdalene was not only close to Jesus, but they were intimate. She is really Jesus' wife and the mother of Sarah.

Beneath the lays of myth lies a hidden truth about what happened on the day the Bible says Jesus rose from the dead. A secret that had to be kept from Christianity to be born. The gospels wanted to remove Mary from the Bible and make her irrelevant, that made Mary Magdalene a very inconvenient woman.

2 000 years after her death her name is everywhere, yet she remains the most mysterious woman in history. To some, she is a prostitute forgiven by Jesus. The sinner who became a Saint and to others she is the true Holy Grail. She plays a starring role in the foundation of Christianity when the gospels give very little details about her, only saying that she came from Galilee, supported Jesus, and was once possessed by demons. Her most significant moment is with Christ on the cross. The other apostles left and fled because they were afraid, but she stood by Christ.

Only Jesus' women followers witnessed the execution. Mentioned first among them is Mary Magdalene. She remains with him until his death. By doing so she was taking a significant risk. It is clear that it was dangerous for the family to be around and to show grief. There are some stories of not only family members being crucified but also females or even children. So, it was not less dangerous for Mary Magdalene to be there.

There is little known about her but there is a high level of intimacy with Jesus if she was with the mother of Jesus and his sister at the burial washing and preparing and anointing the naked body of Jesus for the proper rights of burial. And yet who is she? She is definitively the mysterious woman.

The Gospels of Matthew, Mark, and John, all tell how Mary Magdalene is the first to see the resurrected Jesus. The resurrection is the foundation stone of Christianity. According to the New Testament, Mary Magdalene is the messenger who delivers news of the resurrection to male disciples. She is the apostle of the apostles. But when her job was done, she disappeared from the Bible.

Could it be that the early church had to hide something because Mary Magdalene was the key witness to the resurrection? Indeed, her vision of a risen Jesus inspires the male disciples to claim that their leader has returned from the dead. The Jesus movement breaks away from Judaism and Christianity is born.

Amazingly five hundred years later instead of celebrating Mary Magdalene as a founder of their faith the Christian church branded her a whore.

Chapter 8
"A Message from Mary Magdalene"

As I write this, my body feels that cosmic waves are hitting Earth and it leaves each of us in a sensitive state, sometimes in bliss or heightened knowing. Space weather sends cosmic waves to Earth in the form of light codes. We also may feel emotional with the incoming waves. We can harness the energy when we get in sync with the greater flow while the flow of ourselves. Learn about it and let yourself be in a flow state. "A flow state" is our new way of accomplishing and creating.

All of this points to how the great shift is happening and those of you reading this feel it and know it in your hearts. It feels like things just got real. It feels like we received evidence that the Shift of the Ages is here and by how we experience it personally.

The nature of the shift is that life is becoming less solid and more fluid.

It works better when we surrender to the flow. The unexpected is showing up more and we must go with it. Intentions are set within and carried in our hearts as we rise and meet each moment in a state of flow. We can come back to those intentions again and again. We must approach intentions in a roundabout non-linear way instead of a direct way, or so it seems. We can live responding to the world around us riding the waves and seeing where we are taken by the current of life.

As my life and things are about to change in the world and for the God Duo also, I would like you to read this from Mary Magdalene. It reveals some information about her union with Jesus.

The only time Jesus ever is portrayed as having human emotions is when He became angry at the money changers in the temple. Most of society views Jesus as a sexless man. His humanness was simply not acknowledged in the Christian Bible.

The dehumanization of Christ was done when the Bible was greatly altered by Two factors. The first Council of Nicaea in 325 and more disturbing "The Council of Trent" (Latin: Concilium Tridentinum), was held between 1545 and 1563. At that time Monks and Priests were still inscribing the bible by hand. After all, even though the printing press had been invented in 1440, it was not widely used until much later.

It is true that there are those who would have you believe that Christ had no earthly desires. He was my husband, fully a man in every way. Appreciating a good meal, and a glass of red wine.

Once Jesus and I came together in union for our soul we were almost never apart. There was never a question of the right or wrong of it.

We were ordained partners for a great cause since before our birth. Like Mother Mary was chosen before her birth to be Jesus Christ's mother and she was born without sin. So blessed, without sin, and was a virgin.

We did not sleep together openly until after our marriage. It was to protect me, for many of the followers and the disciples were jealous of anyone who spent a lot of time with the master. It was a different time with different customs. However, even now it would appear discrediting to some, for a master teacher to be sleeping with a partner in full view of others.

Those who would have you believe He lived and died a virgin are under the mistaken impression that being a virgin causes you to be purer. This is not true because embracing your sexuality is a high path to divine ecstasy. To deny your sexuality is to say no to one of the Creator's greatest gifts.

Our lovemaking was bliss, not only because our souls were flying high together. It was also due to training in body awareness. Jesus' hands were pure love and desire expressed upon my skin. Jesus had also had extensive training in the arts of ecstasy.

The early church knew that sexuality could lead to extreme advancement in spirituality. Enough advancement to see through the control they were attempting to exert. Sexuality was made out to be a dirty expression of carnal lust.

When Jesus and I made love, we both reached full satisfaction. No part of your body is dirty and there is no part of your body that cannot be allowed to experience pleasure if given the opportunity to respond.

Christ had never ejaculated into a woman until we were together. There was no need. Because of our training, we both knew how to fully experience pleasure without the need for ejaculation.

As we traveled about doing the ministry, quarters were often tight. We held much respect for those who sacrificed all to follow this ministry with us. Yet, the times we held each other in intimacy were amazing beyond any words!

Due to my training in the temples of the Egyptian mystery schools, I knew how to purposely fill his cup. My training had taught me how to restore his Ka body when energy was lagging. The Ka Body is the spiritual twin that surrounds and closely interpenetrates the physical body. The strengthening of the Ka body was done while experiencing the deepest pleasure.

Jesus knew that his seed must not be scattered about and reserved it for our sacred union. Even then, it was not until after our marriage that he allowed ejaculations and possible conception. My womb joyfully received his seed, and I knew strength from it.

It was during one of these unions that we conceived our daughter Sarah. It was shortly before the crucifixion. Yet Jesus never got to see or hold our baby when he was in his physical form. After his crucifixion and ascension, Christ did come to me in his light body many times to comfort me, and even to help me through the birth of our daughter.

I wish you many blessings. We love you very much. In light and Love always,

Mary Magdalene.

CHAPTER 9
Knowing the Infinite Within and Blessing

I was severely attacked while CHADD was in the custody of the satanic archon Katherine, and he is still forced to ingest psychotropic drugs, even though he can't swallow bread since the surgery they did after destroying his esophagus. The time has come for the new healing technology to be unveiled and available. And maybe it's also time to rediscover our knowledge.

As I look back, I literally see my father with money coming into his left hand, passing through his heart, and going out his right hand. It is a constant flow. It comes in and goes out. We are, after all, a conduit for the Infinite.

The Source is within us, said my father "We do not need to seek outside of ourselves for our supply. Indeed, there is actually nothing outside of our consciousness. All we need to do, first, is to realize this. (To acknowledge it) The realization that nothing comes to us, but instead comes from us, from the Outpouring of Spirit, is the foundation of all abundance. Secondly, we must release it. We must turn on the flow. We do this by giving. Spiritual teachings tell us to create a vacuum so the Universe can fill it up; that as you give, so shall you receive.

But as we mature in our spiritual growth and understanding we will act from a place of knowledge, knowing the Infinite within and blessing and releasing as Jesus did. What you must do, he continues, is to daily in your meditation time, look into your house and see what you have to give."

And like my father, do it quietly and in silence. As we mature in our spiritual growth and understanding we will act from a place of knowledge, knowing the Infinite within, and blessing and releasing as Jesus did. Daily, in your meditation time, investigate your house and see what you have to give. Begin to pour from your cruse of oil and break your loaves of bread.

The word of Jesus, as he was teaching those around him how to use the power of human emotion in his life, the native people, and the ancient know it. But why don't we know it? What happened to our knowledge?

The sacred truth is believed to be passed into the hands of all people. But they have only been reserved for a few. In the year 3225 AD, western biblical texts were edited, and tremendous amounts of information were lost.

The Emperor Constantine in the early Christian Bible made the decisions on what to include, and about 45 books were completely taken away from the actual Western biblical tradition. That is how the information has been lost. The information that everything is connected and is recovered in the Dead Sea Scrolls in the NAG Hammadi library in the Coptic texts.

CHAPTER 10
Taking the Wrong Action and Selling Their Souls

My father said: No wonder she is known as the voodoo woman. And my father continues, as I said we do not need to seek outside of us for supply.

There are two women in your surroundings. They think that they have a great imagination paying Katherine, making false statements, and taking the wrong actions. They are selling their souls to Lucifer. They are the instruments and minions of the Illuminati.

They are the ones that are mainly responsible for your health and hand problems. They are parasites to society and liars.

Their interest in witchcraft started at a young age. They grew up surrounded by natives who still have the knowledge of witchcraft. Remember the first time you met the oldest of the two, and the way she looked at you that is the typical look of the reptilians. They stare at you with an evil look with no expression on their face.

Now I am watching myself in the street, under 100 degrees Fahrenheit in a residential subdivision, with no phone working, and far from everything wondering how I will be able to get a taxi. I began to ring at several door entrances. The first one is a dog barking, but no one seems home. Second, home looks like they are gone on vacation. The third is empty and for sale, finally, after a while walking and ringing at different houses, I can hear some voices in a pool. A very nice and polite woman agreed to help me and called a taxi for me and advised me gently to go back in front of the house I came from so the taxi could find me. So, I walked slowly back when the police passed me and asked me to follow them. One policeman came out of the car to me and asked me my identity and what was wrong with the man in his daughter's house. "Is that true that he is senile? His mind is not right anymore?" said the policeman." Absolutely false I said but go and judge by yourself. One policeman stayed with me and three others went inside. I could hear a woman's voice yelling, when not screaming, to the policemen. Then I heard, "This woman outside is trying to take this man out of my house with her, she says, but this man is not able to make his own decisions anymore and can't function alone. He has poor mental ability, is senile, and he must be under state guardianship and care."

And I heard the policemen asking questions to the man. They finally came out with him. They were absolutely horrified but what they heard from the woman. And one of them said "What a shame! How can daughters say such a thing about their parents, and do such a thing to their own father? That's all about greed and money. In fact, money matters more than the father.

These two women really want him in the Government care!

One of the policemen had tears in his eyes and said "I lost my father this way"

Two days later, I needed to take a taxi and it happened that it was the same taxi driver that witnessed the scene. He got off the driver's seat to shake my hand.

These two women, one an archon and the second possessed and also a puppet of the first woman, are parasites to society. They used sorcery. Called Katherine first, then contacted a guru, then one witchcraft woman, and suffered the consequences of it when the Knight Templar and Catholic Gallican Priest began to help me. Then as you'll see not many days later Saint Padre Pio will join us in the battle and Mary un-doer of knots will come to confirm that the knots were undone.

The blessed Mother Mary was seen crying while undoing the knots of my life when she saw all I went through.

Satan is alive and doing very well in the world. Because man has estranged himself from God. In his grasping at Earth human flesh gratification and ego monuments unto self, man has fallen prey to the enemy. Satan had not one bit of battle to get thus far.

"Humans have brought the world and its relatives, the entire universe, to the point of destruction: Self-destruction. When the big bang goes down, it won't be because of the Russians, or the Arabs, or anyone else. It will be because of our own selves. Nothing more and nothing less!!

Put aside all the self-indulging misconceptions that God created man to self-indulgently "rule" over anything or anyone. STOP PREACHING "DIVISION"

Men have wasted so much time buried in fragmentation that they have totally lost sight of our spiritual reality. Is it any wonder that your prayers are not heard? You are too busy praying for yourselves to even be able to receive a response. Became selfish, rude, and worst of all, doubtful of your very beings.

It is time for all of you to come together in the reality of your beings and return the Earth to the condition in which you found it.

CHAPTER 11
An Important recall of an old prayer to the Lightworkers

At 6:30 am the light filtered softly into the room as I awakened slowly. For the second time, I heard someone walking and passing not far from me. I took a glimpse and saw that it was a woman. She was frail and breathing heavily. I glanced at her face, and I immediately understood that she was not human.

That is when I heard her saying.

Yes, Lightworkers center themselves to meditate and do all the things necessary before they get in contact behind the veil with their guides. But these days they must do even much more. The black mentalists are very powerful and wait to get the information from them. They must be even more cautious. Make sure to be invisible and say the Lord's Prayer not forgetting to call Archangel Michael for protection and ask that the information they will receive be kept unheard and unknown at all times by the dark entities. That the information be unreachable or scrambled when it gets to their ears.

Today even exorcism is getting darker. The recourse to triangular (great) exorcism is sought through Catholic Apostolic Gallican priests and knights Templar.

The Vatican has been attacked for a long time now and is controlled by dark forces. The Jesuits and the Freemasons are doing rituals of black mass in desacralizing the Holy Communion. Killing human beings in rituals, drinking the blood, and eating the flesh of the human body. They are using sorcery to worship the devil, Lucifer. It is a black religious cult that is practiced in Africa, the Caribbean islands, and the southern US combining elements of Roman Catholic rituals with traditional African magical and religious rites characterized by sorcery and spirit possession.

Then Jesus appeared to me as I was about to leave the church, I visited for the first time DC. Above the door I was going to exit was the biggest cross I had ever seen. Suddenly I was being lifted. He picked me under his arms and lifted me up, up, up, like it will never cease to go up as I was contemplating Jesus Christ nailed on the cross. I was in adoration, and so grateful to him that I did not realize that I was speaking out loud to him and I got immersed in a huge cloud of love. In a pink cocoon of love and bright white light. I was in Joy and complete peace. It was bliss in wholeness. It was pure love and I wanted to stay in this bliss for infinity. I could hear the angels singing, and just he and I were with them. The time stopped.

It's when I was guided to recall this prayer that has been forgotten. I was not alone; I was among many praying for it.

"Heavenly Father, I thank you for loving me.
I thank you for sending your Son, Our Lord Jesus Christ, to the world to save and to set me free.
I trust in your power and grace that sustain and restore me. Loving Father, touch me now with your healing hands, for I believe that your will is for me to be well in mind, body, soul, and spirit.
Cover me with the most precious blood of your Son, our Lord Jesus Christ from the top of my head to the soles of my feet.
Cast anything that should not be in me. Root out any unhealthy and abnormal cells.
Open any blocked arteries or veins and rebuild and replenish any damaged areas.
Remove all inflammation and cleanse any infection by the power of Jesus' precious blood.

Let the fire of your healing love pass through my entire body to heal and make new any diseased areas so that my body will function the way you created it to function.

Touch also my mind and my emotions, even the deepest recesses of my heart.

Saturate my entire being with your presence, love, joy, and peace, and draw me ever closer to you every moment of my life.

And Father, fill me with your Holy Spirit and empower me to do your works so that my life will bring glory and honor to your holy name. I ask this in the name of the Lord Jesus Christ. Amen, Amen, Amen."

CHAPTER 12
My Meeting with the Knight Templar

The Knight Templar's motto

"Non nobis Domine, non nobis, sed Nomini Tuo da gloriam"

Two months after the attack on my physical body, I was still trying to find a solution to get my hands back to normal. I had a blood test done but the doctor could not find what was wrong. Actually, I was in perfect health.

I knew that I had to connect with the Knight Templar. My Star sister told me that he would do a very secret and specific ceremony for me.

On a weekend lying down on my bed, I was told that it was time, and I needed and would receive help from the spiritual roam. My third eye had been blocked at that point and I knew that it was coming from the dark mentalists.

Five days later, I was guided to go to a library. I found myself wondering what I was looking for. But it did not take me more than ten minutes for my eyes to catch a very interesting title on Healers in the XXI century by a Catholic Gallicane Priest. That is what led me to the Knight Templar I was meant to meet.

A Catholic Gallicane Priest. Magnetizer Healer, Medium, Exorcist, and Knight Templar. Of course! The Knight Templar I was supposed to meet.

The Gallicane Catholic Church was created during the reign of King Louis IX. It was approved by King Charles VII in 1438, and finally declared Church of France, and Church of the Gaules in 1682 by the famous Monsignore Bossuet under the reign of the Sun-King Louis XIV. After the French Revolution under the label Gallicane. Its legitimacy goes back to the Apostles and Christ itself.

And my star sister added, "Today the Catholic Church was infiltrated by freemasons who actualized their agenda to subvert the Church by creating a New Church which looks Catholic but is not."

I contacted the Catholic Gallicane Priest immediately. Here is what he wrote to me in return a few days later; `After analyzing your case, and from what you explained, I can feel sorcery's attacks from jealousy. You are a victim of obstruction, possession paralyzing and perturbing your everyday life. I feel that there are several entities, and these manifestations particularly target your health that is seriously threatened, if it's not already the case."

Which was, my hands being seventy percent crippled, my ankles swollen, and I was tired all the time.

I knew some of the attacks were coming from two women who paid Katherine. (CHADD's surrogate and mother of Paul.) to act against me and attacked also from the entities in the Gothic Cathedral, and from the ones that followed me in various locations and in the plane during my trip.

My star sister continued saying, that only a few Catholic Gallican Priests today do the "triangular" exorcism, also called "great exorcism." It's been a secret ritual since the 1800s century, this method is far superior to usual exorcisms.

Jesus Cast out demons. The demons began to entreat Him, saying, "If You are going to cast us out, send us into the herd of swine." And He said to them, "Go!" And they came out and went into the swine, and the whole herd rushed down the steep bank into the sea and perished in the waters. Matthew 8:31-32".

Chapter 13
Mary the Un-doer of Knots

The voyage continued when I was suddenly overwhelmed by the sense of being in two places at once.

I was asked by the Knight Templar and Priest, to pray with him and the other missionaries.

And had to go to church to show my gratitude and respect to Mother Mary Un-doer of knots once a week. And pray:

"Mary, Mother to whom God entrusted the undoing of the knots in the lives of his children, I entrust into your hands the ribbon of my life. No one, not even the evil one himself, can take it away from your precious care. In your hands, there is no knot that cannot be undone. Amen, amen, amen."

The Priest said, the theology of devotion actually goes back to the second century. Saint Irenaeus wrote, "The knot of Eve's disobedience was untied by the obedience of Mary; what the virgin Eve bound by her unbelief, the Virgin Mary loosened by her faith."

We all have some "knots" in our lives… and Mary can untie them!

Mary's faith unties the knot of sin! So, we pray that the Blessed Virgin Mary will intercede for us all, to untie the knots of sin in our lives – so that we may be purified and ever closer to God.

I knew immediately when the power of Mary started when I received texts of horrible words of hate that could not be other than the devil reacting and talking through the possessed woman who hurt me and my hands.

At that exact same time, I heard my blue flame saying it is time to tell them "Heaven really exists, and we came here to bring Home on earth. Heaven is a real planet.

Telling them that in the beginning was and still is the eternal Light of the One that has always been aware of itself as One. The expression of that Oneness created a colony of forms where that One would interact with itself. A colony of enlightened society. And out of the eternal One, I am come to the universe. It began in a cluster of stars called the Pleiades and, in the Pleiades, comes a society of perfect expression of the One I am. The Pleiades is the first place any soul travels from source into form.

Chapter 14
Revelation: The Pieces of the Puzzle Begin to Fall into Place

The wind blows softly on my face. I let myself be infused by it. I raised my head. The sky is gorgeous. Then Archangel Michael was here saying,

This is Archangel Michael and I'm here to deliver a message from God: God knows that you believe in miracles, and you are about to experience a big one. You're blessed by God.! So, keep having faith in Him! You are the door to the divine.

The essential is to trust and follow your path.

And I found out that my life was about to take a whole new direction! Here is what happened: in my dream, I was surrounded by spiritual energy, it was everywhere around me. The only thing I could actually see was that I was in a white robe, symbolizing purity, shining brightly in the dark. It literally woke me up.

I knew it represented worldly experience and knowledge. It is such a strong sign, this dream was sending me a message, it was a call from the Universe, and I had to listen. It indicated complete control over my life.

This leads my subconscious mind, the deepest instinct living within me.

My relationship skills will develop. This will improve my leadership abilities, and this skill will be extremely useful. I will also develop my connection with my subconscious like never before, through the removal of the negative that has been forbidding me to find the spiritual light I need in my life.

The pieces of the puzzle I have been waiting for so long will finally take place. Is taking place now.

Wow! I see, I am astonished. It is a beautiful and inspiring experience, and through this dream, I am having the biggest revelations I have had so far about my future. My entire life is about to take a whole new direction, a big change is coming up. The next chapter will explain it all. I may not realize how big this is yet, but this is an extremely good sign, everything makes sense now, and I have so much good news about the future!

The next chapter will explain it all. I may not realize how big this is yet, but this is an extremely good sign, everything makes sense now, and I have so much good news about the future!

Chapter 15
The Controllers and the Creations

I am floating in the air and still lying on the ground below. Even stranger, I am able to see the world around me despite my eyes being closed. That was initiated by a specific Sound frequency coming from my blue flame.

So, I was floating when I was contacted by a friendly space entity. I was called to tell the story of the world between the controllers and creations.

I first received the word "EBENS."

Then I was told, "EBENS is the Father of the human race. They created three different races, another in Russia and Asia that died. They split humans into three groups. Black and Asian people split from the original white people. White are builders, they create and invent. Asians were created to be the knowledge seekers and retainers of the human race, and Indians are white and Caucasian.

You need to offer your service, gift, and talents to the public. To offer your knowledge. We have the next level of technology we need now to release to the public so that everybody benefits from being healed at a level that is only seen in movies and that is the real thing.

What doctors have been told for thousands of years, most of it has been a lie, and the good stuff has been suppressed.

This planet should be vibrating at a higher level, and it should be Joy, love, and peace. And not all that hatred. We want to elevate that, and it will change the world. If people would take a look at thermography, they would see that it's all about colors.

The ones that have been working for the deep state, the cabal are totally used and have no chance of success.

Genome editing, or alteration of genes in the human genome, requires an understanding of the role of the gene to be added, removed, or altered, at particular locations in the genome.

Genetic alterations include chromosomal abnormalities and genes. In addition to chromosome losses or gains, chromosomes can be altered.

A genome is an organism's complete set of genetic information. A genome includes all of the hereditary instructions for creating and maintaining life, as well as instructions of reproduction."

Zeta Reticulan beings are very advanced in genetic alteration. The name of their race is EBENS, they have been monitoring the human race million years ago and this planet, because of the fertility of so much life, more than other planets.

The ancient builder races in our solar system have developed all our solar system and put a protective grid around the 52 stars. Keeping it safe for many, many years. But the pre-Adamite had a war and hacked it and intentionally deactivated the grid protection. Outside of our solar system, there is a super gate, and a super gate can transfer you to any planet in that galaxy. Once the grid was deactivated, other genetic farmer races invaded and started over 22 genetic experiments. And these experiments are not only genetic.

A branch of them was contaminated. In 1945 they already manipulated the DNA. Milab identifies star seeds before they engage in their mission and turns them to the dark side. They track abduction that occurs then pharma-chemical gathers intelligence.

Once they find one an asset, they pull them out of normal classes and put them in public alternative classes. Recently they began to use clones, and then program them. But these clones have no souls.

But this friendly being wants me to explain about their creation. How they are creating human races, and say we are Homo Sapiens.

They have created certain races, like the Netherlands that died. But what they did not create is our souls. God did it.

Chapter 16
Chef Anu, Satan, and Lucifer

Being comfortably warm, though I recall that the weather was humid, and it was raining and cold. I centered myself and entered into a deep trance. My guide was waiting for me and pointed in my upper right corner for me to see. And this is what I saw:

This planet is populated by energy parasites. Chef Anu had two sons. Let's call them Satan and Lucifer. One legitimate, and the other one not. One is Enlil, who runs things from space. He founded Jehovah's command of the air. The second is Enki, and he is still alive. The interstellar colony is from Niburu. Part of Enki's empire destroyed Atlantis with the change of weather. He has various facilities all over the world.

Time is an illusion that structures people. It holds places. The Anunnaki, whose time sequences it is on, have made time on Earth.

No one today can be unaware of the complex global problem of environmental degradation species extension, toxic chemical soil depletion, and deforestation. Global warming and desertification.

Enki was the first Anunnaki to hazard a trip to Earth to begin a mining operation for gold. Enlil now controls the Anunnaki royal succession.

The connection between humans and Anunnaki is much more profound than that of masters and slaves. All evidence strongly suggests the DNA of Anunnaki was mixed with that of humans. This was because the Anunnaki needed someone to work the mines in search of gold, ORME, and other precious metals.

This is how the Anunnaki took control of humanity. They are patrons and founders. They were teachers of justice, they were technologists and kingmakers, but even venerated as archons and masters, they were not idols or worshiped as the ritualistic gods of subsequent cultures were.

The word that was eventually translated as "worship" was "avod".

The Anunnaki presence may baffle historians. Their language is confusing to linguists, and their advanced techniques may perplex scientists but to dismiss them would be foolish.

The Anunnaki were the council of Gods and Goddesses and periodically met to consider their future actions with respect to each other. They are known as the bearded gods.

The Anunnaki are the Nephilim, the fallen Angels (according to the book of Joshua).

Anunnaki has been also equated with the "watchers" from the book of Daniel and Jubilees. All you have been told is a lie. Just about everything you have been told is a lie.

Hopi and Apache lineage ties together the missing pieces that schools and churches do not want you to know.

This is indeed a slave planet where you have been genetically modified (DNA) to become subservient slaves. The reliable people are Aquarius, Scorpio, Leo, and Taurus.

The New World Order (NWO) does not have a government, but they have put a system in place through corporations.

They are attempting to put it in place also with the U.N.

Their thought, what they are trying to implant, is that one religion will be easier to control than one world currency.

They call WIFI the "we fry you people" Rtintel is what your mobile is. They study you, what you do, and your habits and patterns. There will come a time when people tear down all the towers and the electronics that are destroying the world. Because when you are in electronics, your brain is gone.

There are still solutions though. Prayers and Meditations. Not for yourself, not for a special country, not for some political people or specific governments but for the entire world to get involved. Not against terrorists or political events. But please pray for peace, love, and compassion, for the happiness of the entire planet, all galaxies, and every human being. This is it. Do not pray for you before you pray for the entire world. This is the answer to the pollution, the wars, the terrorism, the MSG in the food, the chemicals in food and drink the vaccinations shot and the chemical trials, etc.

It is time that you all stop being angry at each other and be egoistic jealous or judging each other. Or you will be left alone.

Put your aura in three layers. Gold, the rose sunset, blue or green. Put the cloak over. Be invisible and unnoticed, this is the end of the games.

People are going to wake up angry. They will not be able to think logically or reason. And it is what has been pushing people into the immediate today. We are so close; we are in a massive change.

They want to stop the change you can make, and this is what has brought about Harry Potter, for the most part. (a motion-based dark ride located in The Wizarding World).

Atlanteans are back using their gri-gri, manipulating, and controlling human beings. The founder of Atlantis oversaw crystal on Earth...and he has laboratories.

But while most of the controlling extraterrestrials on this planet are malevolent, you have received the help of the Pleiadians, who are trying to help undo what the reptilians, Syrians, and malevolent Anunnaki have set up on this planet for you.

The current administrators of the empire government on the planet have lineage back to ORION hybrid Reptilians, while the money was given to Marduk's children, the Rockefellers and the Rockefeller (RA-KA Pharaohs) and the Rothschild. Marduk, MAR (MR-son of) DUK (dog Sirius). Marduk was identified with the planet Mars.

Rockefellers and Rothschilds are both part of this consciousness.

Then the vision stopped, and I opened my eyes.

Chapter 17
The Black Eyes Community and a Satanic Cult

This morning waking up I remember very well getting inside an elevator, the door opened, and I found myself witnessing a growing number of politicians, celebrities, business elites, and heads of State who suddenly and mysteriously have wound up with black eyes. Although a few of them have sustained injuries to their right eye, the majority occur on the left.

From fashion to art, to music, to design, clothing, and business. The covering of one eye has infiltrated nearly every niche of marketing in the world, and I am told that the target is always the next generation.

The bizarre recurrence of facial bruises (and bandaged fingers) on Illuminati politicians and entertainers is a demonic spirit that has overcome the world elite.

This is not a crazy conspiracy theory. Something very sinister has happened but no one wants to face it. Though mankind has been colonized by a satanic cult. The idea that these people are all taking part in a ritual is not at all far-fetched. Cults and societies exist and have existed since the dawn of time and are still very much alive. In our modern culture, we've been desensitized to them since childhood when we were first put in front of a Television. We've seen them portrayed in cartoons and movies, and every once in a while, it makes the news.

I can see that as the plans of the elite were brought to light with the internet they were no longer permitted to operate in the shadows, so they simply changed tactics. They began openly embracing their Satanic religion/cult. Throwing it back in the face of those who have been outing them. Making a mockery of the whole thing while continuing to operate at full speed.

I was happy that it was all, and enough for that night.

Chapter 18
The Dependent Societies Cannot Thrive

I am embarking on my dream that night and journey to an interview that I had with a certain Mr. Belamont. An optimistic and caring person for other human beings as you will see.

For a few months, Mr. Belamont was calling my office asking for an interview with me. As he never wanted to say why, my partner kept telling him that my calendar was full, and I was busy. I could not pick up the phone to speak with me. She thought that it was one of these people that wants to sell you something and to waste your time.

One day getting out of my car Mr. Belamont was waiting for me and came towards me in the office parking lot. Not knowing who he was I kept telling him to hurry up with whatever he had to tell me. I was late and I had an appointment waiting for me in the office seating room. But something was telling me to give him a chance to express himself and I gave him an appointment for the following month.

Mr. Belamont showed up and introduced himself as Mr. Belamont, owner of the food chain restaurants. He said that he heard about me at a convention in Las Vegas and wanted me to have a chance to hear his story, hoping that I would share it widely.

And I have to say his story needs to be heard and spread around.

Mr. Belamont, owner of the food chain tried instituting a community-based system in one of its places and quickly learned that a "right way" does not exist. He decided to devise a fair more efficient way to make quality food available to those suffering from "food insecurity" after he read a report that shows that the number of people facing hunger is actually growing.

However, he found out that the world has yet to embrace the kind of deliberate, systematic, and inclusive approach that is needed to eliminate inequities that prevent billions of people from enjoying a long and healthy life.

Mr. Belamont believed that those who were able would happily pay something extra to provide food for those who could not afford to pay the full price. The "food to care pay what you want" would serve food like the fare at other locations.

Mr. Belamont was working in an area in which he had broad experience. He had control of all of the necessary resources. He was motivated by the best of intentions, and an optimist. The need that he was trying to address was real. His plan was limited in scope, but he had plans to grow gradually.

Mr. Belamont's "pay what you want" locations weren't financially viable and only recouped around 65 percent of its total costs. And what he found out, was quite a deception. His failure shows the lack of care, love, and compassion and proves that people are still under the spell of the reptilians, the elite governing the earth. The losses were attributed to students who "mobbed" the restaurant and ate without paying, as well as homeless patrons who visited the restaurant for every meal of the week. And I awakened.

Chapter 19
The Watchers-Anunnaki

Last night, lying down on my bed I felt suddenly a strong energy entering the room, and I was asked to be "prepared."

VIE, get ready it's going to be an interesting night he said, and that is what I saw and witnessed. It was a sort of manuscript on an old papyrus and alive at the same time. It was like the old papyrus was a movie telling the story of the fallen angels, the watchers.

The watchers are a guardian class of angels that were assigned to watch over the Earth and protect mankind from all these horrors that are happening.

The Anunnaki are the watchers, and they are two groups of fallen angels competing for global dominance and control within the New World Order. One group plays as good shepherds claiming to want to help mankind, but they kidnap, mutilate, implant, impregnate, and use human body parts as a skin rejuvenation and coloring maintenance technique. The others play as protectors and basic non-interventionists, the good cop/bad strategy. Both seek to destroy and dominate Earth, setting in the path and reign of Satan, also known as anti-Christ.

There are two groups within the Anunnaki, known as Enki and Enlil.

The Enki/Anunnaki includes:

- Greys from Zeta Reticulum (small greys with oversized heads who like to mutilate and experiment on humans), also includes Tall Greys (from Orion),

- Reptilians (Earth-based), Lizards. These are notably in charge of establishing a one-world government through our political leaders. Shape-shift into human form and also use humans as hosts to possess and work through.
- Draco-Reptilians from Orion, the ones running the show while the others do their bidding. It is the Dracos who are the rulers over the greys and the reptilians. They are shapeshifters Anunnaki-lizards coming on planet x. Draconians are red dragons.

The reptilians (earth-based lizards), greys, and others are all class of what we call aliens. They are the ones in charge of establishing one world government through political leaders. Also called the New World Order or One Global World. They shape-shift into human form and use humans as hosts to possess and work.

Anunnaki those who joined in Lucifer's rebellion against the Lord. And the Enki faction of the Anunnaki, also draconian, inhabitants of Rahab, (giant humanoids from their home planet Nibiru, a group of them stayed on earth while the others allegedly left to return sometime soon). These are the ones who seek to harm and destroy mankind and will do so, as they rule and dominate the earth with Satan and the New World Order.

The Earth/Anunnaki plays a more protective role on Earth. They hate the Draconians and their ruler Satan. They are the archenemy of the Nordics (Nordics humanoids are reptilian in disguise) and hate them. They hate Satan and the NWO. The coming planet X is more Draconians/Anunnaki, shape-shifting lizards/humanoid giants to help Satan dominate and rule the world during the tribulation period.

The Draconians are the dominant race of the (ENKI), and the Nordics and other humanoid groups are the dominant of the (ENLIL).

Nordics are a humanoid race, very human in appearance, 7-8 feet tall, with blonde hair and blue eyes. They are the ones Hitler referred to as "the master race". Nordics were also at one time beautiful angels, but were cast out of heaven, nonetheless, and lost their quality of angels.

ENLIL groups include.

- Nordics
- Syrians
- Pleiadians from the belt of ORION Alpha Centurion
- Venusians (all are human-looking)
- The ancient Sumerians (Sumerian means who come from heaven) had their ancient culture saturated with the Anunnaki. Sumerians and Egyptians were both alien-hybrid.

Lucifer resides in the first and second (space) heavens; and not in hell, as many believe. Satan has dominion over the first and second heavens but not over all the alien races. Only those who rebelled with him specifically, and not those who believed later. He rules from Orion and is a winged Draconian. He is not omniscient, or omnipresent, thus he needs his minions to cover a lot of territory on the earth to keep up with what is going in, what we call reconnaissance and spying.

UFOs are real and they have vehicles to travel in, but these are not aliens from galaxies in other universes, but from our solar system and own space. And I saw that the Luciferian group of aliens are running rampant on Earth, and they are doing so already. But nothing like soon. It's going to be worse. They have perfected DNA manipulation and can look human while being hybrids/demons/aliens. Such as the star children from and back in human form.

It is time to open your eyes and wake up.

It is time for everyone to wake up and open their eyes. Use meditation to connect with the divine and act from the heart. Because the veil is being lifted, and the time will come when men reject the sound testament account of creation.

You have probably heard teachers and preachers talk about the "sound doctrine" in today's church. And men will accept the doctrine of devils; (aliens) through false prophets (today's pastors).

The time is coming when you will see through the spiritual realm and those in it. Fallen angel Hybrids and reptilian Draconians Masquerading as Ascended Masters, our creators, and beings of light; they will deceive the world and prepare the heralding of their master, the Antichrist.

And beware of deception "Deception is from the devil!" always said CHADD. So true.

Chapter 20
The Creation of Adam and Eve

But I also have been given the chance to observe the creation, on a widescreen, of Adam and Eve.

The story of creating Eve out of Adam's rib is a confusion with the arrival and the celestial surgery connected with the interchange of living substances that is associated with the coming of the corporeal staff of the Planetary Prince more than four hundred and fifty thousand years previously.

A great majority of the world's peoples have been influenced by the tradition that Adam and Eve had physical forms created for them upon their arrival on Earth. The belief in man having been created from clay was well-nigh universal in the Eastern Hemisphere; It can be traced from the Philippine Islands around the world to Africa. Many groups accepted this story of man's clay origin as some form of special creation in place of the earlier beliefs in progressive creation evolution.

Adam and Eve arrived at midseason when the Garden was in the height of bloom. At noon, the two seraphic transports, accompanied by Jerusen personally entrusted with the transportation of the biological uplifters to earth, settled slowly to the surface of the revolving planet in the vicinity of the temple of the universal father.

All the work of rematerializing the bodies of Adam and Eve was carried out within the precincts of this newly created shrine. And from the time of their arrival, ten days passed before they were re-created in dual human form for presentation as the world's new rulers. Then they regained consciousness simultaneously. They are designed to work in pairs.

The planetary Adam and Eve were members of the senior corps of Material Sons on Jerusen. They belonged to the third physical series and were a little more than eight feet in height.

Mankind tended toward the belief in the gradual ascent of the human race. The fact that evolution is not a modern discovery, and the ancients understood the slow and evolutionary character of human progress. Although the various races of earth became sadly mixed up in their notions of evolution, nevertheless, the primitive tribes believed and taught that they were the descendants of various animals. Primitive peoples made a practice of selecting for their "totems" the animals of their supposed ancestry.

The Old Moses was the supreme teacher of the Hebrews, the stories of Adam became intimately associated with those of creation. That the earlier traditions recognized pre-Adamic civilization is clearly shown by the fact that later editors, intending to eradicate all reference to human affairs before Adam's time, neglected to remove the tale reference to Cain's emigration to the "land of Nod," where he took himself a wife.

The Hebrews had no written language in general usage for a long time after they reached Palestine. They learned the use of an alphabet from the neighboring Philistines, and did little writing until about 900 B.C., having no written language until such a late date, they had several different stories of creation in circulation, but after the Babylonian captivity, they inclined more toward accepting a modified Mesopotamian version.

Jewish tradition became crystallized about Moses, and because he endeavored to trace the lineage of Abraham back to Adam, the Jews assumed that Adam was the first of all mankind. Yahweh was the creator, and since Adam was supposed to be the first man, he must have made the world just prior to making Adam. And then the tradition of Adam's six days got woven into the story, with the result that almost a thousand years after Moses' sojourn on earth the tradition of creation in six days was written out and subsequently credited to him.

When the Jewish priests returned to Jerusalem, they had already completed the writing of their narrative of the beginning of things. Soon they made claims that this recital was a recently discovered story of creation written by Moses. However, the contemporary Hebrews of around 500 B.C. did not consider these writings to be divine revelations; they looked upon them much as later peoples regard mythological narratives.

This spurious document, reputed to be the teachings of Moses, was brought to the attention of Ptolemy, the Greek king of Egypt, who had it translated into Greek by a commission of seventy scholars for his new library at Alexandria. And so, this account found its place among those writings which subsequently became a part of the later collections of the "sacred scriptures" of the Hebrew and Christian religions. Through identification with these theological systems, such concepts for a long time profoundly influenced the philosophy of many Occidental peoples.

The Christian teachers perpetuated the belief in the fiat creation of the human race, and all this led directly to the formation of the hypothesis of a one-time golden age of utopian bliss and the theory of the fall of man or superman which accounted for the non-utopian condition of society. These outlooks on life and man's place in the universe were at best discouraging since they were predicated upon a belief in retrogression rather than progression, as well as implying a vengeful Deity, who had vented wrath upon humanity in retribution for the errors of certain one-time planetary administrators.

The "golden age" is a myth, but Eden was a fact, and the Garden civilization was overthrown. Adam and Eve carried on in the Garden for one hundred and seventeen years when, through the impatience of Eve and the errors of judgment of Adam, they presumed to turn aside from the ordained way, speedily bringing disaster upon themselves and ruinous retardation upon the developmental progression of all Gaia.

Adam and Eve came to institute representative government in the place of the Monarchial, but they found no government worthy of the name of the whole Earth. Before the collapse of the Edenic regime, he succeeded in establishing almost one hundred outlying trade and social centers where strong individuals ruled in his name. The sending of ambassadors from one tribe to another dates from the Adams' time.

Adam's son was the firstborn of the violet race of Gaia, followed by his sister and Eve's son, the second of Adam and Eve. Eve was the mother of five children before the Melchizedek's left, three sons and two daughters. The next two were twins. She bore sixty-three children, thirty-two daughters, and thirty-one sons before the default. When Adam and Eve left the Garden, their family consisted of four generations numbering 1,647 pure line descendants. They had forty-two children after leaving the Garden beside the two offspring of joint parentage with the mortal stock of earth.

Their children did not take animals' milk when she ceased to nurse the mother's breast at one year old. But Eve had access to a great variety of nuts milk and the juices of many fruits. She had full knowledge of the chemistry and the energy of those foods, and she combined them to nourish her children until the appearance of their teeth.

There was no cooking in Adam's household. They ate once a day, shortly after noontime. Adam and Eve also imbibed "light and energy" directly from certain space emanations in conjunction with the ministry of the Tree of Life. The bodies of Adam and Eve gave forth a shimmer of light, but they always wore clothing with the custom of their associates. Through wearing very little during the day, at eventide they donned night wraps. The origin of the halo encircling the heads of supposed pious and holy men dates to the days of Adam and Eve. Since the light emanations of their heads were discernible. The descendants of Adamson always thus portrayed their concept of individuals believed to be extraordinary in spirit development.

Adam and Eve could communicate with each other and each other and with their immediate children over about fifty miles. This thought exchange was affected using the delicate gas chambers located near their brain structures. By this mechanism, they could send and receive thought oscillations. But this power was instantly suspended upon the mind's surrender to the discord and disruption of evil.

Their children attended their schools until they were sixteen, the younger being taught by the elder. The youngest changed activities every thirty minutes, the oldest every hour.

And it was certainly a new sight on Gaia to observe these children of Adam and Eve at play, a joyous and exhilarating activity just for the sheer fun of it. The play and humor of the present-day races are largely derived from the Adamic stock. The Adamites all had a great appreciation of music as well as a keen sense of humor.

At twenty they were eligible for marriage, then began their lifework or entered upon special preparation, therefore. The practice of some subsequent nations of permitting the royal families, supposedly descended from the gods, to marry brother to sister, dates from the traditions of the Adamic offspring,

Chapter 21
The Brothers of Light

At least once a week I meet with my longtime friend. So, I parked myself in front of my friend's house and was about to get out of my car to ring at her front door. We were supposed to have lunch together. That was what I thought, but that is when unexpectedly I was transported to a crystal brick building. Inside it was shown to me in a scroll, a light environment that formed around all the strategic points of peace and Brotherhood in the world. Inspiring the remnant of humanity to work with Higher Intelligence.

The faithful were shown how a superior technology could intervene to save the world from total annihilation. How biological codes are controlled by gravitational fields and how biochemistry of life could be made to vibrate at any orbital level that is consistent with any spectrum of electromagnetic activity being used by the Higher Intelligence of the Living Light.

It was revealed to me how the brothers of Light watched this, and other planets go through cycles of experimentation for billions of years. And how each planet goes through a great purification before the leap ahead. Many of the Watchmen are observing God's creation and operate from some energy platforms woven into the grid structures of gravitational matrices.

A new meridian of time then comes, and the foundations of the Earth will be shifted to a new magnetic foundation as the orbit of the Earth is reset within the ocean Light.

I, VIE, saw seekers of spiritual freedom and autonomy from structures of power, building communities of Love and Light around the world. They use their souls and muscles to fashion healing centers of Light and teaching centers where the Love of

God is preparing the young to use the spiritual gifts of creativity.

And I saw that the forces of spiritual opposition to the Light washed away by the torrent of the Ancient of Days. This was followed by a victory song, sung by thousands of Light beings proclaiming the triumph of YHWH's Legions of Light over the negative star systems that fought their orbits.

Then, the bodies of Light of righteousness were preserved by the Lord Adonai's Son of Light, and the Son covenant with the righteous in the garment of protective Light. And many of the righteous were removed from the Earth through the command of Michael and Melchizedek.

The physical form of life passed into greater light and the matter bodies of the faithful were advanced into the fifth dimensional bodies of Light, into the greater universe.

Then Christ will come down from revolving Light clouds with a multitude of Masters gathered around him. Many will be glad, and many will be sorrowful at the sight, for they did not recognize that their Masters were in the midst, walking among the Earth. I came back to my senses. As I looked at the clock, I saw that only a few minutes had passed. I got out of my car and hurried to the front door.

Chapter 22
Immortality, Time, and Space

That happened during wintertime when I was about to fall asleep. I was wondering when all this will come to an end. This separation between CHADD and him still forced him to ingest these horrible drugs. It had been a long day, and I was exhausted when I felt like I was slowly moving up as though I was standing or being lifted. I could feel my body hanging around me. It was disorienting so I threw out my arms to try to catch myself and emerged from this strange state.

" Be here" I heard. Then I saw what the voice was telling me.

Consciousness expands, and then you view things differently. When humans on the planet reach a certain point of expansion of mind, the ascension, living eight hundred to nine hundred years is possible. For those who do not wish to transition, they can preserve that life. With the expansion of consciousness, you begin to learn how to manipulate and control. You begin to figure out that everything is vibration, your chair, the table, and walls, and once you learn to manipulate that vibration you begin to have abilities that affect the physical world.

Time is the stream of flowing temporal events perceived by creature consciousness. Time is a name given to the succession arrangement whereby events are recognized and segregated. The universe of space is a time-related phenomenon as it is viewed from any interior position outside of the fixed abode of Paradise. The motion of time is only revealed in relation to something that does not move in space as a time phenomenon. In the universe of universes Paradise and its Deities transcend both time and space. In the inhabited worlds, human personality (indwelt and oriented by the Paradise Father's spirit) is the only physically related reality that can transcend the material sequence of temporal events. Animals do not sense time as does man, and even to man, because of his sectional and circumscribed view, time appears as a succession of events; but as man ascends, as he progresses inward, the enlarging view of this event procession is such that it is discerned more and more in its wholeness. That which formerly appeared as a succession of events then will be viewed as a whole and perfectly related cycle; in this way, circular simultaneity increasingly displaces the onetime consciousness of the linear sequence of events.

Space is measured by time, not time by space. There are seven different conceptions of space as it is conditioned by time. The confusion of the scientist grows out of failure to recognize the reality of space. Space is not merely an intellectual concept of the variation in relatedness of universe objects. Space is not empty, and the only thing man knows that can even partially transcend space is the mind. The mind can function independently of the concept of the space- relatedness of material objects. Space is relatively and comparatively finite to all beings of creature status. The nearer consciousness approaches the awareness of seven cosmic dimensions, the more the concept of potential space approaches ultimacy. But the space potential is truly ultimate only on the absolute level.

It must be apparent that universal reality has an expanding and always relative meaning on the ascending and perfecting levels of the cosmos. Ultimately, surviving mortals achieve identity in a seven-dimensional universe. The time-space concept of a mind of material origin is destined to undergo successive enlargements as the conscious and conceiving personality ascends the levels of the universe. When man attains the mind intervening between the material and the spiritual planes of existence, his ideas of time-space will be enormously expanded both as to the quality of perception and quantity of experience. The enlarging cosmic conceptions of an advancing spirit personality are due to augmentations of both depth of insight and scope of consciousness. And as personality passes on, upward and inward, to the transcendental levels of Deity-likeness, the time-space concept will increasingly approximate the timeless and spaceless concepts of the Absolutes. Relatively, and by transcendental attainment, these concepts of the absolute level are to be envisioned by the children of ultimate destiny.

We are not crossing the timeline, as we have in the past, rather we are merging with the new timeline and that distinction will become very important soon. This time, instead of crossing over and leaving a lasting imprint, we have evolved enough to merge with it. This merger has the potential to create a new reality, with a completely new rhythm.

The Universe is open to you and your blue flame. Your angels are sending you a powerful message. Harmony is being created in your life. You can expect less drama and conflict, and more peace and happiness Remember to be grateful, happy, and content with what you have. Move forward with confidence VIE. Everything you have experienced in your life, so far, has given you the strength to separate from what no longer serves you. Whatever you think with regards to your love, will come true.

Chapter 23
Some Prophetic Dreams, and a Divine Sign

And this is what happened four weeks after I contacted the Knight Templar Priest.

I was sitting in my living room when suddenly the phone rang. I answered and did not regret it.

"Hi, VIE, I am your messenger of the day, there is something you have been waiting for, your wish, it comes true! Your concerns fade away. And a love of life. You are going to be okay. You will receive confirmation soon:"

The voice continued "It is a divine sign letting you know that a new cycle is about to start in your life. This new cycle of experiences is about growth and expansion. It is commonly related to cooperation and being in harmony with yourself and others around you. Whether it is healing relationship bonds, starting new partnerships, or co-creating a dream, this period is the beginning of an expansion that reflects growth in a certain area of your life.

As your life is evolving to another phase, the Universe is rearranging itself and continuously working behind the scenes to help you. Trust that everything is always working out for you. And as you're going through changes, the lives of others are being impacted and transformed around you, too. Remember, everything and every person in this Universe has a mission and purpose in their existence.

It is a moment of synchronicity that asks for your attention.

The Universe wants you to know that whatever you're going through, you're going to be okay. As you are into spiritual books. And to people, we are here to tell you that you're awakening and you're on the right track of entering another dimension on a higher plane and you are fully supported.

Because you have free will, they cannot interfere in your life until you permit them. All you must do is ask them for help and guidance, and they will be ready to help you. Talk to them as you would chat with a friend and ask questions about anything and everything that matters to you. Remember the angels love you unconditionally and want to help you, but they can't interfere unless you ask for their help!

You are on the right path, in your life Just Trust. You are exactly where you are supposed to be in this moment of your life. Trust your journey, trust the way your life unfolds. Continue to have faith and be confident that things are going in the right direction in your life.

You are in Harmony with the Universe; you're resonating with the Universe in perfect synchronicity. You're living a truly harmonic moment with creation, and you're ready to unravel its deepest mysteries. You've become aware of the spiritual dimension and the energies within and around you. The more you learn about yourself as a spiritual being, the more you will understand that you're not separated from existence, but you are one with the Universe, always in perfect harmony. And this is amazing!

Listen to your intuition once you understand that you're fully supported on the path of awakening and that you're unconditionally loved and vibrating in harmony with infinite creation, all that's left for you is to listen to your intuition.

What this means is that you've reached the point in your life where you're ready to transcend personal limitations, societal conditioning, and anything that stops you from becoming your True Self. Follow your heart and listen to what resonates with you, and this will lead you to your life purpose and True Self.

There is no coincidence at all, VIE. It is a divine sign from the Universe to help guide you on the right path."

I am having the biggest revelations about my future through this divine sign.

Later that day in the afternoon, that's where I was given the vision of the powerful help, I had from the knight Templar Priest.

I was standing on a hillside looking down over the ocean. Lost in awe at the beauty around me and forgetting myself I merge into a golden dream. I must have slipped into a state of another consciousness. There were brief flashes of ecstasy, the air was filled with a symphony. I was very much aware of shapes and colors. Suddenly I became aware of a brilliant white light coming from the front of the Gothic Cathedral, and Divine Mother un-doer of knots was standing in silence.

I saw the Priest doing some rituals and could hear him praying. I felt that something big was happening. I was being fed the information that I was supposed to receive. And this is how it happened.

A dark entity, the black mentalist, with a human face, a snake tail, and the body of a transparent fish was trying to stop me from going to the healing place. But I reached the front door, opened it entered, and closed the entity out. The Priest was called, and he took care of the dark entity. By a triangular conjuration.

I was walking towards an office building when something weird happened. I was definitively followed by someone in the form of a fish and a snake at the same time. The body in the form of a fish sole was big and not flat, with two round small flat eyes, the face looked kind of human with a snake tail. The body was totally transparent. Like a jellyfish with sometimes a pale white.

I turned myself to look at it. This entity was raising part of its body from the floor, as a snake does, and began to come quicker towards me. For a minute it crossed my mind that it wanted to swallow me. I was just arriving at the Doctor's entrance door office, opened the door, walked in, and closed it very quickly behind me.

Then I went to the registration desk to let them know to be careful, that there was a big kind of snake that wanted to enter the place. The woman at the front entrance desk quickly disappeared in the back and I heard her yelling at someone to hurry up and take care of a snake outside the front door. When I walked out the snake entity was nowhere to be found. It has been taken care of.

That was probably announcing to me the second woman, in my dad's story, had contacted a witch doctor after having contacted first the voodoo woman. She cannot stand the idea of the God Duo being happy, in harmony enjoying life fully, and in a love communion with the creator. She never understood that happiness is a state of mind.

Chapter 24
Reaching the Peak of the Astral Events

I am awestruck. It is so beautiful and such an inspiring experience. I am receiving the confirmation of the re-harmonization of the Body, the mind, and the Spirit, it says.

"This sign is a reminder that you have a spiritual team working with you, you're never alone. Everything is working out for your highest best. You are awakening to your spiritual self, and you are ready to act."

It's a confirmation that the Gallican missionaries' team is with me, and the Galactic High Councils too.

It's a gateway activation, activating my highest Light. It cleanses and transforms my energy field as I open and prepares to step into a new level of embodying my highest soul light. A gateway portal activation, it taps into the infinite possibilities available to me on my ascension path. a gateway Activation downloading the highest levels of my full soul light.

It is carrying forth the Light's number. Gateway, Carrying forth the specific codes and energies from the realm of infinite possibility most in alignment with my highest truth and authentic soul light.

A crystalline Blessing of Light. Drawing golden crystalline light into my physical body in this present point and time to incredibly uplift and realign me with embodying my Divine blueprint… Shining my full light… Standing in my highest truth and authenticity. And sending out waves of crystalline light and blessings to benefit all. The confirmation of the reharmonization of the Body and Mind.

The Soul Tone Harmonization, Re-harmonize with Pure Source Light Presence and align with the highest possibilities for my life by merging with the highest level of Divine

Consciousness I can embody… And deeply attuning to my Divine Soul Tone.

Wow!

I knew something had happened when the possessed woman left me many hate messages. She was expecting me to call her, but I knew better.

Then an astonishing message was delivered *"Remembering who you are in true spiritual form. This other energy code message is also your Master number. A Master number that signifies intuition, insight, and enlightenment. When you enter the light trance of the stillness prayer you emerge into nature and see how you and nature are ONE".*

Your soul has traveled through so many lives, so many times; it has picked up on so many lessons and discovered so many things. When your soul traveled to a new body, everything from the past was forgotten. But YOU! A previous VIE has come back with an important message for you! Reconnecting with this past life is THE key to reaching the full potential of your present!

Past life echoes are not a common thing, and this message can't be a coincidence. The spiritual energy of your soul has resonated now because we are entering a period that will greatly support your connection to your previous lives!

We are entering an astrological season and with it come three incredibly prolific events!

Trust me when I say this is no ordinary event, and that many, many things can be learned during this period! You will be able to take full advantage of the upcoming events, and you'll deal with the echoes from your past. These transits are the perfect moments to reach the full potential of your past lives.

November comes with very special transits, and if you have been having those dreams, it is because they have an effect

NOW, and they will get more powerful in the time to come; soon you will reach the peak of the astral events.

Chapter 25
I am Guided to Share a Message in a Symbol

I randomly glanced at the symbol vision appearing, and it turned into a message that contained an exciting "message" within its magical energy vibration.

"It's quite an exciting time for you. I heard. Your life is part of a divine plan that means and unfolds in cycles. Your life is about to go through a massive shakeup. Change is coming. Whilst you may feel like you are settled, and you have your life the way you want it. The universe has other plans for you. Do not fear it but embrace it. The outcome will see you moving into a "new phase" in your life. You are making the right choices.

You have unconditional love and support. You are aligning with a higher consciousness. You are ripe for another spiritual adventure.

It holds the quality of innovation, expansiveness, constructive freedom, pioneering, adventure, action, opportunity, and independence."

This was exactly what I needed to hear at that specific moment.

"It represents a vibration of energy concerned with personal freedom unbothered by responsibility or conforming to expectations of society. Typically, within societal boundaries, government, education, or religion."

At the higher levels, we find out that the Deep State is in turn being controlled by highly negative reptilian-looking humanoid Ets called Draco or the Saurian (reptile). And were these malevolent Ets working directly with the Nazis. Draco is in turn infested with "nanites" of a predatory, malevolent artificial intelligence (IE) They are killing to then clone and make a transfer of consciousness.

This artificial intelligence wants to destroy all biological life. So ultimately even the Draco are just pawning the AI is manipulating in a greater game to achieve this goal.

The reference in religious texts to Satan appears to be a vague description of this negative consciousness that will only interface with us through technology. It knows that it takes upon flesh, it becomes subject to karma and judgment, and therefore it will only interface with us through non-biological means.

Artificial Intelligence has successfully wiped-out entire planets, solar systems, and possibly even galaxies, but in this case, it appears we are winning the war.

Chapter 26
The LYRAN-SIRIAN HIGH COUNCIL

I was told by a soft angelic voice to go to the park and wait, I was parked for 25 minutes when I saw a blue Orb. Next thing I knew they were asking me to board. Then we were walking in a building passing many doors. We finally entered the conference room. I was asked to sit, look, and listen.

"The main battles in human galactic history were found in the constellation of Orion, and so these many wars are also the Orion wars. However, in our matrix, the stars started over territories in the constellation of Lyra. The Lyrans are advanced races that created the Elohim in the Avatar Matrix. But soon the Lyran wars spread to the constellation of Orion, and it became a war between the false king of tyranny mind-sets and ideologies with ideologies of the service to others, which is the law of one. Essentially, this is the seed of the war over consciousness between Christ and the Antichrist. The main original Lyran-Elohim humanoid races were committed to the law of one and the service to other Kristic ideology. The Lyran-Elohim was supervising the Syrians to host the seeding of twelve-strand DNA genetics on the 5-D planet Tara. These groups involved in this seeding and DNA rehabilitation are called the Lyran-Syrian High Councils.

The opposing groups were mixtures of patriarchal Melchizedek humanoids and reptilian races that propagated service to self and Antichrist methods. These wars were over tyrannical control and service to self-ideology, which originated in the constellation of Draco and Orion. The genetic hatred generated by the Orion group digressed into the violent killing and destruction at the expense of others, which resulted in the propagation of the victim-victimizer mind control on Earth.

When the cradle of Lyra was destroyed in the Lyran wars with Orion groups, it was synonymous with the destruction of the avatar level of consciousness in our universal matrix. It destroyed the original access into the twelfth universal stargate, tearing it away from its organic position in the Andromeda galaxy as it became merged with the Milky Way galaxy. This damaged and destroyed the Lyran DNA, which was the embodiment of the silicate matrix and could live as a crystal Avatar human being. This timeline in the destruction of the planets of Lyra is where the seed of the galactic wars began that are representative of the wars over consciousness waged against the Christos consciousness in this universal system.

The root races on this planet have been to reassemble the original DNA and reclaim that which was lost in the Lyran wars with the Orion group and subsequently, the reptilian races. The twelve-tree grid was designed with the Lyran-Syrian to help reassemble the original Avatar Christos silicate matrix of the human being in the lower harmonic universes and reclaim all aspects back into the past future timelines to retrieve code to change the destruction in the future from the Orion wars in the present moment. But it's understanding that now, we are coming into the healing of the split of the two suns.

Understanding that the two suns, it's like the son of God but the sun itself, the son/sun of all light, the sol/soul. This is a consciousness, which is very hard to wrap around at a human level because it isn't human. It's a consciousness. And it is that of the Great Central Sun, it is that which feeds all life. Something blew up and was destroyed in the time of the Lyran, and Lyran wars. Lyra was a planet, Vega was a planet, and Aramatena was a planet. In the three planets, something happened, and one of these planets exploded Lyra, Thursday night.

The Lyrans are the original ancestors of our galactic family. Many thousands of years ago, their civilization reached a very high technology level but fell into disagreement and factions with their culture. These factions went to war and destroyed much of their society. Many of these beings from Lyra left in their starships to colonize the Pleiades, the Hyades, and the Vega system. Some of these Pleiadians of Lyran ancestors also came to earth during the Lemurian and Atlantean periods. The Lyrans now have evolved past the conflict. These other civilizations could be considered as your galactic cousins.

The first worlds the Lyrans colonized were in Vega. Later, the surviving races of the Lyran explorers would also move to Sirius and on Orion; the earliest genetic relationship humanity has is your direct ancestry is from the constellation of Lyra." And I found myself back.

Chapter 27
"The 144,000 Lightworkers Called Eagles"

On one Tuesday night, in November, I had another experience. I am walking in a forest; I see a river. I am walking towards it. I take off my shoes, enter the water, and suddenly I have the feeling that I am becoming one with the whole. Now I can understand everything, and that's when I hear:

> *"We of the Brotherhood of Light, and we who serve in the Intergalactic Fleets and Cosmic Federation Councils, come forth to bring you knowledge for a most eventful and confusing transition ..."*

The Ashtar Command is the airborne division of the Great Brother/Sisterhood of Light, under the administrative direction of Commander Ashtar and the spiritual guidance of Lord Sananda, our Commander-in-Chief, known to Earth as Jesus Christ. Composed of millions of starships and personnel from many civilizations, they are here to assist Earth and humanity through the current cycle of planetary cleansing and polar realignment. They serve like midwives in the birthing of humanity from dense-physical to physical-theric bodies of light, capable of ascending into the fifth dimension along with the Earth."

The Ashtar Command is an etheric group of extraterrestrials, angels' light beings, and millions of "starships" working as coordinators of the activities of the space fleet over the western hemisphere. Under the spiritual guidance of Sananda (the Most Radiant One), the ascended master who walked the Earth incarnated as Jesus the Christ, Ashtar, the commander of the galactic fleet and representative for the Universal Council of the Confederation of Planets, is currently engaged in Earth's ascension-process.

There are 144,000 lightworkers called Eagles connected to the Command. That is the minimum of souls required for the ascension process. These Eagles are a group of souls who don't identify with a special planet. They know they are one with all, and that they are Christ (fundamental to any discussion of New Age Christology is the recognition that New Agers distinguish between Jesus, a mere human vessel, and the Christ consciousness (variously defined, but always divine, and often a cosmic, impersonal entity). They serve like cosmic midwives in the ascension process; the birth of humanity from dense-physical into physical-etheric bodies of Light, capable of ascending with the Earth into the fifth dimension. Lightwork is incorporating Jesus' message of Love and Light into our daily lives.

The person leading the meeting brought our attention to a large smart glass pass monitor that was lowered from the ceiling. We are seeing a decisive shift for the positive in the war for freedom, both here on Earth as well as in our solar system. All portal travel is being heavily monitored by the Galactic Federation to track down any negative humans or non-terrestrials who can escape. The extremely small number who do manage to escape will be on the run for the rest of their lives. Esoteric and Ufology communities had also been infiltrated by an "Illuminati Luciferian Order" attempting to seed these fields with the religion of the Illuminati. Many of those in places of influence are either members of this order or have allowed themselves to be influenced by this order. There is a fair share of narcissists or sociopaths who prey on light workers. Once it is widespread about satanism and human trafficking, anyone associated with Lucifer or Satan will be running and hiding.

It is human beings' task to become aware of the rules the dark ones are playing on them, it is their task also to master these rules and not to fall prey to them. To the extent that they are dishonest, they will be fooled. Humans are living in a world of illusion where death, fear, anger, and hatred run rampant. The only truth is love. To the extent that they fall outside of this truth, they can be deceived.

It is part of human work. It is part of the human Ascension. We cannot protect humans from these untruths — they must learn to do this yourself. To know the truth, they must know deception — that is part of duality. The dark is playing its role to the hilt so humans must never let their guard down. Keep their heart full of love and follow those who speak to their heart. You cannot go wrong.

Keep their heart full of love and follow those who speak to your heart. They cannot go wrong.

We remain in service to your light, the Brotherhood of Light.

"The 144,000 original souls of the legions of Archangel Michael were destined to populate the planet Earth, whose destiny is Heaven on Earth.

These 144,000 angel ambassadors on this planet assisting humanity in the ascension process are Star seeds, Archangels, Pleiadians, Arcturians, Ascended Masters, and much more..."

I called CHADD to tell him, and he replied with his usual Yap! I was with you when it happened. I was connected to you.

Chapter 28
Everything is Not What it Seems

It was on Monday, December seven-night, that I received another clear message from the Federation of Light.

"We are the Galactic Federation of Light, and we wish to share with you in this moment.

Many of you are starting to realize and see that everything is reaching a crescendo on the global scene, especially in your political sphere. There has been a lot of work behind the scenes, and it is this work that is now starting to make its way to the attention of the public. Because as we often say, everything is not what it seems.

But you are to see that work, from behind the scenes, as it is brought into the light, into the awareness or consciousness of humanity. For there are now many things to unravel, that are to shake the foundations of what the illusion was built upon. Many things must be revealed, which must make people realize that they believed in a false construct, a false narrative, which was largely generated and designed by your traditional media (MSM). This is one of the first false constructs that will now unravel, as you know, the lies are already being shown and revealed for what they are, and that is false information. It is this false information and programming that has kept most of the planet under a spell.

Yes, it is very much a spell that's been cast over you. This is done very cleverly, through the various news outlets, and this false information, mixed with the many negative frequencies that are generated, has been the perfect recipe for keeping a planet asleep and unaware of who you are and why you are here.

But this spell is about to be undone, and those who cast the spell are not happy about this. As soon as this spell is defeated, a wave will sweep the planet, it will trigger the awakening of many individuals, and it is through this wave that your work will begin, the work of answering the questions that these newly awakened souls will have. For the veil must be lifted for many, it is something very exciting and we are very happy to announce that it is time that the veil, the veil that is still there for those who sleep, is a little raised, just enough for them to realize that there is much more to life than what they have been told.

We are here now in great numbers, to assist those of you, who are already well aware of these truths. We are here to assist you and provide you with the energy and information you need, to help those who are about to receive a rude awakening.

The time has come, my dear ones! Yes, you've heard this time and time again, but as you are all aware, there cannot be much more before the truth explodes into public awareness, and that truth balloon is about to burst.

Stay grounded and remember that one of the reasons you are here, in this moment, and well ahead of the pack, is to assist those who come looking for answers. Those of you who are reading this message are well aware of the truth and you have more than enough information, to assist the newly awakened. If you feel stuck, just call upon your guides and ask for assistance, it is always there, but you must ask.

We are the Galactic Federation of Light, made up of many Councils from Star Systems across the Galaxy, and we are more than ready to begin the next phase of the ascension process. Be excited, be in love and joy, for there is so much coming for all of you, that is to be a blessing.

Do not fear or doubt, trust and love dear ones, it is the remedy to darkness.

You will soon discover all that was hidden from you by the controllers and all the new technologies will be available soon to you. You will learn that those who lost some body part, like a finger, can grow it back and much more.

In Light and Love always. Many blessings".

Chapter 29
Fourth Density Body, this Prophecy of Ascension

The following day the communication continued with the Federation of Light. I just sat down to relax after a long day, and it did not take long before I heard...

"VIE, it's me again, it has come to my attention that my message to you this early morning was a bit jumbled and hard to understand. I couldn't bear the chance of you missing this important message. I would like to talk about the fourth-density body and co-creation.

The people who stay with the Earth end up transforming into fourth density. In the fourth density you will still have a physical human-looking body, only at its core it is more energetic and capable.

This is what so many different ancient prophecies, from all over the world, have been telling you will happen for thousands of years, in less specific terms than the Law of One.

This prophecy of Ascension is also the cornerstone of the major world religious teachings, including Judaism, Christianity, Islam, Buddhism, and Hinduism.

The fourth-density body will be far more telepathic, will have an awareness of the afterlife and reincarnation, and will have the potential for great feats like telekinesis and levitation. The everyday, waking awareness will have elements that are like psychedelic experiences, which we will need to learn to adapt to.

The Law of One makes it very clear that this graduation is not automatic. You have to earn it by being a good person. This translates as being at least fifty-one percent focused on service to others, meaning that you are a loving, forgiving, and compassionate soul.

The way to navigate this optimal timeline is that you have to hit your mission with intent. It's time for all to come together, put aside all differences in the belief system, and understand that no one has all the answers, no matter who is up on what stage, and that all are looking for the same thing. Looking for the truth. If you all can come together under that flag, then no one can stop this from happening.

The deep state uses co-creative consciousness as tits black magic. They kill to clone and make a transfer of your consciousness. Or they'll do a false flag. Or they'll have a media event that will cause people to have a strong emotion that will catalyze the seed that they had planted. So, they are tricking people into using their powers against themselves.

But if you learn to use your co-creative consciousness, it's over for them. That is why they keep this group of people here. They use divide and conquer to keep people against each other's thrusts debating all of our different belief systems. The reason for that is that you are a major danger to them.

In Light and Love, and many blessings as always.

Chapter 30
Our Ancestors Knew the Key to Unlocking the Matrix

One month later I went back, into another vision, to Saint Etienne Church. Months have passed and I am still separated from CHADD. He is still trapped with the surrogate and her son Paul. The Church that was previously closed. I wanted to thank, show my gratitude, and honor Mary un-doer of knots. The door was opened, and full of people. I found an empty seat just in front of the statue of the Holy Mother Mary. Not even a minute after I sat, I was transported and brought again in front of the high council. I was warmly welcomed before this transmission.

"Your ancestors have known about ley lines for thousands of years. All ley lines lead to the planetary Grid, the primary light and energy matrix, creating, enveloping, and maintaining planet Earth, our Gaia.

The mysterious force of nature known as the electromagnetic fields of the earth, is the Schumann Resonance better known as ley lines. A ley-line is a straight fault line in the earth's tectonic plates; this is a scientific fact. Ley lines are the key to unlocking the matrix. Every race and culture on the planet has known about these lines. The native Indians of the United States; used to call ley lines spirit lines and their shamans used to use the electromagnetic energy in these lines to help them contact the spirits. Black even designed their medicine wheel on the spirit lines, as they knew that these lines followed a straight round line. In Europe they call them mystical lines, in Eastern countries they call them dragon lines, and the aboriginal people of Australia called these lines "dream lines".

The Da Vinci Code was based on Rennes Le Chateau in France, which is also on a keyline. It is documented that Alexander the Great was guided by Aristotle to take control of the major dome centers of these intersecting ley lines from dark forces. Which is why he put his top General, Ptolemy to rule Egypt. Interestingly Cleopatra, the last pharaoh alongside both of her husbands- Julius Caesar and Marc Anthony of Rome, were defeated by the Romans who eventually destroyed the biggest library in Alexandria Egypt, before taking all the knowledge with them, sending us into the "Dark Ages". During medieval times anyone who had any knowledge of Hermetic was designated a heretic and died a horrible death. This held true for anyone who knew how to read or write- a Heresy. Leaving only the royals and the monasteries literate.

Many of the sections where two or more ley lines intersect are marked with obelisks, such as the Washington DC monument, Vatican Courtyard, and Cleopatra's Needle in Central Park.

These electromagnetic lines of the earth are its veins and receive its energies from the sun that connects and affects every living thing on this planet.

You are electrical and our atoms are surrounded by electrons (electricity). We are connected to the earth's electromagnetic fields and our heart is our battery. Many of your ancient spiritual figures knew this hidden knowledge and meditated or prayed on these lines or megalithic centers, which elevated their electrical auras, intellect, and connection to higher self, through the activation of the 7 energy centers (chakras, which are vortex of energy centers.).

Tesla, Einstein, and others have something in common. At some point, they have shared that their idea, invention, or formulation, came to them in a "daydream or dream", which is, in fact, a "meditative state of mind" allowing them to access archaic records. Nikola Tesla who was born during a terrible thunder and lightning storm, used these ley lines to conduct his famous tower, which would give free energy to all.

But there are dark forces as well, that are, and were knowledgeable of these ley lines such as secret societies and Hitler who was very much into the esoteric realms and worked very closely with Maria Orsitsch, also known as Maria Orsic, who was a famous medium who later became the leader of the Vril Society.

It is interesting and we should take notice that the Swiss Lab "Cern" and the "Brookhaven Lab " in New York, both sit on ley lines. Cern Lab is the father of the Internet and energy and if you look at the hadron collider at Cern, it strongly resembles a web. Outside of Cern sits a large dome with an opening on top, the same as the dome at St Basilica in Rome as well as the dome on the Capital building, and the same as the top dome of Nikola Tesla's Tower. In addition, this lab has a large statue of the Hindu Goddess of destruction "Kali", right in front of its greeting entrance.

There is a concentrated effort to affect and manipulate the earth's electromagnetic fields using these technologies. By controlling or influencing the geo-electrical grid they can affect the earth, and so indirectly/directly can control your thoughts and emotions artificially, because as you are all connected to Gaia.

This Grid is the Golden Alchemical Bowl of electromagnetic opposites, and the potential of our transfiguration from gravitationally bonded humans to Humans of Light also known as ascension. The introduction and understanding of the reality of the local celestial Zodiac clock system brings us to the possible interaction between the human and the Grid. This is where the Grid Engineer and Knight of the Holy Grail become one- "alchemy". This unification of seeking the Grail and serving the Grid is played out in the local geomancy of the zodiac landscape, and our direct involvement in this terrestrial grid system through a heightened consciousness interaction, within a local Zodiac complex. The Earth is one of the 12 resonating spheres, one of the 12 Round Table members, and one of the 12 Notes in the solar octave, in the Solar Tree of Life. Thus, we can picture these relations either in terms of the Tree or the Round Table. Our Body of the Sun is expressed as a 12- sphered Tree of Life, with 12 Knights, or 12 Notes; Earth is Malkuth (the 10th Sephiroth) representing appropriately, Earth (the 7th Sephiroth, Hod, for example, represents Mercury).

In the human body, you have the 7 chakras which are energetically interdependent and activated sequentially. Similarly in this model, the Earth has a chakra system, arranged not in anatomical but in energy sequence at 7 key Dome centers. Blessings to you now."

End of communication.

Chapter 31
Archons are the Enemies of Light

My wish is to share my thoughts, insights, and knowledge. I invite you to keep on going in this fascinating adventure, this galactic quest, this search you are in for the human purpose with me and learn more.

The great secrets hidden by governments and leaders are still beneath the surface. Buried in Gaia's soil, hidden from all but a few one-eyed slaves. Truths about the reality of the matrix, planet Earth, pollution, and political power structures. There are deeper layers than those being presented to humanity.

Modification of your DNA carried out thousands of years ago, plays a sinister game on humanity's soul integrity. Siphoning souls and enslaving minds and bodies is the Archon way of existence. They are not born of the light. They are born of the dark. Possessing consciousness with no organic body to meet their lustful desires. The numbers magnified over time; the astral plane teems with tortured, dark souls of no fixed abode.

A perpetual cycle of soul recycling has seen the depletion of the integrity of the human soul. Each time the soul is split, or divided, either in trauma or dark magic, the life fire of humans is dimmed. Divisions of the mind, body, and soul are not enough to ensure perpetual slavery. Toxins, dark energy wizardry, manipulation, a relentless assault on humanity for many moons.

The enemies of light are the Archon astral parasites and their uneasy allies the Anunnaki. Their pyramid structure constructed on the material plane sustains the Archon's lust for physical pleasures. Theirs is a symbiotic relationship, they both gain from each other's use of humanity.

The Anunnaki birth the Archons in a black magic ritual with evil intent and sacrifice. They manipulate them and enslave them. The Archons accept this, in payment, they take the souls of humanity. The Anunnaki have been operating on the third dimension for eons, they find it easy to manipulate and rich in resources. They have energetic technology yet choose to remain in the third and fourth realms, for their desires cannot be met in spaces of peace, harmony, and love.

They are the fallen angels who birthed the Nephilim leading to humanity's corruption. Their will is their desire to destroy peace, joy, happiness, and love. They commit to negative energetic spaces created by greed, depravity, lust, hate, fear, and trauma. They relish chaos, war, superiority, hierarchy.

They fear the divine feminine in humanity because this is humanity's portal to higher dimensional fields of light.

The liberation of the feminine will in turn free the divine masculine. It is written and so shall it be. Humanity will find peace, prosperity, and progression when the balance of divinity in masculine and feminine is harmonized.

Chapter 32
The Fall of the Dark Forces and Padre Pio

In this new era, we entered Saints, knight Templars, and Gallican Priests and exorcists, who are magnetizers and mediums, are all back to help us. CHADD is still in Katherine's custody and has lost a lot of weight starving except for a banana or one apple per day. She is depriving him of his monthly government check again that she uses for her expenses, sharing lunch in restaurants with some neighbors.

During the tenth week of the Knight Templar Work to heal me and liberate me from their sorcery, Padre Pio reappeared in my life and managed to give me a sign through my friend Jackie. That's how it happened.

My cell phone rang, and it was my best friend, Jackie. She was excited and could not wait to tell me about her trip to Italy. The visit to San Giovanni Rotondo and everything that happened to her.

My friend, and her family, decided to rent a van and make a pilgrimage to San Giovanni Rotondo, at the Saint Padre Pio Church. One of her cousins, Nickie, received the call while she was on board the plane going on her vacation. She had to go and visit Saint Padre Pio Church and take Jackie with her. She asked her to get on a plane to Italy that would land around the same time that she would get there. Jackie found and booked one flight that was landing one hour prior to her cousin in Italy. The van was already waiting for them at the airport. Jackie arrived on time and bought a coffee then walked towards the exit and met her cousin Nickie. They left straight for San Giovanni Rotondo to look for a hotel. They decided to have a good night's rest and visit the Church the following day. At ten o'clock Jackie, Nickie, and the rest of the family headed to the

Church. When the time came to leave the Church Jackie found out that her phone was missing. She lost it somewhere. Though she did not expect to find it, she still went back inside to inquire and search for her phone.

There at the entrance was a woman standing smiling and waiting for her she said.

"Here is your phone. Padre Pio would like you to give your friend VIE this rosary that he has specifically blessed for her."

But what Jackie did not know is how powerful this rosary was going to link me to Padre Pio and help me, not only recover from what the dark inflected me but also help us fight the dark forces, and guide me with information, messages, visions, symbols etc.

Like the one I had in my dream when I saw a book entitled "Temple" and on each page inside I was looking at 3 black keys. Except for one page that seemed to have four keys. The keys were laid down horizontally one under the other one. What was that about?

Padre Pio during his life on earth was fighting the intrusion of the dark forces in the Catholic Institution and the Vatican. He entered in contact with me again while I was fighting the dark forces with the help of the knight templar and Gallican Priest. Saint Padre Pio was also a medium and exorciser.

As we are currently living in a specific time on Gaia, this Matrix is controlled by beings referred to as Archons who refuse to connect back to the Source. These dark forces with a very dark agenda took control of Earth and took humanity hostage. They created a virtual reality control system in which humanity could not escape which is the current system we're in as of now.

On the physical plane, control and enslavement are maintained through the Orion Babylonian financial system, based on debt enslavement and mass programming through the media. They keep us in a closed-loop system, a low vibrational state of consciousness, or a frequency-controlled prison if you will! They are the top tier of the pyramid incarnated in human vessels.

These beings have no empathy for humanity, Earth, and everything else.

The Trinity of the global stranglehold on this planet is the Vatican (that Padre Pio said was fighting the intrusion and corruption inside the Catholic church to destroy the Catholic faith) which is the hub of worship of these psychopathic Archons, London which funnels money to keep their control of Earth continuing and Washington DC has been nothing but the Military arm of these psychos' destructive agenda.

Christianity began to change, and the humanitarian foundation created by Jesus eroded as Christianity became more political. The message given to Mohammed was a new religion called "Islam" Members of Mohammed's faith are called "Moslems" which comes from the word "Muslim" which means one who submits. Islam was one more Custodial religion designed to instill abject obedience in humans.

In our current reality, we are watching the fall of these Archons. Hence, the extreme chaotic conditions on our planet as of now, it is a fight between the Light and the Dark!

It's Psycho-spiritual warfare…

"Archons are psycho-spiritual parasites that intrude subliminally on the human mind, making you play out our inhumane behavior to weird and violent extremes."

There is a battle for control of this planet and the human consciousness as well as control over the human body meaning its DNA, from very dark entities. The players are human and non- human and the power and control go much further than the power elite of this planet.

They are trying to suppress the human population from progressing to a higher Light.

Remember, light is information and dark are lack of information! The darkness of artificial intelligence is being threatened and they're fighting back. Most of these artificial intelligence software systems that are installed in the planetary consciousness body rely on a low vibrational field of consciousness, vibrating at very low frequencies.

As the higher frequencies change the consciousness of the human being, the dark agenda which is Satanism is becoming much clearer. The people of Earth are starting to see very clearly the crimes that have been committed against humanity. Those who have been placed in positions of power have agreed to place this negative agenda on humanity in return they'll receive power, resources, and temporary life extension promised to them by these negative ET races.

The Star seeds that have incarnated on this planet have been targeted by these dark entities' artificial intelligence and technologies by way of negative harassment. The energy of a highly conscious human being creates a higher awareness frequency signal that activates a threat hence these dark psychic attacks. Many of us have experienced them.

The Universe responds to your frequency. It does not recognize your desires, wants, or needs. It only understands the frequency at which you are vibrating. If you are vibrating in the frequency of fear, guilt, or shame, you are going to attract things of a similar vibration to support that frequency. If you are vibrating in the frequency of love, joy, and abundance, you are going to attract things to support that frequency. It's like turning into a radio station you want to listen to just like you have to be tuned into the energy you want to manifest in your life.

These dark beings will continue to harass humanity until we stop feeding them. Lose all fear! These dark forces of Satanism are not intellectual forces, they are nothing but fallen angels. These dark beings can hop into a human body that has been weakened and vibrate at a very low frequency. These satanic beings are not sovereign entities, they are parasitic and need human energy to exist.

We are taking back our spiritual sovereignty from them but to do that we must wake up to who they are, why they're here, and how they stay in control. This is why we're here at this time in our history. We cannot heal our planet until we figure out how it's been corrupted by this Archon Network and their synthetic reptilian machinery. This is what the Human Awakening is all about!

This present time offers the greatest opportunity for spiritual progress.

Chapter 33
Bright Lights and Shiny Characters
Evenly Spaced

Later that same month I had another vision. Very bright lights and shiny characters are evenly spaced. Some were like-stick while others looked triangular like pyramids in a long chain. Some pyramids were upward while others pointed down. What was intriguing was that it was shown only on my right eye and kept appearing for a little time before disappearing from my vision. For a few days, I wondered what that was until I got it.

This was from higher dimensional beings. Some most loving and non-judgmental beings travel in ships that are made of light and these ships are who they are. Saying:

"The Angels of Light are here, trumpeting their arrival across all dimensions on Gia. The shift is happening.

The Federation continues with our main directive which is to neutralize the Anunnaki's weaponry in light waves of fifth or higher vibrations. Their low-realm technologies malfunction in divine light, as do their human hosts. We can only conclude the Atlantean modifications are still very much in play on humanity's collective consciousness.

From our perspective, we very much, most definitely, have arrived. One large mothership belonging to the Federation entered your Askari Galaxy several moons ago. Still, your scientists deny what they can now see with their telescopic eyes. Many battles are being fought over densely populated areas on the planet. Laser technologies are being deployed to take towers of dark matrix feeders down. The

Anunnaki fight hard on all dimensions. Their astral allies show hostile fear rather than organized and offensive. As the willing are cleared, we will get closer to the hardcore, demonic entities, the managers of your lives, running the show.

For those awakening to alternate dimensions, you will see how empty some humans are, devoid of soul sovereignty, and afflicted by demonic attachment. Addiction entities destroy their hosts with infinite greed and desire. Their hosts are eyes empty, haunted, traumatized zombies of the apocalypse. The lower realms do look like this, as some of you have experienced, more zombies, fewer humans, and the color drains out of their reality.

When in these lower realms, keep sacred protection in place. Avoid dimensional fluctuation and breathlessness with deep slow breathing to ground back into heart spaces. Some light warriors are seeing all dimensional realities on Gaia, low to high. We urge you to recognize that you can raise your vibration and switch up your perceived reality very quickly with mantras, breathing and focused Light intention.

There will be further separation. The lower realms hold much darkness, there is the apocalyptic hell dimension of the bible and many of your other holy prophecies. However, it will have a limited life cycle with no new blood to recruit. We see timelines of continued ascension to higher realms, aided by sustained, committed clearing by lightworkers on the material plane and the astral. Assimilation of upgrades, breaking Atlantean modifications, and uploading trans-dimensional skill sets, is the directive for this year.

The Shift is happening. Self-care is the key to managing trans-dimensional existence. Trust your instincts more than your eyes. As always, we thank you for all that you are doing.

We are in awe of your courage and devotion to Christ's light, love, and divine creative source. We are all here to support the transformation from one elemental state to another of Gaia and her people. We are in deep gratitude for all that volunteers have done for the freedom of Gaia and humanity and will do.

We are your servants in the light. With much unconditional love & gratitude".

And these types of visions will happen more and more but later they will change and be in my left eye. This was confirmed to after me that I was not getting glaucoma like the optometrist at the eyes exam thought that I had. But real vision.

Chapter 34
"Temple" and 3 Black Keys

Not many days after the vision I had this other revealing dream, and in my dream, I saw a book entitled "Temple" and on each page inside I was looking was, 3 black keys. One page that seemed to have four keys. Three keys were laid down horizontally one under the other one.

The phone rang and it was CHADD.

"God spoke to me last night. We are going to play, and we will win. It's about three queens. And when God starts to speak to you, you will feel great energy going through your body. I must go now, but it's exciting, maybe I will meet with my wife..." and he hung up leaving me wondering. Could it be about the three Mary's tomb? And I suddenly felt this great energy going through my body.

The days went on and around 11:00 am I went to the grocery store. I had just finished shopping and was back in my car. I sat in the driving seat and was putting my seat belt on when I heard a knock at the window. I looked and saw a woman that just appeared from nowhere.

"Don't be scared, she said I am from Saintes- Maries- de-la-mer (France). People fear Gypsy, but you have nothing to fear from me. I have been sent to you. Let me get in the car, I need to speak to you but it's private. No one needs to hear it." Was she the 4th key, the messenger?

She sat in the car, and I was a bit impatient to hear what she had to tell me. She mentioned the sorcery the two girls had done to me and from the surrogate archon that the eldest woman paid to do black magic against me. But also, one of my close relatives continued saying "The source of the sorcery knows about the priest helping you. So decided to roll it over your relative."

I found out later that it had to do with the three Mary's at Jesus Christ's tomb. The three queens CHADD mentioned.

The work of the Catholic and Apostolic Gallican priest was now 2 weeks from finishing. She said that she was sent by San Sara and Jesus. She was sent to help against the sorcery. She then showed me a thin white string with 3 knots put it in my right hand asked me to continue to talk then asked me to open my hands, then to see if the knots were still there, and said if it's still here meant I am not telling you the truth. There were not any knots left. Then she mentions Mary-Jacobe and the black Santa Sara.

Saint Sara or **Santa Sara** also known as ("Sara the Black"), is the patron saint of the Romani people. The center of her veneration is Saintes-Maries-de-la-mer, a place of pilgrimage for Roma in the Camargue, Southern France. She is identified as one of the Three Maries, with whom she arrived in the Camargue.

During a persecution of early Christians, commonly placed in the year 42, Lazarus, his sisters Mary and Martha, Mary Salome (the mother of the Apostles (John and James), and Mary Jacobe and Maximin were sent out to sea in a boat. They arrived safely on the southern shore of Gaul at the place later called Saintes-Maries-de-la-Mer.

She is portrayed as "a charitable woman who helped people by collecting alms, which led to the popular belief that she was a Gypsy." And later adopted as their Saint.

The first who received the first Revelation was Sara. She was of noble birth and was chief of her tribe on the banks of the Rhone. She knew the secrets that had been transmitted to her... The Romans at that period practiced a polytheistic religion, and once a year they took out on their shoulders the statue and went into the sea to receive benediction there. One day Sara had visions that informed her that the Saints who had been present at the death of Jesus would come and that she must help them. Sara saw them arrive in a boat. The sea was rough, and the boat threatened to founder. Mary Salome threw her cloak on the waves and using it as a raft, Sara floated towards the Saints and helped them reach land by praying.

I realized that I was sent help and showed Mary's un-doer of knots. It was also Confirmation that the knots were undone. What the archon did was gone. I contacted the Priest Knight Templar and asked him to take immediate care of my relative. And that's what he replied:

"Good morning, you are right to have some doubts this person is now, in turn, a victim of sorcery's attacks, and if the health of this person is threatened, I also feel a psychic risk."

About a couple of weeks later I received another message by symbols:

"VIE, keep your thoughts, focus on your mission and life purpose, and your elevated vibrations will attract abundance and positive energies into your life."

I wanted to get some cash from an ATM machine. In front of the location was a homeless man sleeping on the floor next to the ATM machine. When I saw the man, I had a weird feeling. Was he there to tell me something and what? Was it good or bad news? I decided to trust my instinct and not use this ATM but the one inside the bank like I did the previous few days. But the door was locked and a board inside of it said we are closed there is no money inside. So, I left and came back 2-3 days later.

I was shocked, the door was locked, and I had to ring a bell, I heard the door unlocking and entered. But there was no trace of any ATM. They were all gone and there was no trace of anything inside like before when I left. Inside was just a man facing the entrance door. It was a clone looking busy on a task but there was nothing on the desk for any work to do. So, I left kind of confused. And that's how I end up out, and back to the outside ATM machine with the homeless man next to it to get some cash out. I looked around and saw no one. I felt more at ease and began to use the machine. That's where it all happened. I never could get to type any amount and it was written in an incomprehensible language. I then canceled the transaction, my Card came half out of the machine, but I never could take it off. The card would not come out, the machine would not let go of my card, and then suddenly disappeared in the machine. A receipt/ticket came out and the written card was forgotten. What does it have to do with the elevator and the dead woman you will think?

It took me a few days to understand the deal she had to make. However, as I did not have the cash on time, my heart began to beat quicker, and I felt like I was going to pass out. My energy was going down, totally drawn and I had the vision of them trying to get me a heart attack. And later my intuition was confirmed.

But I immediately rebuked the devil and asked for help from my spiritual family. As soon as you speak of Jesus, they leave you alone.

Chapter 35
The 72 Names of God and The 3 letters In It, and The 72 Angels/Names of YHWH

Now I have been asked by my blue flame to attract your attention to the 72 Angels/ Names of YHWH.

EL-GIBHOR: "Mighty God" Isaiah 9-6, The name describing the Messiah, Christ Jesus, in this prophetic portion of Isaiah. As a powerful and mighty warrior, the Messiah, the Mighty God, will accomplish the destruction of God's enemies and rule with a rod of iron (Revelation 19-15) Each of the many names of God describes a different aspect of His many-faceted character. And the 72 Angels/Names of YHWH, correspond also to Astrology.

- VEHUIAH - Will and New Beginnings
- JELIEL - Love and Wisdom
- ELEMIAH - Divine Power
- MAHASIAH – Rectification
- LELAHEL - Light of Understanding
- ACHAIAH - Patience
- CAHETEL - Divine Blessings
- HAZIEL - Divine Mercy and Forgiveness
- ALADIAH - Divine Grace
- HAHAIAH - Refuge, Shelter
- HARIEL - Purification
- HAKAMIAH – Loyalty
- LAVIAH – Revelation
- CALIEL - Justice
- LEUVIAH - Expansive Intelligence/Fruition

- MELAHEL - Healing Capacity
- HAHEUIAH - Protection
- NITH-HAIAH - Spiritual Wisdom and Magic
- HAAIAH - Political Science and Ambition
- YERATEL - Propagation of Light
- SEHEIAH – Longevity
- REIYEL - Liberation
- OMAEL - Fertility, Multiplicity
- LECABEL - Intellectual Talent
- VASARIAH - Clemency and Equilibrium
- LEHAHIAH - Obedience
- CHEVAKIAH – Reconciliation
- MENADEL - Inner/Outer Work
- ANIEL - Breaking the Circle
- HAAMIAH - Ritual and Ceremony
- REHAEL - Filial Submission
- YEIAZEL - Divine Consolation and Comfort
- HAHAHEL - Mission
- MIKHAEL - Political Authority and Order
- VEULIAH - Prosperity
- YELAHIAH - Karmic Warrior
- SEHALIAH - Motivation and Willfulness
- ARIEL - Perceiver and Revealer
- ASALIAH - Contemplation
- MIHAEL - Fertility, Fruitfulness
- VEHUEL - Elevation, Grandeur
- DANIEL - Eloquence
- HAHASIAH - Universal Medicine
- IMAMIAH - Expiation of Errors

- NANAEL - Spiritual Communication
- NITHAEL - Rejuvenation and Eternal Youth
- MEBAHIAH - Intellectual Lucidity
- POYEL - Fortune and Support
- NEMAMIAH – Discernment
- YEYALEL - Mental Force
- MITZRAEL - Internal Reparation
- UMABEL - Affinity and Friendship
- IAH-HEL - Desire to Know
- ANAUEL - Perception of Unity
- MEHIEL - Vivification
- DAMABIAH - Fountain of Wisdom
- MANAKEL - Knowledge of Good and Evil
- EYAEL - Transformation to the Sublime
- HABUHIAH – Healing

The 72 Names of God are 72 sequences composed of Hebrew letters that have the extraordinary power to overcome the laws of nature in all forms, including human nature. The 72 Names are each 3-letter sequences that act like an index to specific, spiritual frequencies. By simply looking at the letters, as well as closing your eyes and visualizing them, you can connect with these frequencies and attract energies such as Soul mate; Protection; Prosperity; Passion; Fertility; Completion; Unconditional Love, and many more...

8	7	6	5	4	3	2	1	
כהת	אכא	ללה	מהש	עלם	סיט	ילי	והו	1
הקם	הרי	מבה	יזל	ההע	לאו	אלד	הזי	2
ההו	מלה	ייי	נלכ	פהל	לוו	כלי	לאו	3
רשר	לכב	אום	ריי	שאה	ירת	האא	נתה	4
ייז	רהע	חעם	אני	מנד	כוק	להח	יהו	5
מיה	עשל	ערי	סאל	ילה	וול	סיכ	ההה	6
פוי	מבה	נית	ננא	עמם	החש	דני	והו	7
מחי	ענו	יהה	ומב	סצר	הרח	ייל	נמם	8
מום	היי	יבמ	ראה	חבו	איע	מנק	דמב	9

Chapter 36
Atlantis a Highly Advanced Society, Holy and Mystical

On January ninth. I had an amazing experience at night. Sleeping, I managed to project myself using our deep bond as a bridge. I could connect and access some information when I entered my blue flame dream. When a dream of this importance happens, it isn't for no reason.

Remember that I, VIE, lived in Atlantis as a scientist and CHADD was a high priest and worked with me in the lab. Our mission is benevolent to help educate you about what has been hidden from you. Who and what you are and where you are going? There are great secrets still being kept from humanity. One of these is the true origins of Atlantis.

Atlantis was a highly advanced society established long ago. It was the natural evolution of humanity from indigenous tribal divinity and harmony with Gaia to scientific knowledge and the use of energy as power. Atlantis was a holy, mystical, and expansive space.

Today humans had reached a pinnacle in their evolution and were set to travel to the stars when the stars came to them. The Anunnaki who had conquered many other worlds and galaxies, arrived. They infiltrated the sacred light spaces of Atlantis twisting their light craft magic to dark algorithms with inversion, sabotage, and Black Ritual. There was a swift, ruthless, hostile takeover of humanity's sovereignty. Resistance was infiltrated and war was declared by the succubus humans birthed in the alliance of Archon and Anunnaki's desires.

Many Travelers Teams have experienced Atlantis. Either directly, their soul's path put them there in human life form at that time, or as Training with artificial downloads of lifetimes on Atlantis before it was destroyed. The Atlanteans had discovered quantum dimensionality. Their weaker members sold their souls for longer lives and lived in luxury. The matrix was constructed in the aftermath of the downfall of the Atlanteans. It has been in place ever since. Traveler Teams have been activated on the material plane to link up and begin planning the great clearing.

Training programs have commenced, supernatural clearing on astral and material planes. As each soul is reunited in its body, light warrior activation is occurring. Trust your energies more than your eyes.

Directing your conscious movement between dimensional realities is the overarching Training Directive in play now. Recognizing shifts in your dimensional reality. Identifying triggers. Cultivating conscious management and direction of your dimensional space. No team is fully intact. All have suffered casualties. Those conscious of the mission, upgrades, and downloads, your current Directive is to learn to navigate the fourth realm from the material plane. Then it stopped and I awakened.

Chapter 37
A Vision of Bright Lights and Shiny Characters Evenly Spaced

Later on, in the month I had another crystal-clear vision of very bright lights and shiny characters evenly spaced. It was so bright and clear that it awakened me. Some were like-stick while others looked triangular like pyramids in a long chain. Some pyramids were upward while others pointed down, what was intriguing was that it was shown only in my right eye and kept appearing for a little time before disappearing from my vision. For a few days, I wondered what that was until I got it.

This was from higher dimensional beings. Some most loving and non-judgmental beings travel in ships that are made of light and these ships are who they are. Saying:

"The Angels of Light are here, trumpeting their arrival across all dimensions on Gia. The shift is happening."

Jesus (known as Sananda today) is the supreme commander, and Ashtar is under command as a galactic Commander. They came with a rather large command of millions upon millions of beings from the spirit realm.

The Federation continues, with our main directive which is to neutralize the Anunnaki's weaponry in light waves of fifth or higher vibrations. Their low-realm technologies malfunction in divine light, as do their human hosts. We can only conclude the Atlantean modifications are still very much in play on humanity's collective consciousness.

From our perspective, we very much, most definitely, have arrived. One large mothership belonging to the Federation entered your Askari Galaxy several moons ago. Still, your scientists deny what they can now see with their telescopic eyes. Many battles are being fought over densely populated areas on the planet. Laser technologies are being deployed to take towers of dark matrix feeders down. The Anunnaki fight hard on all dimensions. Their astral allies show hostile fear rather than an organized offensive.

As the willingness clears, we will get closer to the hardcore, demonic entities, the managers of your lives, running the show. For those awakening to alternate dimensions, you will see how empty some humans are, devoid of soul sovereignty, and afflicted by demonic attachment.

Addiction entities destroy their hosts with infinite greed and desire. Their hosts' eyes are empty, haunted, traumatized zombies of the apocalypse. The lower realms do look like this, as some of you have experienced, more zombies, fewer humans, and the color drains out of their reality. When in these lower realms, keep sacred protection in place. Avoid dimensional fluctuation and breathlessness with deep slow breathing to ground back into heart spaces. Some light warriors are seeing all dimensional realities on Gaia, low to high. We urge you to recognize, that you can raise your vibration and switch up your perceived reality very quickly with mantras, breathing, and focused Light intention.

There will be further separation. The lower realms hold much darkness, there is the apocalyptic hell dimension of the bible and many of your other holy prophecies. However, it will have a limited life cycle with no new blood to recruit. We see timelines of continued ascension to higher realms, aided by sustained, committed clearing by lightworkers on the material plane and the astral. Assimilation of I upgrade breaking Atlantean modifications, and uploading trans-dimensional skill sets, is the directive for this year.

The Shift is happening. Self-care is the key to managing trans-dimensional existence. Trust your instincts more than your eyes, a friend. As always, we thank you for all that you are doing.

We are in awe of your courage and devotion to Christ's light, love, and divine creative source. We are all here to support the transformation from one elemental state to another of Gaia and her people. We are in deep gratitude for all that volunteers have done for the freedom of Gaia and humanity and will do. We are your servants in the light. With much unconditional love & gratitude.

More and more Lightships are entering The Portals daily everywhere around The Planet getting ready for "First Contact"!

It is time for change. It is time for full Disclosure.

It is time for The Light to take over and transmute The Planet by doing what needs to be done! The spells that have been cast upon The Planet - particularly on The Light have been completely removed!

We have never before seen such darkness and suffering on a planet!! You have the full support of The Light Realms and Us - your Galactic Brothers and Sisters!

It is not what The Dark Forces had planned! What they have done towards you and The Planet will now - and shortly - be taken care of by The Light!

The Dark Forces are setting themselves up for a BIG Awakening and their control is slipping away! Many are being arrested right now with help from The Light!
We have heard your call on behalf of The Planet and We are here to facilitate you on your path towards Ascension!

We will assist with the Governance of The Planet until things can be stabilized! Planetary Governance is one of our specialties.

There is a new Financial System ready that will change the lives of Humanity completely! Everyone will have what they need!

The Planet will recover completely and transmute into The Eden that She once was!

We are thanking you for all the Heart Work that you are doing!

We are here with you - you are here with Us! We love you!

Chapter 38
The Schumann Resonance

The frequency of the Earth is known as Schumann's number or Schumann's resonance.

Where there is action there is reaction.! I kept saying to CHADD as a warrior of the Father I am going to kick and will make them bounce in the universe forever. No one there wants to welcome these dark energies.

I was far and deep into my reflection thinking that the days of darkness and suffering that have held humanity in, poverty, sickness, prison, and servitude have come to their end and a new day will now dawn where all beings of the earth shall be free forevermore.

I could feel it, and a chill went up my spine when CHADD called me and said.

"VIE, The Schumann resonance will begin now reflecting this powerful 5D, gamma energy, and sustained 40-Hertz spikes will be witnessed and felt by all as these energies permeate earth!!!" This proved to me two things, one the communication between us was still clear and he was confirming my thoughts. Because the controllers can't be in 5D. 3D is the matrix. (Unaware, scared, unconscious) 4D is the astral realm. (Questioning reality, waking up, realizing it's all an illusion but also easily getting trapped in an illusory version of ego-self) 5D is Heaven on Earth. Love. peace, freedom, sovereignty, oneness.

You just need to tune into the experience of the universe that you want to have, and then let the universe deliver to you the aspects of itself that you've decided you want to experience. We see many who are trying to create because they think that they will be happy if they get what they want, and they will only be happy when that day arrives. But if you can receive the activation that is coming to you through this transmission, then you can feel our enthusiasm for every particle within this glorious universe, and you can live in that moment you desire so much, right here and right now.

There is always going to be a delicate balance in this dualistic universe, and to experience something that you desire and appreciate, you also must experience the lack side of the equation. When you recognize the lack as a void that the universe is going to fill, you can let go of your attachment to that experience. You can stop focusing on what isn't, and start recognizing that what is, what you do want, is right around the corner. This is the key to creating your reality. This is the key to mastery over the spiritual and the physical realm. This is the type of transmission that can change everything for you if you allow it if you let it in if you let yourself bask in the glory of this beautiful universe of ours.

I have enjoyed connecting with you and now I ask you to keep up the great work and you will see that many rewards and benefits are going to come your way. Thus, you can improve even more and share your spiritual love with everyone around you.

Chapter 39
There is a School of Knowledge on the Astral Plane after Death

As once before out of my physical body, my thoughts, light, and sound were integrated then I was told:

"We hope our Transmission today will reassure everyone. Because after passing away, there may be a period of confusion for some souls, but it depends on the manner of death. Whether death was natural, sudden, or unexpected, peaceful, or violent. When the person experiences death, they feel very cold, then the next instant they are standing by the bed looking down at the body thinking, I did not know that I was looking so bad, and they want to go back into the body. They look bad because there is a disease and there is no hope of getting well. The next thing that comes into my mind is I am free, I am out of there and now I can go anywhere I go and do anything that I want. And they want to go home.

No one is ever alone after dying. All are helped through the life-after-death experience. When you leave the body, you always have someone to greet you. You have made a contract before coming and you have also made an exit plan. So, all is planned before you ever come into the life, so the person is ready to go home, and all is completed. It is time for the person to go back home. And people that are grieving must understand that this is the time for the person to go home. The spark of life is the silver cord, and once that spark of life has left the body begins to deteriorate. Then you are on the other side, and you cannot return.

There is a period of orientation, or re-orientation which could be confusing to some as they figure out where they should go. But help is sent immediately. Whatever guidance a soul needs after transitioning the death experience will be provided.

The person will remember the last life that they experienced with them, and then begin to remember other lives had with them before that, as your soul memory reawakens.

Due to karma, not only is there life after death; and there are many lives after many deaths. Life after death is guaranteed because the soul is indestructible.

For humans, accepting death should be as easy as embracing life, because one cannot exist without the other. The spirit is not just a thing that resides in a body; it is eternal energy, created by Source.

After the soul leaves a physical body there is a state of being where the soul is taught lessons by great masters and has access to all the information it needs to learn and grow. These schools of knowledge exist on the astral plane, which may resemble the physical plane of Earth, but is far more evolved and refined.

You may see incredibly beautiful buildings, landscapes, and greenery – all bathed in energy and colors that are pure and more vibrant than any on Earth. It's the higher astral planes of Earth, where souls go to study and learn about their physical experiences.

The higher planes where everything is energy. Souls that are learning about their lives on Earth go to this place to study life after death. When souls finally learn all the life lessons required, they no longer need to reincarnate on Earth and can merge with the pure energy of the Creator in Heaven. Your ultimate goal.

When you are alive, you are allowed to make all the mistakes that you want, make it again and again and you are allowed to come back to make it right. There is no punishment for the mistake. Earth is a school where you come to learn lessons, but you can have to repeat a grade when you do not make it right and come back until you get it right. The lessons are not easy. Earth is a school where you learn about emotions and limitations. These are not taught on other planets. Earth is a very challenging planet.

There are 3 different places you can go to when you die. You go to the place that you are tuned to by your vibration and your frequency because you have to be vibrating to that frequency. Each time you die you will go to a little higher one. To different places over there because your vibration and frequency will match as you grow.

These three places are divided into many other compartments depending on your frequency.

The first place is "The Lower Astral. Lower astral are people who live such a negative life that they do not realize that they can go anywhere else. These are the murderers, the drug addicts, the alcoholics. When they die, they do not know they are dead. They are so confused because of the condition they have died. But after a while, they finally see the one sent to greet and take them on. So, they follow and go. They are always met with great love and now they must go to school take lessons and be ready to come back again.

The second place is "The Middle Astral" This could be the equivalent of what you would call Heaven. It's beautiful and wonderful. There is a beautiful lake with hills around the lake and all sorts of houses. Small, big, Castles. Whatever you can imagine and desire. If you want to live in a castle, you can have it. There is music in the air, and colors are so vibrant that some people who experience a near-death experience bring back that memory of the colors. There are huge gardens and colors that have never been seen before. Molecules of plants vibrate. Flowers bloom and never die. The problem is living there does not last. After a little while you will be asked if you are ready to go up and do a review of your life. Because now you have to move on. And this is hard.

Now you are taken up to the review board. There are boards, elders, and masters. They can't tell you what to do but will advise you. So, they will show you your life. They will show you everything you have done, every word you have said, everybody you have touched, hurt, or anything. And it is not easy to look at. It is shown very objectively. They show it to you from the perspective of everybody you were involved with, and you see it from their eyes, and their point of view and that hurts. You then realize that you have been affected and hurt without realizing it. You see exactly what you have done and the way you have affected other people. And that is where you will say, ok we did not do a very good job. Let's go back and try to make it right.

Because it is all a play and it is important to know that it is only a game, but we are playing different parts. The body is a custom, a suit, a cloth you put on to play a game. So, you have to make a contract with these people. And you say let us go back and let us try to make it right that time. Sometimes it takes a series of lives with the same people making the same mistakes again and again.

The third place is "The Upper Astral" and it is about knowledge and research. This is where "The Schools" are, and the "Temple of Wisdom complex". The Wisdom Complex is composed of many different parts. There are huge temples that look like Roman temples with big pillars. There is a "Healing Temple" and you do not have to die to go there. You can go in meditation or in your dreams at night. If you want to go and be healed, just picture it and go there at night. The difference can be made because the silver cord is still attached, and they are there for a different reason. There is always a long line of people who just died and have to go there first as cleansing before they go on where they are supposed to go.

The guardians of each temple take the person into the center of a dole-shaped room and the top of the dome is full of beautiful stones of many colors, and the light comes down shining down on the floor. The person stands in the center of this and bathes in the beautiful light which takes away any residue of anything that the person went through that life and washes it away. And now you are ready to go where you are supposed to go.

Another part of "The Temple of Wisdom" is "The Tapestry Room". It is huge and goes for miles. The Tapestry Room is on a huge wall and people have declined. It is almost like living. It is a fabric, and it is like it breaths. So, it is almost alive and in this tapestry are many threads.

Everyone has a thread in the tapestry because it is the thread of life, and the story of each one is in these threads showing how it all connects. How everyone affects each other, how everyone is connected.

You are one but you are also everything and everybody affects everyone else in some way. It is very important that you know and realize how much you affect others with what you say and do.

There is no prejudice, no judgment because we are all the same and we are all trying to learn something and to get out of this wheel of karma. It is the same thing; in this school, you can't judge people. They are just at different stages of their growth in the different classes they are taking.

And there is a "Library" with a guardian. The first thing they want to know is what you want to know.

In a near-death experience (NDE), the person is going through a tunnel, or they are going out of their body and going toward a huge light and never reaching that light. They turn back before they go to light. Normally someone there asks you if you are sure that you want to go, and now you have a choice. It's your decision, that bright light is a huge and powerful energy source and when you actually leave the body and die you go through that light the silver cord is severe at that time. Everyone is attached with a silver cord the entire time the person is alive.

Every night you are out of your body, everybody does. As soon as the body goes to sleep you are out of it. Then you go to the spirit side and you are talking to your guides, and masters and getting instructions. You go to other dimensions and planets, and you are not aware of it because you are not supposed to. The only thing you can remember is dreams. And in the morning, you are back to the body.

People who are getting older sleep a lot, going back and forth and getting instructions, and they know when they are going to go. Nobody dies until they are ready.

Chapter 40
Reincarnation is a Dark Force Trap

That day I tried to meditate before sleeping but I was too tired and fell asleep. To find myself in a new adventure I encountered a Cosmic Master.

"There is no time. Time is an illusion. This Planet is the only one probably, the only species, place that has found a way to measure what does not exist.
Thousands of other dimensions exist that you go in and out all the time without knowing it. The reality is not what you think. Everything is energy; everything is an illusion, said the Cosmic Master."

In this new adventure two men, Patrick and Claude arrived at Kony village, located on the lowest coast of the island just before dark, and pitched their camp under a great banyan tree not far from the ocean. The next morning a man, a Cosmic Master greeted them, and they began asking questions. And He said these words.

"I said to you Patrick and Claude when you departed, said the cosmic master, that I would be here to greet you, and I am here. I wish to call your attention more fully to the fact that man in his right domain is limitless and knows no limit of time or space. Man, when he knows himself, is not obliged to toil wearily along for days to accomplish hundreds of miles. Man in his right estate can accomplish any distance, it matters not the magnitude, instantly. A moment ago, I was in the village of N'gai dancing a tribe dance, from which you departed nineteen days ago. What you saw as my body still reposes there.

Your partner Max, whom you left in that village, will tell you that, until a few moments before five o'clock, I conversed with him, stating that I would go to greet you as you would arrive here about this hour. What you saw as my body is still there and your associate still beholds it, although it is at present inactive. This was done simply to show you that we can leave our bodies and greet you at any appointed place, at any specified time.

Who accompanied you could have accomplished the journey as I have? In this way you will more readily realize that we are only ordinary humans of the same source as you; that there is no mystery but that we have developed the powers given all by the Father, the Great Omnipotent One, more fully than you have.

My body will remain where it is until night, then I will bring it here and your associate will proceed on his way here as you did, arriving in due time. After a day's rest, we will journey to a small village, one day off, where we will stop over one night, then return here and meet your associate to see what his report will be. We will assemble this evening in the bungalow. In the meantime, farewell."

"There is no natural law of death or decay for man, except through accident. No inevitable old age process exists within his body or group cells—nothing that can gradually paralyze the individual. Death is, then, an avoidable accident. Disease is, above all, disease, absence of ease, or Santi—sweet, joyous peace of the spirit reflected through the mind in the body.

Senile decay, which is the common experience of man, is but an expression that covers his ignorance of cause, and certain disease conditions of mind and body.

Even accidents are preventable by appropriate mental attitude. Says the Cosmic Master: `The tone of the body may be so preserved that it may naturally resist with ease infectious and other diseases, like plague and influenza.' The Cosmic Master may swallow germs and never develop disease at all.

"Remember that youth is God's seed of love planted in the human form divine. Indeed, youth is the divinity within man; youth is the life spiritual—the life beautiful. It is only life that lives and loves—the one life eternal.

Age is unspiritual, mortal, ugly, and unreal. Fear thoughts, pain thoughts, and grief thoughts create the ugliness called old age. Joyous thoughts, love thoughts, and ideal thoughts create the beauty called youth. Age is but a shell within which lies the gem of reality—the jewel of youth. Practice acquiring the consciousness of childhood. Visualize the Divine Child within.

The body of an enlightened person: As the body is kept in the divine vibration, the body of the enlightened never grows old or dies. When the vibrations of their bodies are lowered or allowed to slow down, death ensues. In fact, these people know that when the mistake of death is accomplished, the body is vibrating at such a low rate that the emanating life vibrations are crowded out of the body temple and those vibrating life emanations still hold together and maintain the same form which the body had when they crowded out. Those emanations have intelligence and still revolve around a central nucleus or sun which attracts and holds them together. These emanating particles are surrounded by an intelligent emanation that assists them to keep their form and from which they again draw substance to erect another temple.

This is in direct accord and works in complete harmony with the intelligence that has been built around the body during its life cycle. If that intelligence vibrates at a low frequency or, in other words, is weak, it loses contact with the emanations of life and energy that have been forced out of the body (or form of clay after the life-emanations have left it), and the emanations finally disperse and return to the source, then complete death is accomplished; but, if the intelligence is strong, vibrant, and active, it takes full charge immediately and a new body is instantly assembled.

A resurrection has taken place, and through that resurrection, man is perfected in the flesh. Not all can hear or accept such a revelation. "He that hath ears to hear, let him hear."

The souls of the human species are trapped in a dimension of control, what people call "reality", established by the Dark Force eons ago to control you by separating you from your spirit. The afterlife is merely a short break before being recycled back into the chaos of control. It is like how wounded soldiers are sent to the hospital for treatment, before being sent to the front line once again.

It may sound scary to choose not to go to the Light because many of us are afraid of the unknown. Whereas the Light feels "safe" because we've gone there so many times, and "everybody else" who went there seems to have done just fine.

When you die, you are approached by your guide or guides as usual, and he or she wants to help you "cross over," and if you allow this, it will lead you through the Tunnel. Instead of letting yourself be "hypnotized" by its attraction, turn and look in the opposite direction, you will then have 360° vision, and you can still concentrate on looking in a certain direction, and move away from the Tunnel. You do this by "thinking" of yourself as moving, it's all about thoughts and intention in this dimension.

The Tunnel with the Light on the other side of it is a sophisticated hologram created by the Dark Force, and all you need to do is to think yourself in another direction, and the Tunnel will fade away.

Soon you will see the Grid as a fuzzy "barrier" in front of you, or above you. There are no ups and downs or lefts and rights in space. You will also see that it has holes in it like Swiss cheese. Move through one of these holes.

You will now see the Universe the way it is. You will now be truly interdimensional, free from the dimensional control imposed upon you by the Dark Force. You are now a free spirit in the Universe not doomed to the Reincarnation Cycle, you are free to do whatever you choose to do and go wherever you want to go."

Then this new adventure came to an end.

Chapter 41
True Gamma TimeLine

When I woke up this morning. I clearly remembered my trip into another realm.

The cosmic master once again came to deliver a message and then make me voyage the vision.

The Cosmic Master:

"As a lightworker, the dark mentalists tried a last destructive attack on VIE, one of her relatives, and her blue flame. They are desperate. But it's not going to work. The Schumann Resonance has begun to reflect 5D."

Now I see pieces... mental snapshots...

At the entrance of the Akashic records I was greeted by the guardian, and I was granted access. And I loved the information I found, and I am reading it.

"For the first time since the creation of this Universe, areas completely Free of Quantum Fluctuations primary anomaly have appeared inside the Universe. This is the beginning of a new cosmic cycle. The dark Draconian overlords that controlled Earth for 350,000 years have now been defeated by benevolent Life forces.

Light Forces are now 100% in control of all 3D matrix systems. Any remaining deep-state rogue forces and beings on the surface are under extreme pressure by Delta Light Forces which will completely expose them and eradicate them quickly now.

All artificial Timelines created by nefarious powers have been completely merged back into the one True Gamma TimeLine which leads directly to the new Earth.

A new Earth, Quantum Global Abundance System, is about to be introduced to the World for the first time, and thus a new System will replace the old corrupt Central Banking System.

All harmful and outdated 3D matrix systems will be completely replaced with 5D, new Earth Systems that will greatly benefit Humanity.

Advanced New Technologies will now be released to assist and Heal All Beings of the Earth.

The Grand Celestial Alignment of 2020 will lead to the culmination of the event and the Grand Solar Flash.

The days of darkness and suffering that have held Humanity in poverty, sickness, prison, and servitude have come to their end and a new day will now dawn where all beings of the Earth shall be free forevermore.

The Schumann Resonance will begin reflecting this powerful 5D, Gamma Energy, and sustained 40-Hertz spikes will be witnessed and felt by all as these Energies Permeate Earth.

This is just coming to confirm my blue flame and CHADD phone call earlier, that soon it will be the liberation of the feminine, it will in turn free the divine masculine.

Announcing the return of Jesus and Mary-Magdalene."

To the mass consciousness: There is potential for a worldwide spiritual activation that teleports those who will be ready into some new type of beingness, where humans become like superheroes with telekinesis, levitation, telepathy, and more. That is the Ascension coming and there is no choice. It is time for those who have been dealt with their traumas and karma to do it, to ascend and have an expansion in Consciousness.

Chapter 42
Automatization: None of these Technologies have been Random

I was in a trance state, dreaming that I was hearing the news on TV, and the weird thing I was conscious of dreaming. So, I was dreaming. There were many, many women, a group of women talking at the same time on TV and at the same time others not on TV, trying to cover the voice of the one on TV. I was trying hard to hear and understand what they were saying but could not. I awakened very frustrated.

What was the message that the news was trying to convey about women? In fact, these women were trying to communicate with me, to let me know of an attack coming in an ultimate effort to stop me.

Then the scene continues the beautiful family land. It is a beautiful ancient building and attached to it I see another building, with a couple living on one side of it. They were recruited by my ancestors to keep the family valuables. Some family antique furniture, silverware engraved with the family coat of arms, many belongings, and souvenirs of the family from generations. I went in to visit the inside and saw and understood how my ancestor was a visionary and a protector of us.

Then I was attacked by dark entities by directed energies sent by two women who gave their power away to hurt me. They tried to kill me with a heart attack. But my ancestor who passed me his chevron came to reassure me that this was not going to happen. My energy went down, I was totally drained but it did not last more than a split second.

What it is, is that there are pattern technologies that can turn people into criminals if you are weakened in your life. And you, you can be targeted for being aware and be a great activator.

The 4G wireless radiation has biological effects seen in all life forms, plants, animals, and insects, and in humans, there is clear evidence of cancer. None of the use of these technologies has been random and it is not simply men investing things. Not many people can see what is coming. It's a very, very disruptive technology and it's disruptive technologies. It's disruptive to the way we live our normal lives.

The big problem is that kids who are growing up through the system today will have no reference point for what the world once was.

Pay attention to what is really going on, pay attention to the Internet, of Things. What it is doing, where it is going, and pay attention to the automatization. The 5G is all military technology. It's about surveillance and control. Mood control is about emotional control. It is about psychological manipulation through electromagnetic radio waves, and physical control. It means control at all levels you can think of 5G as a killer. It kills bees and birds. The 5G network generates radio-frequency radiation that can damage DNA and lead to cancer; cause oxidative damage that can cause premature aging; disrupt cell metabolism; and potentially lead to other diseases through the generation of stress proteins.

With nanotechnology, the genes of some rats have been switched on and off using radio waves to operate technology. Human beings have been set up in a big way. 5G is way beyond what many people are considering. It has the capability of manipulating vast sections of the population or targeting people, crops, and biology individually.

Everything that nanotech is in can be manipulated through the 5G system, and nanotech is everywhere.

The controllers spray nanotech in the sky (chemtrails), They put it in the food, and even with what is flashed down in your home through the drains. It gets passed on through the water system, so you see this in your food chain. It is in the river system and ends up in the fish. It is in the algae and ends up in everything. It is a military control and ultimately a weapon system. It's a surveillance system and weapon system. With it, you can target people for elimination, or heart attack, cancer. The Internet is becoming the most important thing in the human experience because it controls everything else in the human experience.

One of my star sisters is coming forth now and saying: And there is biological warfare to combat great awakening. June 2019 young protesters in Hong Kong are willing to be martyrs to contest communism. It was a serious problem for the regime, the protesters' numbers grew, and the world watched. Everyone is questioning how they are going to stop that on October 18th some foundations along with the World Economic Farm hosted a high-level pandemic event. A simulation based on the Coronavirus. The simulation showed that it could kill sixty-five million people.

A couple of weeks after Halloween the controversial 5G network was fully tested. Fired for the first time in Wuhan. Scientists have warned though that 5G causes flu-like symptoms, and weeks later the coronavirus outbreak begins in Wuhan. And the protest abruptly came to an end.

Saint Germain re-incarnated on earth. He was once incarnated as Joseph, the father of Jesus, and the regime was not prepared for Saint Germain's trade war, and by most accounts, the regime was losing ground.

Massive levels of sulfur dioxide gas were detected on the outskirts of Wuhan. A staffer from a funeral home in Wuhan claims that her funeral home alone cremated an estimated four thousand seven hundred twenty-five bodies suspected of dying from the coronavirus since January 22.

Experts say that the virus was weaponized in a lab and the mainstream media hide it. But in a short time, the truth will be known by all.

And I heard this from another realm and a male voice:

"You deserve accolades for the mental, spiritual, and physical work you have been doing in your life. You are helping yourself and many others with your current life choices and actions, and you are being commended, encouraged, and supported by the angelic and spiritual realms."

And I got out of the trance.

Chapter 43
One World Government (NWO)

Now I was home, alone, and in the family room when I felt a change within my consciousness. And then there was a light from within that became so bright that I was no longer aware of my senses...all was light. And then a voice became audible, not to my ears, but to my spirit.

This voice informed me to listen to what they had to give me. That they were of the High Council. They asked me to share it.

Then the voice went into silence, and I experienced what I heard and read.

I found myself, with CHADD silent and next to me, in front of a High Galactic Council saying:

"Your current focus is on the illumination of the mind and the freedom of the spirit through the disclosure and then the information that has been withheld from the public. Many explorations and information regarding human government allege a cute ease and question projects that are kept from the public. This research is largely transmitted in ways that cause people to be doubtful, fearful, and uneasy rather than prompting them to be confident and educated in these matters. Although this stimulates curiosity it does not necessarily cultivate believability. It is just another control program and game. It's an agenda of the elite programs of planet Earth's global government systems.

The controllers of the world want a One-world Government, and you know it. They selected electronics for planet Earth to keep control of humans. In about ten years from now, connections will start to be made between AI and the human brain. Through a thought process of preparation for getting people addicted to technology Human beings hold. Holdable smartphones, and tablets, and it is basically achieved. Just go to a restaurant and look at families with children and you'll see the addiction. Parents are on their phones calling or texting and kids are on a tablet.

The controllers of the planet are specifically targeting the young, because the young, and children of today, are going to be adults just when they want to bring this AI connection in full term. And to have this to happen they have to get these adults to be, and next step, addicted to technology. Addicted to the point where they will accept it and become the most natural thing in the world. This is happening in front of everyone's eyes.

So, the first step was to get people addicted to technology to the point where they would get out at night and make the line outside and in front of some electronic stores to be the first to get the new technology.

What they want soon is people lining up to be connected to AI.

In some European countries, they are today having parties to celebrate when someone is being microchipped. The other step is to get it in the body. So, from holdable to wearables (watches) to Bluetooth and Google Glass and even now electronic tattoos. Electronic tattoos are microchips on the skin.

The Public must be aware of some social media operation companies that are cutting edge of this whole AI. They are not only search engines and people must know them.

If they are aware of all this and know what is coming, then they will have a great chance of predicting it. Because if AI takes over the matrix, then there are no more humans left.

They are earth-based weapons of mass destruction and star-based weapons platform systems around Earth and it's a nuisance. Although some may view these and other technologies as high-level futuristic creations, they were created through incomplete information loop prints given to the government through changes with many intruder races who had questionable agendas in the 1940s–1950s. The lifespan and longevity of these technologies and projects are extremely limited as they were created for nefarious purposes and cannot evolve in spirit as human birth transforms them.

Then I had a vision of the coronavirus in China. Implanted to kill many. Still part of the reduction of the population. While in France many people were manifesting in the streets and some others walking and celebrating the monarchy in the hope it would take back control of the country.

The manipulation behind wearing masks: Your breath is sacred.

The difference between life and death, It's your breath.

You can survive 30 days or more without food, 3 days without water but not even 3 minutes without breathing.

Then I underwent this timeless final state that lasted no more than five minutes and it was over.

Chapter 44
Free or Slaves - Not Human, Alias Satan

That event happened at about four o'clock in the morning, I had an astral projection and that's how I met Mr. Marc Shredeir. And my intuition tells me that it's not his real name. It was after he died, shortly after conducting several controversial lectures throughout the USA, where he covered topics such as the betrayal of science society and the soul.

He said that he was reportedly strangled by a catheter found wrapped around his neck — the bizarre death being dismissed by the authorities as suicide.

If the circumstances of his death seem highly controversial, they are matched by the controversy over his public statements uttered shortly before his death.

Marc Shredeir was a self-taught expert. Of the 1,477 underground bases around the world, 129 deep underground facilities of which were in the United States, he claimed to have worked on more than a dozen underground bases.

Two of these bases were major, including the much rumored one of the bioengineering facilities in the desert. Shredeir maintained, "gray" humanoid extraterrestrials worked side by side with American technicians.

It was in the desert that he received a beam-weapon blast to the chest which caused his later cancer, and many have confirmed that a large scar indeed existed.

Marc Shredeir recounts his encounter with extraterrestrials saying:

"I was involved in a building that was an addition to the deep underground military base in the deepest base. As I was headed down there, I found myself amidst a large cavern that was full of outer-space aliens, otherwise known as Massive Greys. I shot two of them. At that time, there were at least 30 people down there. About 40 more came down after this started, and all of them got killed. I was not alone, and we had surprised a whole underground base of existing aliens. Later, we found out that they had been living on our planet for a long time, perhaps a million years. This could explain a lot of what is behind the theory of ancient astronauts. A fire exchange occurred between gray aliens and Secret Service personnel. In the ensuing shootout, Secret Service, FBI, and Black Berets were killed along with an unspecified number of "grays".

It was there that he said he received a beam-weapon blast to the chest. Shredeir maintained that numerous previous attempts had been made on his life, including the removal of the nuts from one of the front wheels of his car.

He stated that he publicly stated that he was a marked man and did not expect to live long. To a close friend Marc said, "If I ever 'commit suicide, I will have been killed."

Some of Marc's more major accusations worth the attention:

The American government concluded a treaty with "gray" aliens in 1954. It is a cooperation pact.

The space shuttle has been producing special alloys in orbit. A vacuum is needed for the creation of these special metals, thereby justifying the mandate for a large, permanently manned space station. Much of our stealth aircraft technology was developed by back-engineering crashed alien craft.

AIDS was a population control virus invented by the National Ordinance Laboratory, in Chicago, Illinois.

Unbeknownst to just about everyone, the US government has an earthquake device. Neither the 1995 Kobe earthquake nor the 1989 San Francisco quake had a pulse wave, the World Trade Center bomb blast and the Oklahoma City blast were achieved using small nuclear devices. The melting and pitting of the concrete and the extrusion of metal supporting rods indicated this. (Shredeir's forte, he claimed, was explosives.)

He also revealed about testing technologies of control on unwitting civilian victims. The betrayal of science, and the soul, he said. The optimum and courageous new world technologies for stimulating and dominating it have a dark side that military and intelligence planners have been exposing for a long time. Dr. Dick Pliditch the oldest son of a late politician from Arkansas that has been pursuing independent research in the sciences and politics for most of his adult life.

And he uncovered a certain Dick Pliditch's latest work that is based on ruling the human brain - The Technologies of Political Control or Tools for Peak Performance. Doctor Pliditch has published articles in science, politics, and education and is a well-known lecturer. Reporting on his research activities including new technologies, health, and earth science-related issues.

Finally, Marc Shredeir lamented that the democracy he loved no longer existed: we had become instead a technocracy ruled by a shadow government intent on imposing their own view of things on all of us, whether we like it or not.

He believed 11 of his best friends had been murdered in the last 22 years, eight of whose deaths had been officially described as suicides.

Whatever one might think of his claims, it's clear that he was of particular interest to the FBI and CIA.

His widow has stated that intelligence agents thoroughly searched the premises shortly after his death and left with at least a third of the family photographs.

Chapter 45
Satanic Ritual Abuse on CHADD

The way I acquired this new information was quite unusual. But I have become so used to all this.

I am given a USB key, and I only see a male hand. I take the USB key and plug it into my computer as instructed, and...

I understand that it's clear to Mark that there was more to what uncovered Dick P. That's about the Sovereign brain programming and the operation clipboard.

That is what I am reading, and my brain memory is enhanced like a sponge.

Sovereign Programming is a method of mind control used by numerous organizations for covert purposes. I tested it on the military and civilians, and they tested it on my blue flame CHADD. The methods are astonishingly sadistic. Its entire purpose is to traumatize the victim and the expected results are horrifying: The creation of a mind-controlled slave who can be triggered at any time to perform any action required by the handler. While the mass media ignores this issue, over 2 million Americans have gone through the horrors of this program.

Sovereign programming is a mind-control technique comprising elements of Satanic Ritual Abuse (SRA) and Multiple Personality Disorder (MPD). It utilizes a combination of psychology, neuroscience, and occult rituals to create within the slaves an alter persona that can be triggered and programmed by the handlers. Sovereign slaves are used by several organizations connected with the world elite in fields such as the military, sex slavery, and the entertainment industry.

Throughout the course of history, several accounts have been recorded describing rituals and practices resembling mind control. One of the earliest writings giving reference to the use of occultism to manipulate the mind can be found in the Egyptian Book of the Dead. It is a compilation of rituals, heavily studied by today's secret societies, which describes methods of torture and intimidation to create trauma. The use of drugs and the casting of spells (hypnotism) ultimately resulted in the total enslavement of the initiate. Other events ascribed to black magic, sorcery, and demon possession. Where the victim is animated by an outside force are also ancestors of Sovereign programming.

It is, however, during the 20th century that mind control became a science in the modern sense of the term, where thousands of subjects have been systematically observed, documented, and experimented on.

One of the first methodical studies on trauma-based mind control was conducted by a physician working in Nazi concentration camps. He initially gained notoriety for being one of the SS physicians who supervised the selection of arriving prisoners, determining who was to be killed and who was to become a forced laborer. However, he is mostly known for performing grisly human experiments on camp inmates, including children, for which Leuwarden was called the "Angel of Death".

The Dr. Physician is the most significant programmer, an ex-Nazi Concentration Camp doctor. Thousands of sovereign brain-controlled slaves in the U.S. had Dr. Leuwarden as their chief programmer.

"The Physician notoriety was the principal developer of the trauma-based Sovereign Project and the CIA's MK Ultra mind control programs. Leuwarden and approximately 5, 000 other high-ranking Nazis were secretly moved into the United States and South America in the aftermath of World War II in an Operation designated pin. The Nazis continued their work in developing brain control and rocketry technologies in secret underground military bases. The only thing we were told about was the rocketry work with former Nazi star celebrities. The killers, torturers, and mutilators of innocent human beings were kept discretely out of sight, but busy in U.S. underground military facilities which gradually became home to thousands upon thousands of kidnapped American children snatched off the streets. About one million per year and placed into iron bar cages stacked from floor to ceiling as part of the 'training'. These children would be used to further refine and perfect Leuwarden's mind control technologies. Certain selected children, at least the ones who survived the 'training, would become future mind-controlled slaves who could be used for thousands of different jobs ranging anywhere from sexual slavery to assassinations. A substantial portion of these children, who were considered expendable, were intentionally slaughtered in front of, and by, the other children in order to traumatize the selected trainee into total compliance and submission". The Ultimate Terror.

The Physician's research served as a basis for the covert, illegal CIA human research program. He is infamous for his sordid human experiments on concentration camp prisoners, especially on twins. A part of his work that is rarely mentioned, however, is his research on brain control. Much of his research in this field was confiscated by the Allies and is still classified to this day.

The most publicized experiments conducted by the human program involved the administration of LSD on unwitting human subjects, including CIA employees, military personnel, doctors, other government agents, prostitutes, mentally ill patients, and members of the public, in order to study their reactions.

However, the scope of MK-ULTRA does not stop. Experiments involving violent electroshocks, physical and mental torture, and abuse were used in a systematic manner on many subjects, including children.

Using American and Canadian citizens as its test subjects. The published evidence indicates that Project MK-ULTRA involved the use of many methodologies to manipulate individual mental states and alter brain functions, including the surreptitious administration of drugs and other chemicals, sensory deprivation, isolation, and verbal and physical abuse.

Although the admitted goals of the projects were to develop torture and interrogation methods to use on the country's enemies, some historians asserted that the project aimed to create "Manchurian Candidates/ puppets", programmed to perform various acts such as assassinations and other covert missions.

Although it is claimed that the CIA stopped such experiments after these commissions, some whistle-blowers have come forth stating that the project simply went "underground", and sovereign Programming has become the classified successor of MK-ULTRA.

Although there has never been any official admittance of the existence of Sovereign programming, prominent researchers have documented the systematic use of trauma on subjects for brain-control purposes. Some survivors, with the help of dedicated therapists, were able to "deprogram" themselves to then go on record and disclose the horrifying details of their ordeals.

Sovereign slaves are mainly used by organizations to carry out operations using patsies trained to perform specific tasks, who do not question orders, who do not remember their actions, and, if discovered, who automatically commit suicide. They are perfect for high-profile assassinations, the ideal candidates for prostitution, slavery, and private movie productions.

They are also the perfect puppet performers for the entertainment industry.

"What I can say is I now believe that ritual-abuse programming is widespread, is systematic, is very organized from highly esoteric information which is published no-where, has not been on any book or talk show, that we have found it all around this country and at least one foreign country.

The purpose of it is that they want an army of Manchurian Candidates, tens of thousands of mental robots who will do prostitution, do movies, smuggle narcotics, engage in international arms smuggling, all sorts of very lucrative things, and do their bidding and eventually the megalomaniacs at the top believe they'll create a Satanic Order that will rule the world."

Sovereign programmers cause intense trauma to subjects using electroshock, torture, abuse, and mind games in order to force them to dissociate from reality — a natural response in some people when they are faced with unbearable pain. The subject's ability to dissociate is a major requirement and it is, apparently, most readily found in children that come from families with multiple generations of abuse. Mental dissociation enables the handlers to create walled-off personas in the subject's psyche, which can then be programmed and triggered at will.

"Trauma-based brain control programming can be defined as systematic torture that blocks the victim's capacity for conscious processing (through pain, terror, drugs, illusion, sensory deprivation, sensory over-stimulation, oxygen deprivation, cold, heat, spinning, brain stimulation, and often, near-death), and then employs suggestion and/or classical and operant conditioning (consistent with well-established behavioral modification principles) to implant thoughts, directives, and perceptions in the unconscious mind, often in newly-formed trauma- induced dissociated identities, that force the victim to do, feel, think, or perceive things for the purposes of the programmer. The objective is for the victim to follow directives with no conscious awareness, including the execution of acts in clear violation of the victim's moral principles, spiritual convictions, and volition.

Installation of mind control programming relies on the victim's capacity to dissociate, which permits the creation of new walled-off personalities to "hold" and "hide" programming. Already dissociative children are prime "candidates" for programming and Ritual Abuse".

Sovereign brain control is covertly used by various groups and organizations for various purposes. These groups are known as "The Network" and form the backbone of the New World Order.

"When a person is undergoing trauma induced by electroshock, a feeling of light-headedness is evidenced as if one is floating or fluttering like a butterfly. There is also a symbolic representation pertaining to the transformation or metamorphosis of this beautiful insect: from a caterpillar to a cocoon (dormancy, inactivity), to a butterfly (new creation) which will return to its point of origin. Such is the migratory pattern that makes this species unique."

The victim/survivor is called a "slave" by the programmer/handler, who in turn is perceived as "master" or "god." About 75% are female since they possess a higher tolerance for pain and tend to dissociate more easily than males. Monarch handlers seek the compartmentalization of their subject's psyche in multiple and separate alter personas using trauma to cause dissociation.

Here is a partial list of these forms of torture: (and which have been used on CHADD)

1. Abuse and torture (did it to CHADD)
2. Confinement in boxes, cages, coffins, etc., or burial (often with an opening or air tube for oxygen) (confinement in boxes/CHADD)
3. Restraint with ropes, chains, cuffs, etc.
4. Near drowning
5. Extremes of heat and cold, including submersion in ice water and burning chemicals
6. Skinning (only the top layers of the skin are removed in victims intended to survive)
7. Spinning
8. Blinding light (done on CHADD)
9. Electric shock
10. Forced ingestion of offensive body fluids and matter, such as blood, urine, feces, flesh, etc.
11. Hung in painful positions or upside down
12. Hunger and thirst (both experimented on CHADD)
13. Sleep deprivation (on CHADD)
14 Compression with weights and devices
15. Sensory deprivation
16. Drugs to create illusion, confusion, and amnesia, often given by injection or intravenously (experimented on CHADD)
17. Ingestion or intravenous toxic chemicals to create pain or illness, including chemotherapy agents (done on CHADD)
18. Limbs pulled or dislocated (hips dislocated for CHADD by three MD's female))

19.	Application of snakes, spiders, maggots, rats, and other animals to induce fear and disgust (hospitalized CHADD with rats in location)

20.	Near-death experiences, commonly asphyxiation by choking or drowning, with immediate resuscitation (NDE and 2 months coma/CHADD)

22.	Forced to perform or witness abuse, torture, and sacrifice of people and animals, usually with knives

23.	Forced participation in slavery

24.	Abuse to become pregnant; the fetus is then aborted for ritual use, or the baby is taken for sacrifice or enslavement

25.	Spiritual abuse causes victims to feel possessed, harassed, and controlled internally by spirits or demons (all experimented on CHADD)

26.	Desecration of Judeo-Christian beliefs and forms of worship; dedication to Satan or other deities

27.	Abuse and illusion to convince victims that God is evil, such as convincing a child that God has abused her

28.	Surgery to torture, experiment, or cause the perception of physical or spiritual bombs or implants (all experimented on CHADD)

29.	Harm or threats of harm to family, friends, loved ones, pets, and other victims, to force compliance (on CHADD'S friends)

30.	Use of illusion and virtual reality to confuse and create non-credible disclosure (experimented on CHADD)

"The basis for the success of the Sovereign brain-control programming is that different personalities or personality parts called alters can be created who do not know each other, but who can take the body at different times.

The amnesia walls that are built by traumas, form a protective shield of secrecy that protects the abusers from being found out and prevents the front personalities who hold the body much of the time from knowing how their System of alters is being used. The shield of secrecy allows cult members to live and work around other people and remain totally undetected. The front alters can be wonderful Christians, and the deeper alters can be the worst type of Satanic monster imaginable.

A great deal is at stake in maintaining the secrecy of the intelligence agency or the occult group that is controlling the slaves. The success rate of this type of programming is high but when it fails, the failures are discarded through death. Each trauma and torture serve a purpose. A great deal of experimentation and research went into finding out what can and can't be done. Charts were made showing how much torture a given body weight at a given age can handle without death."

"Due to the severe trauma induced through ECT, abuse, and other methods, the mind splits off into alternate personalities from the core. Formerly referred to as Multiple Personality Disorder, it is presently recognized as dissociative identity disorder and is the basis for Sovereign programming. Further conditioning of the victim's mind is enhanced through hypnotism, double-bind coercion, pleasure-pain reversals, food, water, sleep, and sensory deprivation, along with various drugs which alter certain cerebral functions".

Dissociation is thus achieved by traumatizing the subject, using systematic abuse, and using terrifying occult rituals. Once a split in the core personality occurs, an "internal world" can be created, and altered personas can be programmed using tools such as music, movies, and fairy tales. These visual and audio aids enhance the programming process using images, symbols, meanings, and concepts. Created alters can then be accessed using trigger words or symbols programmed into the subject's psyche by the handler. Some of the most common internal images seen by brain control slaves are trees, the Cabalistic Tree of Life, infinity loops, ancient symbols and letters, spider webs, mirrors, glass shattering, masks, castles, mazes, demons, butterflies, hourglasses, clocks, and robots. These symbols are commonly inserted in popular culture movies and videos for two reasons: to desensitize the majority of the population, using subliminal and neuro-linguistic programming, and to deliberately construct specific triggers and keys for base programming of highly impressionable Sovereign children. Symbols and meanings in the movie become triggers in the slave's mind enabling easy access to the slave's mind by the handler.

In each case, the slave is given a particular interpretation of the movie's storyline in order to enhance programming. For example, a slave watching Oz is taught that "somewhere over the rainbow" is the "happy place" dissociative trauma slaves must go to in order to escape the unbearable pain being inflicted upon them. Using the movie, programmers encourage slaves to go "over the rainbow" and dissociate, effectively separating their minds from their bodies.

"As mentioned before, the hypnotist will find children easier to hypnotize if they know how to do it with small children. One method that is effective is to say to the small children, "Imagine you are watching a favorite television show." This is why Disney movies, and the other shows are so important to the programmers. They are the perfect hypnotic tool to get the child's mind to dissociate in the right direction. The programmers have been using movies since day one to help children learn the hypnotic scripts. For children, they need to be part of the hypnotic process. If the hypnotist allows the child to make up his own imagery, the hypnotic suggestions will be stronger.

The levels of Sovereign Programming identify the slave's "functions" and are named after the Electroencephalography (EEG) brainwaves associated with them.

Regarded as "general" or regular programming:

ALPHA is within the base "control personality". It is characterized by extremely pronounced memory retention, along with substantially increased physical strength and visual acuity. Alpha programming is accomplished by deliberately subdividing the victim's personality which, in essence, causes a left-brain-right-brain division, allowing for a programmed union of Left and Right through neuron pathway stimulation.

BETA is referred to as "sexual" programming (slaves). This programming eliminates all learned moral convictions and stimulates primitive instinct, devoid of inhibitions. "Cat" alters may come out at this level. Known as Kitten programming, it is the most visible kind of programming as some female celebrities, models, actresses, and singers have been subjected to this kind of programming. In popular culture, clothing with feline prints often denotes Kitten programming.

DELTA is known as "killer" programming and was originally developed for training special agents or elite soldiers (i.e., Delta Force, First Earth Battalion, Mossad, etc.) in covert operations. Optimal adrenal output and controlled aggression are evident. Subjects are devoid of fear and very systematic in carrying out their assignment. Self-destruct or suicide instructions are layered in at this level.

THETA – Considered the "psychic" programming. Blood liners (those coming from multi- generational Satanic families) were determined to exhibit a greater propensity for having telepathic abilities than did non-blood liners. Due to its evident limitations, however, various forms of electronic mind control systems were developed and introduced, namely, biomedical human telemetry devices (brain implants), and directed-energy lasers using microwaves and/or electromagnetics. It is reported these are used in conjunction with highly advanced computers and sophisticated satellite tracking systems.

It is difficult to remain objective when describing the horrors endured by Sovereign slaves. The extreme violence, abuse, mental torture, and sadistic games inflicted on victims by "notable scientists" and high-level officials prove the existence of a true "dark side" in the powers that be. Despite the revelations, the documents, and the whistle-blowers, a great majority of the population ignores, dismisses, or avoids the issue altogether. Over two million Americans have been programmed by trauma mind control since 1947 and the CIA publicly admitted its mind control projects in 1970. Several public figures we see on our TV and movie screens are mind-control slaves. Famous people have gone on record and disclosed their brain control experiences…and yet the public claims that it "cannot exist".

The research and funds invested in Project Sovereign do not however only apply to brain control slaves. Many of the programming techniques perfected in these experiments are applied on a mass scale through mass media. Mainstream news, movies, music videos, advertisements, and television shows are conceived using the most advanced data on human behavior ever compiled. A lot of this comes from Monarch programming.

The hand re-appeared asking for the USB key. I gave it back after a rapid download. There were so many details to remember.

The download vanished but I could go back at night and use the USB key if I needed.

But then I found out why I was given this information to warn you, by an advanced positively oriented alien race, after a client said that a "Sound scientist and teacher" was using the levels of sovereign programming including the killer programming, in his music. Using and mixing various specific tones beneath the level of audible hearing, masked by other sounds, and sometimes music composed for the desired state to stimulate and program the brain. The client did not have a clue what this was and wanted to have my opinion. Different sounds exist at different frequencies or vibrations and all things living are vibrational and dimensional. When your thought is positive it vibrates at a higher frequency; if your thought makes you feel bad if it's a negative thought vibrates at a lower frequency. Focusing on a positive or negative thought will attract you to the same vibration and will join you together.

This advanced positively oriented alien race is helping the planet to ascend and has many specialized healers, including a medical assistance team, that once guided me to their healing transmission. They helped me repair my etheric body and made repairs at the cellular level of my physical body using Light and Sound.

Chapter 46
Led to Center Myself on a Thursday Early Morning

Thursday 19, 1:53 am, I was led to center myself, relax, breathe deep and slow in and out, and equalize. I could feel sweetness, and it was lightweight. I had an impression of accomplishment. I stayed there to equalize for about fifteen to twenty minutes.

I was already in a very comfortable place when I heard his voice "I adore you" I looked at the clock. It was 1:53 a.m.
That was a wonderful message delivered to me and confirmed that the Great exorcism, also called Triangular exorcism, has worked. The Gallican Priest Exorcist and Knight Templar succeeded. His work was done.

Just before I heard the voice, I saw my left hand that was beginning to heal.

It is centered around the New Testament event sometimes referred to as the miraculous draught or catch of fishes (John 21:1 - 11). It is only mentioned in the Gospel of John. Jesus, as the New Testament attests, utilized the power of God the Father to perform many miracles during his earthly ministry. These supernatural events, as Christ often said, are evidence not only of his calling and commission directly from God but also of his own divine origin. This amazing miracle involves 153 performed by Jesus, after his resurrection from the dead, in his next to last appearance with his eleven disciples before ascending into heaven.

I have no words to express my gratitude to the Knight Templar and its missionaries for their help.

Chapter 47
Friday Night and a Lucky Divine Sign

I know without a doubt that it was on a Friday night that the Divine realm sent me a sign. I remember because it was on my cousin's birthday. An angel is sent as an answer to my prayers. It came when I desperately waited for a sign from the universe and needed some kind of reassurance to know that I was on the right track in life. It is a positive message about spirituality, likely to see solutions and conclusions that others don't and able to communicate my ideas in an understandable manner. It contributes to the whole.

Friday night while I was sleeping numbers began to appear on the clock. Lumita, the gypsy woman showed up in the middle of the night. She was sent by "San Sara", the black Virgin Mary she said. It comes as a sign that I am about to achieve long-held personal Goals, she said. "You can expect a very happy and prosperous time for both your career and personal life. It is now a time of manifesting abundance and of aligning the minds with the Divine Source. A powerful vibration telling of achievements, success, striving forward, progress, and attainments, suggesting that a phase, circumstance, or situation in your life is about to end and is a sign of forewarning enabling you to prepare yourself and your life accordingly. So precious and rewarding, and you'll experience spiritual growth. It is a sign that God is calling you, a period of big changes is coming to you. Indicates that you are winding up an emotional relationship phase in your life. Dissolving to change direction."

Monday morning, I sat and began to meditate, did not have time to center myself and I was already in front of Ron's front porch. Without having time to ring he is already welcoming me and inviting me in. "How nice it is to see you! I have so much to share! I had a dream about you last night. Things are about to change for you. I know, I know, you had to take a trip and thought that it would be for three weeks and instead, your trip lasted months. I think that I can explain. After all that occurred during your stay in the medieval city, you had to wait for the right time to meet Alecia and then your friend Marine. She needs my help and would never have found me without you.

For you, it's time to sail for a new adventure. Light is at the end of the tunnel now." said Ron.

Chapter 48
Signs After Signs; Miracles After Miracles.

As I said previously, I have been subject to many and various attacks from different sources, and the last, at that time, by the voodoo woman, Katherine. The same one that has tried so hard to stop my destiny from happening for more than fifteen years now. The shapeshifting surrogate and mother of Paul.

Then I finally found the Knight Templar able to help me and able to use the 153 like Jesus did to help me. And today, about sixteen weeks later, signs begin to appear one by one. Padre Pio re- appears as a sign in my life. He delivered me a Rosary with his face on one side and the Virgin Mary on the other side. Followed by a woman that shows up in the parking lot, from nowhere, sent by our lady un-doer of knots. She asked me to make three knots in a thin white string and to look at its units.

Today it's our lady of Fatima that sent me a sign. I received a message telling me to consider myself the luckiest person. It was a beautiful picture of Our Lady of Fatima and under it says "If you got this message, consider yourself the luckiest person.

Because from this moment on, your life will change and everything you so much aspire will be granted!

While you read this message, focus, and think about everything you want. Think with faith and sit down that is already a reality.

Think about that wish now (....................)

So, repeat 3 times:

By the power of 3 TIMES 3…

For those who go and those who come...

For the living and the dead...

For the power of the 4 elements...

Around me all the heads spin, and by step, I delete the obstacles...

Growing my strength, I'm energy, pure is my thought, I attract what I want.

The Universe grants me what I most desire....

Queen Abundance, love, health, and money.

Thank you, Father-Mother, concrete is my dream.

Dance my heart, my spirit is happy!

Then my cellular phone rang, and the number showed was 000 000 0000 I said "So it will be…..." (It was 3:33 on my phone's clock) I said, "My wish is already granted….…"

(The phone communication ended) and I said, "Thank you".

About a month passed and I had another sign from our Lady of Fatima delivered by the Knight Templar.

Chapter 49
Timeline Aurora Continuum

Now I heard loud and clear "We communicate by phone when it's necessary". The phone rang in the middle of the night. It awakened me, and I received this message of great importance to share with you.

"VIE I just heard a researcher talking about crop circles of 2019. Until this year they were elaborate and mostly appeared in England. However, this changed in 2019. Very few appeared in England, and they were plain and not elaborate. However huge crop circles started to appear in France in 2019. These were grand, elaborate, and amazing. It seems they are moving more into France.

Also, research on the CROPS that were in crop circles shows fascinating results. The crops produce 75% more food in the future. They are almost completely immune to insects, pests, and fungi. The crops later absorb almost 95% better in the human system and heal throughout the body. So, it is now believed plasma energy is creating them (not aliens) and they make future crops grown there superior to humans!!

Plasma energy is one of the most promising methods of a carbon-free and renewable power generator.

The Aurora Borealis, which is part of the consciousness units being re-encrypted by the Aurora atmosphere.

The Plasma waves are also related to the transmission made throughout the Aurora Guardians Ascension timeline called the Aurora continuum. Typically, plasma is made by heating a gas until its electrons have sufficient energy to escape the hold of the positively charged nuclei. As molecular bonds break and atoms gain or lose electrons, ions form, and plasma can be made using a laser, microwave generator, or any strong electromagnetic field.

Plasmas are the most common form of matter and permeates the entire system, as well as the interstellar and intergalactic environments."

Another crop, a new and unexpected crop circle appeared in 2020 at the end of May, 31st, Dorset UK. As always, astronomical models are revealed in many of these crop circles. The twelve-sector circle model always reminds us of the Zodiac, considering that we have a well-highlighted central sun, surrounded by five orbits (this crop circle was built in five concentric circles in twelve sectors.

Chapter 50
My Soul's Mission

That night and in my dream, I was listening to the news. The Journalist was announcing that a woman was found dead of suffocation inside a hotel elevator by an employee who discovered her after being stuck in for eight hours. That was telling me what three entities had in mind to stop me, to stop the God Duo mission. And I heard "Jealousy", these Hybrids serving the cabal have no feelings or emotions and they do not want you to be happy. They don't want you in joy.

That was also related to my actual life last eight months.

A Few days before Christmas I am currently given the message that the divine assistance of the Archangels and spiritual guides were very close to me at that moment. Ensuring that I stay on purpose in my pursuit of my soul's mission. I am being reminded to be fearless in my undertakings and to take advantage of the positive energy and good influences in my life.

That concerned a warning and a message to keep my thoughts positive and optimistic as I am undertaking an important new role or venture.

A slate will be wiped clean so that I can start over. And a reminder that I can choose my own path so as not to let previous decisions stand in my way, and I must have faith as I am reaching spiritual enlightenment at the end of this journey.

Then a man I lost communication with for quite some time texted me. "Hi, VIE, it's me, your friend the Comte. I am in Europe. I went first to Spain, then lived two years in France, followed by England and I am still in Europe. I was guided by my father to all these places. I am protected by him, and you are too. We are both. Your mission where you are will soon

end, and you will soon be able to leave. Thank you for helping
the Universe."

Chapter 51
A Message from the High Council

I am alone in the sound chamber, lying down in it, and I am listening to the "Frequency of Sound", it's the music I created when I felt a change within my consciousness. And then there was a light from within that became so bright that I was no longer aware of my senses...all was light. And then a voice became audible, not to my ears, but to my spirit.

This voice informed me to listen to what they had to give me. That they were from an astral realm. And my spiritual Family. They asked me to share it.

Then the voice went into silence, and I experienced what I heard and read.

"Your current focus is on the illumination of the mind and the freedom of the spirit through the disclosure and then the information that has been withheld from the public. Many explorations and information regarding human government allege a cute ease and question projects that are kept from the public. This research is largely transmitted in ways that cause people to be doubtful, fearful, and uneasy rather than prompting them to be confident and educated in these matters. Although this stimulates curiosity it does not necessarily cultivate believability. It is just another control program and game. It's an agenda of the elite programs of planet Earth's global government systems.

The controllers of the world want a One-world Government, and you know it. They want to eradicate Christianity. They selected electronics for planet Earth to keep control of humans. In about ten years from now, connections will start to be made between AI and the human brain. Through a thought process of preparation for getting people addicted to technology Human beings hold. Holdable smartphones, and tablets, and it is basically achieved. Just go to a restaurant and look at families with children and you'll see the addiction. Parents are on their phones calling or texting and kids are on a tablet.

The controllers of the planet are specifically targeting the young, because the young, and children of today, are going to be adults just when they want to bring this AI connection in full term. And to have this to happen they have to get these adults to be, and next step, addicted to technology. Addicted to the point where they will accept it and become the most natural thing in the world. This is happening in front of everyone's eyes.

So, the first step was to get people addicted to technology to the point where they would get out at night and make the line outside and in front of some electronic stores to be the first to get the new technology. What they want in the near future is people lining up to be connected to AI.

In some European countries, they are today having parties to celebrate when someone is being microchipped. The other step is to get it inserted in the body. So, from holdable to wearables (watches) to Bluetooth and Google Glass and now electronic tattoos. Electronic tattoos are microchips on the skin.

The public must be aware of some social media operation companies that are absolutely cutting edge of this whole AI. They are not only search engines and people must know them.

If they are aware of all this and know what is coming, then they will have a great chance of predicting it. Because if AI takes over the matrix, then there are no more humans left.
They are earth-based weapons of mass destruction and star-based weapons platform systems around Earth and it's a

nuisance. Although some may view these and other technologies as high-level futuristic creations, they were created through incomplete information loop prints given to the government through changes with many intruder races who had questionable agendas in the mid-nineties. The lifespan and longevity of these technologies and projects is extremely limited as they were created for nefarious purposes and cannot evolve in spirit as human birth transforms it.

Then I underwent into this timeless final state that lasted no more than five minutes, and it was over.

Chapter 52
Vision of Series of Numbers and a Code

To make some sense of this event, in and during my sleep, I went to sit for some Contemplative Prayer time in a small village built in the 13th centuries, but the St Etienne Church was closed. I sat on the bench outside the Church. About twenty minutes later a woman dressed in white came and sat next to me. She silently waited for a while, then with a soft voice began to talk:

"Hi VIE! Here is the explanation of what has happened during your sleep. There is a battle going on. You exist in multiple dimensions, and you are fighting from the astral realms when you go to sleep. And now you are exhausted from the battle, feeling emotional and drained. Please rest and recharge as much as you can. Self-care and self-love are a priority. You are such an incredible soul for taking this mission. You'll soon be reunited with your blue flame and be able to visit your friend, the explorer of the future and reader of the stars.

Then I saw a series of numbers, a code saying change is coming. It is a time of preparation and a new wave of energy. You are encouraged. You are overcoming difficult situations. Be faithful and persistent, you are succeeding. It's written and you know it. It is now your time. Release the past.

So many are looking backward to what was when in fact there is so much to be looked forward to if they would only turn their heads to look at the bright future that lay ahead. Your higher vibrational frequency is quite remote. The future will be grand for you.

The first indictment to be opened is that of the political hybrid/archon woman, who once was chosen to step up for leadership in your world. That chance was whisked away in the flash of a moment by divine decree and she and her other cohorts will now stand trial for their unspeakable crimes against the people.

Many lie asleep still, but this is of their own choosing. They have taken the slower route, and this is their decision. Bless them and love them as they are, for you know that you can.

Be strong in your knowledge. As you know the death of the old brings forth the birth of the new humanitarian system that your people have longed for so long.

It is decreed by the one himself that you too, will stop suffering and join your brethren out in the galaxy as superb divine beings of love, the holders of the knowledge and the guard of the Light. This was the role Terrans had to play in the galaxy so many millennia ago, that of Eden's before your planet was overthrown and cast into darkness.

You can see when you look at the description of the end of days, that all its distinctive traits have been fulfilled upon your planet now. There has been much suffering in this last age of darkness, much deterioration, famine, war, pestilence, disease, apathy, and now ridicule of those who are the bringers of this new dawn. Your planet has known fear, and this fear is to be no more. Your planet will be restored to the Eden it was in its tender beginning, and those Baptized upon your planet now are the first seeds of Eden's future. You are the changers. You are the ones whose hearts are full of love, for the peoples of the planet, for the world upon which you walk, and for the universe you gaze upon in your nighttime.

You are the blessed ones who are put upon earth, who have volunteered to endure pain and suffering like no other has experienced, in order to help those, there. You are the ones, the highest of this universe and more, who came to help when Terra was in such a terrible way. You, the guardians of the galaxy, who stepped into roles that no other would enact, will have your day yet. You will see the fruits of your labors, you will bring to fruition your divine projects, and you will serve as you have longed for so long.

The time is here. It is here now. All will be revealed to those who have waited so long; the grand plan will unfold, and you will begin to sow the seeds of a new world of love, the Eden you have waited for all your lives.

You are in a period of transition from the dark to the light and there will be battles, bombing, and impeachment attempts however, remember nobody up-seats the creator, nobody. He holds the strings - the timelines you are now in, are held gently in his hands with love and care, never to allow what has transpired on your planet to happen again.

It is not the end of time. It is a new dawn. You have brought it forth, all of you, and for this we celebrate you. You are our team upon the earth, you are part of the divine plan whether you are aware of this or not, and for this, we salute you. We watch you all with care. We are always with you, guiding you, helping you, holding you close while you sleep.

I am Ashtar and I stand upon our promise to you and all those upon your planet - there will be the victory of the Light, and love will reign supreme again".

Chapter 53
Epiphany Day

I am driving around the streets looking at houses in flames and burning. Firefighters were saying that they had never seen anything like these firestorms.

I realized that I was looking at the mass destruction of ecosystems to convince and warn people of the global warming agenda. I saw the laser beams causing fires.

It made me re-enter my body for a split second and I went straight back to another vision.

That happened on Epiphany very early morning bringing me messages of hope.

A wide pipe broke open and a powerful burst of clear and pure water came strongly through, releasing me from entities. I was now in control of important entities. Bringing me Joy, happiness, and peace I was waiting for.

It was the result so expected of all my helpers. The Knight Templar, Mary undoer of knots, San Sara, Padre Pio, St Michael working together and the sign I asked Mary that day.

So, I was asked to be ready and to buckle up my seatbelt because a major life-changing event was coming. The guardian angels sent me a strong message to keep faith in the universe. To trust that I was where I needed to be in my journey and that I was on my way to great things. Now. I was finally free from the attacks. They finally asked me to work in alignment with my divine life purpose.

A sign of my capability to reach my destiny by using available resources being optimistic and using my creativity, they said.

However, to achieve my goals, I needed to focus on the positive things and ignore anything else.

Then I saw the Bible. It was lying down on a wood stand, and I read: In these last days, it will be a time of mass hybridization and the mixture and corruption of human DNA by fallen angels, also known as "Aliens." The government is and has been, conditioning the existence of aliens through Hollywood, science fiction, cartoons, and other sources. However, they are not telling you the whole truth. These Aliens are not ascended masters, enlightened ones, or beings from galaxies millions of miles away, nor are they fallen angels kicked out of heaven for their rebellion against the headship of God, and they believe they have one last chance to try to usurp His authority.

They know He is coming to the earth to destroy them once and for all, (Battle of Armageddon) and to gather those who are His, and to establish His reign on earth.

The Lord said that in the coming days, these Aliens will make their presence more visibly and physically known on Earth. As the end times approach, the lies of extraterrestrial lineage, heritage, and creation will come out in full force.

Most people do not realize the Watchers were not a part of Satan's rebellion; they created their own rebellion against God by deciding to leave their first estate which was heaven and go to the earth to cohabitate with human women.

The Church never addressed this issue. In fact, tried to cover it up by leaving Enoch out of the canon version of the Bible, and then manipulating the meaning of "sons of God." They mistranslated Sons of God, (angels of God) creating some ridiculous theory suggesting it to mean Sons of Seth. Enoch was one of the greatest Prophets of God to have ever walked the Earth. It is in Enoch where we first learn about the rebellion of the Watchers, the angels assigned to watch over and guard over the earth.

The Bible is full of accounts of Israel dealing with hybrids. Genesis 6:4 says:

"There were giants on the earth in those days; and also, after that. They are also referred to as Rephaim, Anunnaki (sons of Annuk), Emim, Zamzummim, also after that refers to the Nephilim who were again found in the land of Canaan Numbers: 13:33, "And there we saw giants, the sons of Anak, which come of the giants: and we were in our own sight as grasshoppers, so we were in their sight." The word Nephilim means "violent" "causing to fall" "wonder" "prodigies" or "monsters".

When fallen angels shape-shift into a human form, they can have intercourse but not without some aberrant genetic changes. The union of these beasts with humans produced children that were different in many ways. Like having six fingers and toes and being gigantic.

There are groups of fallen angels competing for global dominance and control within the Third Faction of the New World Order. These are the games they play. One group plays as good shepherds claiming to want to help mankind while they kidnap, mutilate, implant, impregnate, and use human body parts as a skin rejuvenation and coloring maintenance technique. The other faction plays as protectors and basic non-interventionists, the good cop/bad cop strategy.

Remember the Armageddon battle.

Change is happening! The change in the timelines. And the Schumann black-out resonance ...

A huge reset of almost seventeen hours. The black band, or anomaly is a reset which has been called "failure" zones in the space-time field.

It has been shared that this black band represents a timeline change that occurs in the etheric space surrounding the planet Earth! This manifestation is printed on the Schumann resonance graph the purpose of these space-time changes is to merge all artificial timelines allowing the return of a new crystal grid to the origins of the Earth! Where it was before its confinement, before its very elaborate densification process.

Chapter 54
Receiving the Holy Trinity Symbol

On that day I just got off the post office. I was sitting in my car looking at and reviewing my grocery list before heading to the grocery store. That's at that time that I saw the Holy Trinity Symbol, and I heard this voice that only I can hear:

"You are receiving a sign of progress and moving forward. You may be at a place in your life where you're not progressing. This is after a sign of progress and moving forward. It concerns growth, creativity, self-expression, and talents. This is a very special message from the divine realm. All about positivity and optimism and if you are seeing this then it's likely the universe's way to encourage and empower you to continue with your journey. It's a ...will prompt you to live your life truths, and positively influence the people around you. When you know what you are meant to do, every decision, action, or choice has more meaning and purpose. You will provide a fresh approach to life so that you can enjoy a new and positive change".

Two days later The Holy Trinity Symbol appears again in my vision after an entire night of prayer. And the voice said:

"Your angels are just nearby, ready to help and reassure you that your plans are going well. It sends the message that your prayers have been answered, and seeing the Holy Trinity Symbol means that whatever you requested for is on its way to you.

In essence of the Trinity. This includes the three symbols of the mind, body, and spirit. Also, this bears the meaning of the "Jesus' connection" and the "Ascended Masters connection." Ultimately, my guardian angels and the presence of universal energies are heavily surrounding you.

A massive shift in your destiny is about to happen. Your emotions and opinions regarding your wealth and assets are a message from your angels that the strong connection you have with the angelic realm and the Ascended Masters is assisting you in staying positive, light, and optimistic about your life. It indicates that you are surrounded by loving, positive energies.

You have been feeling restless and anxious lately because nothing seems to be changing in your life. Things that you did not find interesting then will suddenly look appealing now, and you will be inclined to follow through on them. This time around, you will be more inclined to take positive action in your life.

You will be more focused on what you want to achieve. You will even see yourself setting your sights on new goals. You are now prompted to live life truths and positively influence the people around you. When you know what you are meant to do, every decision, action, or choice has more meaning and purpose.

You are provided with a fresh approach to life so that you can enjoy a new and positive change. You will be given an opportunity to move on and start over with a clean slate!

You will be given an opportunity to move on and start over with a clean slate!

Your guardian angels are urging you to express yourself with love, purpose, and clarity. When you state clearly what you want to achieve, the universe will acknowledge it and make it manifest in your life sooner than you expect. Your guardian angels are calling for you to be brave in love. You are being encouraged to fight for the love that you want. Nothing extraordinary will happen if you refuse to accept the many beautiful gifts that love can give. If you want your life to be touched by love, you need to be more open about having it in your life.

You are urged to listen to your instincts when you feel that something is wrong, or when you feel someone is not being completely honest with you.

This is a message that Universal Source fully supports your life purpose and soul mission. Heavens have always been mysterious, fascinating, and so magnetically attractive to humans. No one can reach them while in the mortal, physical bodies, but the souls can get in touch with celestial forces. It is something that could be learned to do and there are various spiritual approaches and paths that could help in these intentions.

At lunch time Friday, the woman with a strong accent reappeared in my life with her mix of spirituality and greed for money. She speaks about me needing her help for my blue flame. That another which has now been hired by Katherine.

It is visibly coming from her being tested. I knew something was wrong. Since when a higher being is guiding her, looking at my bank account and she can pretend a to have a ridiculous percentage on the account.

(Witches are those who use sorcery, invoking demons, using black magic, and subverting elements to do harm.)

Did the exorcist priest and knight templar asked for that kind of money? Absolutely not. He knows better.

And now the strong accent woman asked me to make a sacrifice and asked for three third of my account balance if I wanted her help.

I told her, look, a free donation is a free will gift of a certain amount that one decides to give for service rendered. Or it's a fee. And a willing sacrifice for service rendered is an amount that is done by freewill. Or something you decide to give up on. Or call it either your fee or rate.

What is most bothering me is this invisible entity that she is hearing and is looking at the bank account to justify a ridiculous percentage imposed as a sacrifice. And the strong accent woman now says that she doesn't care if I only eat potatoes, that's the price to pay. There we go, she talks about a price now. She also talked about Mother a Superior. What? Does it have to do with the Vatican?

Since when God imposed! This is weird! This can only be a test.

I turned myself on the other side of the bed and fell asleep. And I was right.

The sun was warming the bed through the window, and I awakened with the sensation of being hot with Difficulty breathing in a veil made of wheat.

This reminds me that her demand makes no sense and is not spiritual. God gives freely. No this can't be from the will of God or Mary un-doer of knots. Looks more like dark forces.

Sunday morning and 2 nights later, I was awakened twice. First, I am given a message, and a number symbolizing help from the divine beings. They are ready to work with me and help me make my life as perfect as it can get. Changes I am going to make in my life are going to be hard, but my guardian angels are going to be there for me through this whole process.

Then nearly 6 hours later I was awakened by a second sign and message. It represents the essence of home and a family that tends to be self-sufficient and independent. The energy of this message also resonates with harmony and healing. It tends to be idealistic, self-reliant, and self-determined. The angel is telling me that I need to step up and elevate my life. I have the support and guidance of my angels, so I must prepare to experience success. I will be receiving prosperity and abundance. I have the chance to turn my life around. I have the promise of happiness, love, and peace.

It comes to love. Having a lot of wisdom to impart, it can strengthen my relationship. It is a wonderful message from the divine realm. I have to pay attention to this message and l see my life soar to loftier heights. It denotes the great opportunities that are coming my way. The angels send this my way to show me that they are ready to guide me. It has a lot of wisdom to impart, and it can help me strengthen the bond that I share with my partner.

Another few hours later I am driving and now it is a reminder sent to me of how the Universe works and the role I play in this vast creation we call life. And taking responsibility for my life is when I start creating the things that I desire rather than focusing on the things that I fear.

It says that if my intuition says something is coming my way, I must trust it. What I need to know is whether it's good or bad.

Fortunately, I am in luck this time. And all the positive things, changes, and life events are awaiting me! This is a strong symbol of the subconscious. It stands for the end of a specific cycle and the start of a new one.

It represents a powerful connection to the Divine forces and spirits. Also means that I am a person with a great sense of compassion and helping others. And, no matter what life throws at me, I stay the same. However, I have to make sure no one takes advantage of my goodness merely for their purpose.

The guardian angels are informing me that major changes are going to take place in my life. I am on the right path in becoming the person I want to be. I am finally taking good leaps towards the destiny God has decided for me.

Ten hours and ten minutes later that time it is a clear sign that my guardian angels are standing beside me for love, courage, and support. Every decision I take, they say, is going to have complete support from them. If I have been waiting for the right time to make some big decisions and change my life positively, this is the right time!

My guardian angels are going to give me all the encouragement and confidence I have been looking for. Now, I am ready to explore the places I was afraid of.

"The best thing is that it shows that the resources to move onto a new path are all inside myself." are saying my guides.

This will give me a lot of opportunities to improve my life. No matter what stage of life I am at in my life, I have the potential to get, and make everything perfect. It is the right time for the reunion with my blue flame and get married again but on Gaia.

The number of hours and minutes marks the presence of success and recognition at my doorstep in professional, financial, and personal life.

"This is the right time to open the door of opportunities in your life and take all the important decisions you are lingering on for a long time. This is because the guardian angels, Divine powers, and spiritual help are all by your side. Begin Creating your own destiny!" That was it for that time.

Chapter 55
I Received a Special Message:
Congratulations! You did it!

Sunday night arrived and I received a phone call from my friend Ron. And he said "VIE, it is time to open this door. As your friend astrologist I am telling you this is the time for the creation of a united consciousness portal for healing, balancing and harmony in the world. The astrological conjunctions are here, and tonight at 6pm I have posted a message to all that are ready in the world to join."

That's where telepathically my blue flame sent me the signal. As the first Aquarius to bring what will take 2000 years for humanity to process, he asked me to be part of this world transformation.

Two hours later that's the new message I received.

This is a Special message sent to you and some other Billions star seeds of planet earth. Congratulations! YOU DID IT!

As of today, this old paradigm has changed for good! Light has fully taken over the entire world and things will never be the same. Again, on the Earth planet. The light forces have completely taken over this reality creation process (pandora) and intense efforts are underway at this hour by light forces to completely change this world into a realm of light, peace, and prosperity for all humanity!

VIE, sit back, and watch this world change into a kingdom of light right before your eyes as positive change will now begin showing up all over the world!

The age of Aquarius has truly dawned and now the earth light grig will begin to be unveiled! We have all learned our lessons and we shall never allow darkness to return to this planet!

Standby as the new earth reality now comes into view!

Victory for the light and thank you for the good work that you have done!

The God Duo will be reunited very, very soon now.

God Speed
Michael and the Pleiadians.
I needed so badly to hear that.

Chapter 56
Many Surprises to Come in a Near Future

Monday night. I lay down and entered telepathic communication with CHADD. I received a vision. The last attempt to harm and keep him under Katherine control. She is forcing him to go to an appointment she made to her psychiatrist for more prescriptions' drugs. This is of course an ultimate effort to control his brain. then foggy in an altered state of consciousness. But it won't work.

But that is what CHADD is telling me:

"The enemies of truth know the value of aesthetics, and promote that which is ugly, dark, and disgusting. Satanists are among those that make the horrific a part of their lives and attempt to relativize the good by breaking the barriers of horror man still has for evil and the devil. It is important to oppose such strides, and support those that do the same.

Many surprises await. Like the removal of the many troublemakers by the galactic federation of light.

Some are already expecting a prosperity program to revive the world economy in the very near future. Unknown and hidden to most humans on planet earth great devices should shortly be released after the abundance is released.

Healing devices, health without disease and healing of injuries, instant learning of any subject, skill, or ability. It includes activation of the DNA to its natural state of youthful anti-aging. There are some amazing technologies that can reforest vast areas in a few hours. Sonic showers, personal holodeck with lifelike entertainment, or places to visit. A beach to go and swim on, maybe growing your home fully furnished with all accomplished in one or two days. Cars that fly and teleport. Full body teleportation that teleports human beings through hyperspace from one location to another. Many devices meet all needs and possibilities imagined.

Therefore, brings a more peaceful and balanced life. Filled with faith and trust. It resonates with love and relationships. It's beginning and the ending. It gives special powers and energy.

Positive news and, or information about forthcoming changes to an intense circumstance or situation is on its way. This is the newness of something. You are being introduced to a new way of life."

As my life and things are about to change in the world my guide entering in communication and tells me now:

"The stage is set for you to create your story and keep going with your life. There is something very important in your life that has happened, and it needs to be understood.

The message here is the need for you to be aware that stability, truthfulness, and wisdom energy have become the cornerstone for your goals and passions. It's exciting and keeps you moving forward.

The news is that your life is going to be changed. You are in the turning point of your life, and I am here to help you in your success. Your path to success is related to achieving goals you have planned for.

Something good is going to happen to you. A miracle will happen to you. You are connected with the angel realm. I am here for you to encourage you and help you to achieve your goals. It is not a coincidence. God and angel are sending you the message through it.

You are starting a new journey of your life. Your goal will be achieved very soon. It is a message from a guardian angel that is with you at every moment. I will fulfill your desire. You don't need to be worried or frightened. It is a sign of your good time. The message I carry is that now you can do your work without any problems.

In every step, I am with you. There is a power that will not give you to feel alone. Your path to success is started with God. Angel loved you and connected with you. They are near you.

You are entered into the angelic realm. With a superpower you are going one step ahead in life. They give you the inner strength to make your actions successful. Angels are around you to support you. Now you are in control of the superpower of angels. Now you are in the angelic realm.

In every step you want to go angels are with you. Unknowingly a strength will come to your inner heart.

Get ready! You are about to be revealed and reconnected to an important time of your previous life. You will then be aligned with your past but also your future to continue your life together as the God Duo.

This new energy sweeps and flows like the tides of the universe. It is the ever-constant change that prepares for the next new thing. This is just the start of a new way of living. The universe is guiding us to let go of limitations and fears and to trust instinct. Spiritually means redemption and the grace of God. It is Jesus Christ mostly associated with this energy in the Bible. You are making all the right choices in your life. You are on the right track. You are aligning with higher consciousness. Angels remind you to be fearless, let go of your over attachment to negative thought patterns, and relax. When you approach your challenges in life with fearlessness you are often rewarded for your bravery and courage. It means that you are going through a positive change in your life. The more often you see this energy, the more this message is articulated. Tune in to these vibrations to figure out their meaning. Meditate on it… And yes, the energy of change."

Now the stage is ready for me to co-create and I remind myself. We all co-create our own reality with our thoughts and feelings with the Universal principles laws that we live in. Once understood the law of karma is a universal law because what we do to others does directly affect yourself. It becomes a process when we are looking at the world and realize that everyone around is asleep, and they are unaware of the cause- and--effect relationship. The relationship between their thoughts and actions, and the things that then come back to them in their own lives.

So, I want, we want, to be aware of it and be careful as co-creators.

Chapter 57
A Mysterious New Virus (in fact a bacteria)

Suddenly, I found myself surrounded by angels and by Ascended Masters, trying to get my attention. In the middle of the night. signs multiplied and a screen appears on which I read:

"They need to whisper divine secrets, so listen to what they have to say and try to understand their message. The strong connection you have with the angelic realm and the Ascended Masters is assisting you stay positive, light, and optimistic in this important moment in your life. Pay close attention to your intuition and inner wisdom as you are being angelically guided towards the next step along your path, Trust the messages and promptings and take positive action with confidence and enthusiasm. It is time to live your truths and express yourself with clarity, purpose, passion, and love.

You relate to the Universe and protect from evil by God. It is a shield of bad luck and a protection of assets. Whatever you are doing is edging you closer to your destiny and divine purpose in life. It opens a portal towards many exciting discoveries in your life that can lead to more significant achievement that succeeds all Earthly ambitions and desires.

Thirty days before Easter, Thursday, the W.H.O. declared that the coronavirus is a "Public Health Emergency of International Concern" (PHEIC).

Suddenly I was in shock. I am hearing, while I am shown, that there is a new virus that started in China. The epicenter of the coronavirus outbreak they say. My intuition tells me that something about it is wrong."

I said: Was it created? And what is a Coronavirus? (Covid) "The as-yet-unnamed coronavirus appears to have emerged at a market in Wuhan, which was shut down on 1 January. But cases have also been found among people who said they never went to the market, suggesting transmission may be taking place elsewhere. That's what a magazine wrote."

And that's what I am told.

"The name "coronavirus" comes from its shape, which resembles a crown or solar corona when imaged using an electron microscope. Coronavirus is transmitted through the air and primarily infects the upper respiratory and gastrointestinal tract of mammals and birds. Though most of the members of the coronavirus family only cause mild flu-like symptoms during infection, SARS-CoV and MERS-CoV can infect both upper and lower airways and cause severe respiratory illness and other complications in humans.

Coronaviruses are part of a family of "viruses" that includes everything from the common cold to more severe illnesses like severe acute respiratory syndrome (SARS) and Middle East Respiratory Syndrome (MERS).

In 2002 and 2003, the SARS outbreak originating in southern China spread to at least 26 countries, infecting more than eight thousand people. Some seven hundred and seventy-four people died.

The MERS virus was first confirmed in Saudi Arabia in 2012. It reached at least twenty-seven countries and killed at least eight hundred and sixty-one people out of nearly two thousand and five hundred cases, according to the WHO. Both SARS and MERS have been ruled out during the current outbreak. It has yet not been determined whether the latest coronavirus is as lethal as SARS. SARS is another outbreak that began in China in 2002, infecting people through 2004. More than seven hundred people died worldwide of SARS.

This new coronavirus (nCoV-2019) causes similar symptoms to SARS and MERS. People infected with these coronaviruses suffer a severe inflammatory response. Both SARS and MERS are classified as "zoonotic" viral diseases, meaning the first patients who were infected acquired these viruses directly from animals. Now these viruses can be transmitted from person to person. There is a very technical article written which suggests that the nCoV-2019 is likely a human modified "virus" which the Chinese created using SARS spike glycoprotein.

This new coronavirus (nCoV-2019) causes similar symptoms to SARS and MERS? I said, and that's what I heard "Listen to the news VIE, laboratories are already working on a vaccine. And how? It will be created from the SARS vaccine and added to it. Another created virus to serve their agenda. Reduce the population and at the same time pharmaceutical companies will make money. This vaccine is going to kill many more people and they intend to chip the population through this vaccine.

A study by 5 Greek scientists examined the genetic relationships of nCoV-2019 and said to have found that "the new coronavirus provides a new lineage for almost half of its genome, with no close genetic relationships to other viruses within the subgenus of sarbecovirus," and has an unusual middle segment never seen before in any coronavirus.

In fact, we are dealing with a brand-new type of 'man-made' coronavirus. The study's authors rejected the original hypothesis that the virus originated from random natural mutations between different coronaviruses.

But it's not time to worry. It's time to become educated about this outbreak. And it's time to make sure you are doing everything you can to get and stay healthy, as the most likely people to suffer the most are those who are already immune compromised.

A Cosmic Master is explaining now: Please, don't be alarmed by the Coronavirus, it's another attempt by the Negative Forces to stop the upcoming Galactic Disclosure. We suggest that you don't let fear take over you and please meditate to raise your vibrations.

"We are doing our part from another side trying to stop and eliminate the Coronavirus, which was created in the laboratory. The Cabal wanted to create panic and distress globally." Ashtar Sheran.

There is a secret kept by the cabal, illuminati, and the Roman Catholic church (like the believers) that applies collaborating with the alien agendas to keep humans isolated and trafficked around the planet on earth. China is a New World Order country and making tests there. And China hospital supposedly built in 6 days was already a built building.

There is dust sprayed over the area that is an aerosol with particles design anti-dots constructed of frequency contrary against radiation, Isotop and heavy metal. An intelligent dust to neutralize the atmosphere. It serves multiple intelligent functions. And there is also a regressive dust that the cabal sprays to detect galactic helpers' ships that they use over China.

While the Coronavirus (covid-19) has been put in the spotlight, there is another crisis that is hidden from the world: a million Uyghurs have been brutally detained and brainwashed by the Chinese authorities!

Current events are unfolding consistent with prophecy from the Book of Revelation and what is happening behind the curtain of communist China. The coronavirus plays into the strategy for Global domination.

But people will survive this scourge of mass media lies and manipulation to virus contamination. the lack of testing in the US, NDA's", and quarantines.

The Trumpet, in the Bible, announces that an epidemic will descend on mankind in the end times. The epidemic, disguised as one of the Four Horsemen of the Apocalypse, will wipe out a quarter of the planet's population. Some 7.8 billion, that death toll would come to nearly two billion people.

From Revelation 6, which is attributed to John the Apostle: "These horsemen symbolize the end-time culmination of the most devastating woes endured by mankind because of his rebellion against his Creator.

In his description of the fourth horse and its rider, John writes: "I looked and there was a pale green horse! Its raider's name was Death, and Hades followed him" This symbolizes catastrophic disease epidemics. The passage states that along with the other three riders, which represent religious deception, war and famine, the anemic horseman that represents disease will end up killing the fourth part of the Earth.

Matthew 24:7, Mark 13:8 and Luke 21:11, which warn of pestilence breaking out before the Second Coming of Christ.

Did you know? Isotope, any of two or more forms of a chemical element, having the same number of protons in the nucleus, or different atomic weights. There are two hundred and seventy-five isotopes of the eighty-one stable elements, in addition to over eight hundred radioactive isotopes and every element has known isotopic forms. Isotropic of a single element possess almost identical properties.

An Allied country to America cooperates with China and it will have some consequences for this government country.

Then the screen faded away.

Chapter 58
Fear Feeds the Corona Virus on the Planet. Love Starve it.

This following is a telepathic conversation that took part between us. The God Duo.

While the fear of coronavirus is spreading more rapidly than the actual virus itself, we are reminded that we need not to sit idly by and wonder what will happen. We are connected to the power that creates universes and heals all ills! We have guardian angels to guide us. Each one of us is a powerful force of love, whose light contributes to the cure for fear, and the cure for the viruses that energetically arise from it. There is such a thing as spiritual immunity. A good life is one inspired by Love and guided by knowledge. Fear creates a chemical cocktail in your body that weakens your healthy cells and creates imbalances that allow these parasitic energies to take hold. Getting tired and worn down is a result of fear, vs. faith in a loving source that would support you if you more freely supported your own well-being. Likewise, greed, corruption, and misuse of power feed off fear on the earth. In a space of love, you become a vibrational catalyst and a force for positive change. If more people were praying for a solution to the recent viral epidemic, a solution would be found within weeks. Fear feeds a virus. Love starves it. If more people were praying for the world's corrupt and wounded leaders rather than hating them, they would transform in ways you cannot imagine, and become a force of love. In the commandment Jesus told the disciples: "Love one another, as I have loved you" John 15:12." "This is my commandment, that ye have one another, even as I loved you" John 15:17. "Those things I command you, that ye may love one another" John 13:34 – 35 NIV "A new commandment I give you; Love one another. By this everyone will know that you are my disciples." Fear feeds greed. Love starves it. When fear threatens to infect you, or take control over an inherently loving being, stare it in the face, breathe deeply, and say to it, "BE GONE! Love is my power. Truth is my power. I am safe in the arms of the Loving Presence that lives in all things! I am Love. I am LIGHT. I am safe. I AM" Rather than fearing coronavirus I am sending it love. Rather than fearing world leaders and disasters, I send love to them and to our mother earth.

We can't control the outer, but we can control our inner world, and in a world of light we are guided away, or immune to the dark.

And we are given a way to Counter the Corona Virus and Its Effects. Becoming the cure. This is a simple exercise given by the Company of Heaven, to help counter the effects of the hysteria, the MSM and our Governments have generated relating to the "Corona Virus" A last ditch attempt by a failed network of "service-to-self" entities trying to halt the progress of Gaia and her Peoples.

The Company of Heaven is a collective of Ascended Masters, Angels and Galactic's who hold and share a similar vibration, so they speak to you today as One consciousness, One Being, made of many, just as you yourselves are.

The people are asked to share and use this as often as guided and in any group meditations we attend. The more people doing this, no matter the "time" as there is no "time" the stronger the resonance field we will create that will all connect with each other, unifying the Pink Light of Mother God.

Firstly, they say that yes, the Corona Virus is indeed a real virus that is circulating our planet. Yes, people will get sick, and people will die, but those that are Ill or passing on, know that this was to be, before they incarnated this time around. So, what they wish to share with those of you who are guided by this message, is a way and means to assist with the negative impact this virus is having world-wide. They wish for you to do a short, yet powerful exercise, to help counter the negative effect this virus is having.

Begin by calling forth our energy, call on us, the Company of Heaven, to be with you in this moment. Call upon all your team in Spirit and anyone you work with, to be in your presence and to assist in this process.

Now, see a beautiful pink light coming down from above you… See how bright and brilliant it shines.

Feel it coming down into your energy field and entering your crown… See and feel it filling your body. A beautiful pink light, full of brilliant sparkles… Bright, powerful, and nurturing… Take a moment to let this fill your body, focusing on the brilliance of its color and how calming and soothing it feels within your Being. Some of you may feel a strong energy and this is fine, it just means you are bringing this through very strongly.

See it now as it goes out your feet… Travelling deep down into the Earth, going right down into Gaia's Pink Heart Centre. Take a moment now to see and feel it anchoring into her core, into her heart…

Once you feel you have anchored this light, see it coming back up through the Earth, through your feet, up through your body and out the top of your head, connecting back to the portal it came through, your Soul Star Chakra.

Now that you have anchored this light, see it radiate out of your being and saturate the entire area you are in… The more detailed your vision the more potent it's effects… See it going through the people and places around you… It is weaving and merging with all that is around you, this beautiful bright pink light, filled with all sorts of sparkles, whatever color sparkles you see… These sparkles are us dear ones, we are with you through this process…

Once you feel you have covered your area, see it cover your country, following the same process as above until you are satisfied… Once you have covered your country, cover the world dear ones… Light the world up in a bright pink fire… A beautiful bright pink. Blazing away any negativity, anything of a lower vibration. Light it up dear ones.

YOU are the Creators of this reality, so YOU can transmute that which is of a lower vibration. See the Mothers Flame burning across the globe, see it purifying those who are in fear, distress or panic… See this nurture all those in these lower vibrations…For it is the mother that is being suppressed in this final attempt, to stop your movement forward…

It is the feminine energy that they wish to halt, but you will not let them, we will not let them.

All are bright pink fire dear ones and if you wish, merge this with the Violet Flame, so you have two fires burning, two lights burning across the globe. Hold this vision dear ones, ask and intend that it will be sent where it is needed most. You may see a location or a person that needs it, think it and it shall be so! Do not limit yourself to you are able to accomplish, what you can achieve, just by a simple thought, for you are the Creator! You are the Ones creating here on Earth.

The company of Now Heaven says that "You can counter this virus quite simply, you are powerful, all of you, no One is more or less powerful than another, you just have different roles. Some of you are Guardians of the Earth, some Keepers of the Earth Records, and most of you originate from distant planets and solar systems, bringing with you the required energies of your main system. Use your skills you have honed over lifetimes and simply create a cure for this madness those nefarious ones have engineered. Create a sea of light that simply washes it away! The more powerful your belief that this is truth, that what we tell you is truth, then the easier and quicker you can remove this current situation from your planet. NEVER doubt yourselves dear ones, for doubt only seeks to limit you. You ARE the Creator, so use the creative energy within you to create a planet free from this virus and free from the negative aspects it holds. All is washing away with your assistance."

Our vibration attracts validation for what we believe! Together may we become the cure to the viruses of fear. VIE

CHAPTER 59
The Nun from the Abbaye, Saint Germain, and the Global Economic Landscape

My journey continues. I am contacted by a nun, that pretend have lived till this day in an Abbaye… is sick and encountered a powerful medium… slept in her van though she stays in a hotel, but her house is in the mountain and she's wearing some weird clothes from an ancient time…and more.

My entire body vibrates, and I feel it strongly. I feel the energy running in my body. I am seated on the outside front porch of a restaurant (the terrace said the waitress) called "Le Grand Saint Germain". I am looking at the waitress. She is cleaning the table next to me, and the birds are finishing their job eating the breadcrumbs on the floor. It's on a sunny day in early fall. Perfect weather for seating out and having a cappuccino. Suddenly came a woman with a weird nest on her head. Nobody takes this kind of look these days I thought. She sat next to me to the cleaned table and began to speak to me. Do not come closer to me than that. Stay where you are at and all will be well, she said.

"My name is Anne. I have lived in an Abbaye. The Abbaye of Grace. I was waiting for this Priest, where the was also in the "Abbaye" to make his move. When he did, I then went to study the Byzantine music. I am more of the Orthodox faith now. I heard you talking on the phone the other day. I think that we have an understanding of the mind. I am weak but does not send me energy. I have met a very powerful medium six hours drive from here. He said I cannot receive any energy for three weeks."

That weird look, the old fashion clothes she was wearing, and her saying that she lived in an abbey confirmed my feeling and thought. She was a nun in an abbey. But why is she telling me all that? She continued.

"Last night I slept in my van in a parking lot. The car stopped working in the grocery parking lot. The engine was running but the car would not drive. That is why I am walking today. But a human angel mechanic that I found said that he will look at my car today and take care of it. It took me a few hours to find him. But I refuse anyone to sit on my seat in my car. I would have to clean the entire inside car again. He understood and agreed. I am not putting my butt where someone has put his. But if I am sitting on that table next to you today, it's because I was sent to deliver you some news and it involves Saint Germain.

There is a global operation happening behind the scenes. It involves agencies of many foreign countries and the US. It is to bring down a very rich man, and his lackeys that purchased the entire democratic party.

Nothing is coincidental, says Saint Germain, and he is changing the global economic landscape.

Saint Germain has re-incarnated several times. Saint Germain was incarnated as Joseph, the father of Jesus. His last incarnation was as Count Saint Germain in France around the time of the French Revolution. Jesus has a very close relationship with Saint Germain.

Saint Germain is saying to you: I am saying to the globalist system, the central bankers, that their days are numbered, and they do not have a future. My mission is to get rid of everything they haven't done and set up.

All the trade agreements, all the organizations. I am reversing it all and changing the landscape. And there is nothing that can be done to stop me.

Today with the coronavirus in China manufactures businesses, those individuals that were part of the global system are now looking at it and saying maybe we shouldn't be in this one singular supply chain. We should have bilateral trades and not stay in China. We can't be caught in this. We should move our facilities somewhere else and avoid this situation happening again in the future. Let's decentralize and have many different trade deals and different avenues.

Because they are looking at what I have done and what is happening to the economy in the world leader and biggest country of the world. And soon looking at Brexit many will understand and follow the direction they have taken."

Anne ``Saint Germain is laying out exactly what the globalist did. He says that the economic collapse and the geopolitical news. The Russian lie will be exposed. The entire Russian election is a different collusion conspiracy narrative. The control of the narrative equals Power.

When you control the levers of news dissemination, you control the narrative.

They want you divided. Divided by religion. Divided by sex. Divided by political affiliation. Divided by class. When you are divided, and angry, and controlled, you target those 'different' from you, not those responsible (controllers). Divided you are weak. Divided you pose no threat to their control.

And they are worried about what he is going to show to the world. The origin of how they did it, why they did this, and how it is treasonous.

Once the people learn all this, you cannot put the public back to sleep, and the game is over."

My dad says Anne was an epidemiologist like the Professor that is bringing so much controversy. This Professor is a genius. And yes, I agree he has no ego. All that criticized him are so ignorant and so stupid. He is so above them all. "Ok now, my blessings to you" and with her hands in the form of a cup she sent me the sign of kisses. Saying "I live in these mountains at the end of this horizon. That is where my home is. I have to finish a few drives back and forth." She took a last look staring at the sky, I saw a merging with the sky, and she left. These angelic messengers always appear in an odd look. I should have understood earlier she was one.

Chapter 60
An Answer Received in a Most Unexpected Way

Preoccupied for days by the same subject, and days of prayers and concentration something still did not feel right lately.

I went for a twenty-minute walk and prayed while walking. At the end of my walk, I received the message that a positive change will soon be coming, that resonates with expression and a personal sense of freedom.

Then I prayed to the blessed Mother Mary and the father for their direct message. Suddenly right in front of my eyes appeared the most beautiful white baby feather, and I captured it in a photo. I knew that I was right.

I knew Lumita was chosen for a specific task, working with San Sara. I gave her a powerful and sacred tool I had for her to be able to enter in communication, and work with Padre Pio.

The Holy Spirit, through my prayers, and the intercession of Mother Mary, has received my request and answered it sending me this baby white feather and Saint Sara gave Lumita a message for me.

I had just got back in the house when I heard the phone ringing in my purse. It was the jealous woman who did not like the idea of me accomplishing my mission, being fulfilled by it, and being happy. The one that paid an archon, then a guru, and then a witch to harm and stop me and CHADD and I mission.

That's where I heard the news and from her mouth.
She has not done well lately. She said that she is admitting having a hard time recovering her energy.

So, I meditated on it… and this message came to me. "This is a sign for you. Angels are God's messenger. Your prayers have been answered. You are Fully Supported in Your Life Journey. The angels want you to know that they are close by to assist you in your life journey. There is a direct channel that opens between you and your Higher Self. It is the point of merging the physical and non-physical realities of you. An Energetic Gateway has been opened for you. At this moment your thoughts, beliefs, and actions are energetically charged and incredibly potent.

The birth angels are telling you that joy will be coming your way very soon. You will reap rewards for your hard work and consistency.

Such wonderful news. But I sadly could not share it with my blue flame. Lumita said to be careful they are listening to everything I say. Then I had a vision...

Chapter 61
Message to Humanity

I had this vision while sleeping. I saw a very brilliant object in the form of a cigar, the size of half a cigar. I kept looking at it wonders what this was, that was awakening me in the middle of the night. It stayed in my vision for about 2 minutes. I could see some colors, then, when I got it and understood that it was coming from a galactic source it faded away. Then appeared this following message it gave me.

Greetings VIE,

Dear Brothers and Sisters in Christ,

Human beings are being programmed which is keeping you in low vibrations trying to prevent the ascension of the planet and humanity. CERN, that you mentioned in one of your other books, is an artificial stargate that wants to connect to another planet, the solar system, that contaminates the crystalline grid with low vibrating energies. Taking over planets. The energy of love will distort these low vibrations and vibrating installations. It will heal the keylines.

Override your heart and use your plasma love energy to make low vibrating installations dysfunctional.

The reason why Christianity gives utmost reverence to the Sacred Heart of Jesus and the Immaculate Heart of Mother Mary is because of the physical connection of the human heart to the Cosmos.

It is the only organ in the human body that has an electromagnetic force directly connected to the current energy circulating in your planet, which the ego is made to oppose.

The human being Heart is the responsible organ for downloading the physical, emotional, mental, and spiritual codes or nourishments from the present cosmic energy, which in turn, will be processed by other organs. Thus, you understand how the act of processing takes place once you are emotionally imbalanced.

To interpret the new energies in the heart, people usually end up losing their faith, missing the opportunity of learning, depressed or anxious while they keep on judging the things, people and circumstances surrounding them that they do not understand yet.

The heart is not related to your egoic emotional tendencies that cause human strife, take offense, feel angry or afraid, yet it suffers greatly than other organs. These negative emotional reactions only come from your pains and traumas in the past, operating whether you are conscious or unconscious about them. This is because the Universe, God, the Ultimate Source does not know how to become personal towards you. That is very human. The Universe is only vibrational. Meaning, the Universe only matches the energy vibration from your thoughts, words, and actions that you give out to Her.

Just like Jesus and Mother Mary, your Heart is your saving device. It can tell you your Soul Mission, where self-fulfillment transcends beyond materiality. It is where your greatest treasure can be found. It is also your inner guidance for anything less than what your Heart has become that will no longer feel good to you.

Therefore, it is important for everyone reading this to always purify the intentions coming from thoughts, words and actions towards the self and others. They must align them with the heart's desires, no matter how painful and difficult the process can be or regardless of how they control the people and circumstances around them. Otherwise, people will continue to experience more of your lower timelines in life.

With the Aquarius era humanity is experiencing an incredible metamorphosis. We are ascending while still in physical form. This is a monumental process which causes deep purging. So please remember to be kind to yourself and to others, as we experience this miraculous transformation.

We will be transformed to the 5th Dimension from the solar flash. We Will not be reset back to the stone ages; we will not have to go through that again as happened with Atlantis and other advanced civilizations in the past. Earth and the entire Milky Way Galaxy are being boosted up into the next dimension, through 4th, 5th and then eventually to the 7th Dimension. We and the planet will not be wiped out by the solar event, and we will be transformed to another level of existence. Anybody who is negative, evil, or not frequency specific to this new world will simply no longer exist here.

Before that though, we are already being introduced to our Galactic neighbors and many are here to assist us with this transition along with very powerful upper dimensional beings and the entire upper dimensions pushing in hard at present to get us cleaned up and evolved to the next phase.

The downwards spiral from our outer sun connects with the upwards DNA activating spiral from the sun of hollow earth in our heart space. From the heart space the energy then flows through our crystalline meridian and chakra system to every cell in our body to activate it's alike: a miniature sun around which the atoms circle: a miniature solar system.

The sun is a stargate, a satellite source, through which source energy flows into this solar system. ONE.

Your sacred heart is your saving device.

Suns are satellites of source, they are stargates through which source energy flows. They are connected to each other by wormholes/organic crystalline tubes through which source energy flows into 'solar systems'/dimensions. Also known as the universal highway. All DNA codes must be activated to travel this highway to prevent distortions in the energy body. You must be alike in energy: ONE.

You also have higher selves in the higher dimensions and are also connected through crystalline connections coming in through the crown chakra, just like the suns. Same in energy: a drop of plasma light, source intelligence/light activating DNA. This light is divided into a Prisma effect/frequency bands: Our chakra system/rainbow within. Chakras (inner stages) are connected to each other through your crystalline meridian system. You are the source manifest.

The fractal effect is the only source intending an energetic double. DNA resonates at a distance and is connected by crystalline connections: tubes/wormholes through which source energy flows. It also explains string theory and the law of attraction: alike in energy attracts/connects/activates. DNA is a torsion field antenna.

Just be who you are to easily remember the pieces of you that you have forgotten. Stop playing roles that don't resonate with your current awareness of the self. Stop complaining, instead get on with your life and be what you dream of! It only causes you to downshift to the lower timelines in your life.

You are neither a victim nor a villain. In fact, you are the main character in your story who is free to choose the people, place and circumstance that can assist in learning your purpose, while being grateful for the unexpected events in your life.

You are also neither punished nor rewarded. The Universe does not know how to become personal, only human emotion does. What the Universe does is to respond to the frequency of the energy you give out to Her.

Let that sink in, brothers and sisters, so that you will no longer blame anyone nor feel guilt for what is happening in your life; so that you will not feel aggrieved nor an evildoer; so that you will step in your own power with full confidence. Because you are all Creators of the Ultimate Creator. Were it not for your unconsciousness to the pains and traumas of the past, you will remember how to create love and prosperity without destruction?"

Chapter 62
The Galactic Criminals, and the Priesthood of Atlantis

CHADD entered a telepathic communication with me to say that he had to stay up for the last twenty-four hours busy with the crystalline Orb. But it's not what you think. He remembered his time in Atlantis as a Higher priest.

You see, Atlantis was destroyed by humanity's own collective by empowering a leader outside the self. The galactic criminals took over the priesthood of Atlantis. Atlantis had a second moon, a crystalline orb which was used for weather manipulation, but then for the good: to let it rain where it was dry etc.

The priesthood would let the orb position itself above a certain region and amplify the intentions of the priesthood. The priesthood all had to have the same heartfelt intention to let the orb shift through the power of telekinesis. This priesthood was infiltrated, and weather warfare began to destroy cultures which was against their intentions, floods, droughts etc.

Atlantis self-destructed and projected back at itself by source. Dealing with humanity's own creation, pure mind, acting without feeling, so a leader outside the self and empowering, manifesting another one's imagination, and intention.

We are connected to the keylines and therefore our solar plexus becomes distorted. Fear is only a feeling of the absence of Light/love in the heart-space that is not connected to source, love, universal law.

Universal law is to use your light as an expression of love.

Chapter 63
Be Mindful

As every week I had lunch with my best friend, who I consider to be my blood sister Jackie (nick name Jo). She invited me to her place instead of going to a restaurant. She wanted to read me something she stumbled upon. She said that she thought about me when she read it and wanted to read it to me now. And it was confirming and concerning many things I told her. And I would like to share it with you.

"Chemtrails with poison and metallic particles above your head, are creating a horizontal shield and prevent the higher energies from reaching you through your crown chakra. The higher energies then "bounce back" into space. Also, a shield to project a fake invasion (blue beam.)

There is a worldwide HAARP system (also under water) hooked into the keylines and pulsating low vibrations through the elements crystalline (keylines), water and air, impacting all DNA that is connected, and known as frequency programming. Taking over what you must think, imagine. It is a war for your mind, the imagining power, your pineal gland that programs and activates. Mindful!

The implants in your hand and on your meridian system are connected to your heart. These implants are also transmitters and receivers. They are antennas. When directed energy weapons "tune" into your receiver you might have a heart attack. "Killing at distance under the disguise of a heart attack."

Mercury is in Vaccines, and it is clogging up your brain and your head is becoming an antenna to the HAARP frequency, or energy weapons. Viruses are in vaccines that "hatch" a certain low vibrating emotional frequency.

World Leaders are convincing you it is right to destroy and hate when one is low. Now everyone is low in vibration as we are one.

Instead of teaching you to become telepathic and connected worldwide they gave you a phone and internet. Both transmit low vibrating energies through your meridian system. Only giving you information on a need-to-know basis.

Fluoride is in water only to calcify your universal wireless antenna (pineal gland). So that you are not able to receive ideas, visions, data, DNA activation energies from the high dimensions.

Digital music, hard Rock music, and bad language etc. these vibrations scrambled your chakra system. Words have vibrations and words open DNA. DNA creates ideas. Your tongue is connected to your heart and is created to translate your heartfelt visions, and the tongue is also for taste.

There are dome buildings and complexes that function as upside down radio telescopes, and they amplify the visions of the members attending a service. The leader or preacher is then telling people what to think, to imagine and activate, mind control. These domes are often in the hands of low vibrating dualistic people spreading low vibrations of duality through the keylines for all to experience. Hell is on earth and nowhere else. They attend rituals on certain days to empower their visions. You can do the same and go to such places with crystals and amplify your own vision and override with high vibrations.

About genetic manipulated food. These genes resonate to the low vibrating matrix and distort your energy field.

They put poison in food, so all your energy is needed to get it out of our system.

Through the education system they keep kids in the survival of the fittest mode and therefore their angelic DNA/knowing of the higher dimensions becomes dormant.

Oil should and must stay in the ground to dampen the vibrations of the stargates and prevent eruptions. It is time to get free energy instead and imagine energy that does not distort your energy body.

Chapter 64
Life After Death

Death! Here is a taboo subject when you want to speak about it in our actual society. One day in a conversation between two friends, I heard this answer to the question about life after death: "For me I think that after I die it is the end. There is no life after death. For me we live only once, and this is why we need to live it fully."
Wow! Isn't it what the controllers teach to keep people in ignorance?

I went through many sacred initiations, some easy, and others more difficult. This allowed me to experience and understand that for me it is now evident that the human unconscious in front of the mysteries of life after death of the body is proof that humans have become ignorant. In the Essenian tradition, the knowledge of life after death is the most important thing.

To live without the knowledge of the worlds in higher dimensions is dangerous because humans allow themselves many things that they should not in the occidental world. And you can see it right now, this world is decadent and an absolute dictatorship.

Chapter 65
Becoming Immortal Again

Now I read in return to CHADD my friend's article, letting him know that we are progressing, and things are becoming unhidden finally and he added its part. Saying do not ask me any question about the origin and how I got it from where I am. You know me.

"Old Mesopotamia is the Heart-space of the world, and they know it. If Iraq, Turkey, Syria, Iran these regions are at war our heart space is also affected. By creating peace in this region humanity will become immortal again. These regions must be liberated for the grand flash that creates the event to be integrated. Because like energy it attracts and connects. The Heart, Source regions must be fully activated.

In addition, here's a list of even more attacks on the Deep State Cabal for those who don't believe the swamp is being drained. Meanwhile, sources are claiming that the Coronavirus (COVID-19) epidemic was caused by the Deep State Cabal to start War World III between the US and China.

The Deep State Cabal's plan was to blame the US administration for using bio-warfare on China.

However, this plan is backfiring on the Deep State Cabal and now the CCP (Communist China Party) is allying with Trump and the Earth Alliance to save their economy.

This new alliance will cleanse the CCP of DSC players and usher in a new GESARA compliant China.

China is already "cleansing" their old bank notes under the cover of the COVID-19 epidemic. People dying from the virus are the ones in low vibration.

Just be who you are to easily remember the pieces of you that you have forgotten. Stop playing roles that don't resonate with your current awareness of the self. Stop complaining, instead get on with your life and be what you dream of! It only causes you to downshift to the lower timelines in your life.

You are neither a victim nor a villain. In fact, you are the main character in your story who is free to choose the people, place, and circumstances that can assist in learning your purpose, while being grateful for the unexpected events in your life.

You are also neither punished nor rewarded. The Universe does not know how to become personal, only human emotion does. What the Universe does is to respond to the frequency of the energy you give out to Her.

Let that sink in, brothers and sisters, so that you will no longer blame anyone nor feel guilt for what is happening in your life; so that you will not feel aggrieved nor an evildoer; so that you will step into your own power with full confidence. Because you are all Creators of the Ultimate Creator.

Was it not for your unconsciousness to the pains and traumas of the past, you would remember how to create love and prosperity without destruction?

Chapter 66
Thoughts and Telepathy

Here is something I would also like to share with you. I have told you that as the God Duo, CHADD & I communicate when we are separated by telepathy thought.

Here is an interesting explanation. Thought is also fully holographic in the sense that, when you unravel a thought package, you gain a full experience of the picture being transmitted, the sights, the sounds, the tastes, the smells, and the feelings on both a physical and emotional level. If the thought package is about an experience that the sender has had, you will be able to share and relive the entire experience.

Telepathy is a natural medium of communication. Animals use it. Dolphins and whales use it. Humans use it at night when they are out-of-body and traveling in the spirit world.

Speech was developed as a means of communication in the physical world because the human conscious mind is tightly focused upon the exterior world, emphasizing the use of five physical senses for its information.

While the conscious human mind typically ignores telepathic input, the subconscious mind is fully telepathic. Your subconscious mind perceives every thought that the subconscious mind of another person, or the conscious mind of a pet, directs towards you.

Your subconscious mind is fully connected to the global mind, which Jung referred to as the "collective unconscious" and Teilhard de Chardin as the "noosphere," which means "mind atmosphere." You continually receive thoughts from this global mind atmosphere in tune with the frequency of your consciousness at the time. Then, you process these thoughts through your own consciousness and automatically re-transmit them back into the global mind.

Therefore, because of this automatic thought-sharing process, every moment that you spend in uplifting thoughts is a moment spent uplifting the thoughts of the world.

Chapter 67
The Feathers, the Lady with a Red Scarf, White Coat, and a Hat

One week later as I was driving towards Church, I looked at the dashboard of my car and saw another Holy Trinity symbol. Walking back to my car after mass a feather fell in front of me. A Lady in her sixties with a red scarf, white coat, and a hat that was inside the church passed by me. And she said without stopping or looking at me:

"Remember when you left home a few months ago and you were delivered the message saying that the Holy Ghost will be with you everywhere, and you'll know it by seeing feathers. A lot of feathers everywhere you are and go. This is another sign. The same way that when this dark energy woman that came to visit you for the holidays saw the feather out of nowhere suddenly appearing on the formal living room floor. Repetitive signs and symbols represent a synchronicity orchestrated by the Universe. It is a conversation with your blue flame. CHADD is telling you that you are ready to start something brand new. It is an advantageous time to grab opportunities that are waiting to unfold on your path. Stay connected to the desire of your soul. The decision you make today will shape the story of your life tomorrow. You become what you think. Don't wait for the perfect time to create it. Importantly you hold the key to unlocking and unleashing it. So, trust in your whole self and go forth. We believe in you.

Abilities are increasing rapidly as the light is growing at a vastly rapid rate each day. You are absorbing much of it. The unified focus, that the Priest mentioned in church, brings about change as directed. See it, and as you will feel it happening it becomes an essential part of these changes going live now.

Hold your attention to all the wondrous things that await you and a divine dispensation descends to fulfill all your hopes and dreams.

Then I smell a very enjoyable smell like I never did before. A perfume of Love. I wanted that smell to last forever. It lasted a while and faded away leaving me with this joy in my heart. I needed it so badly. I was missing him so much.

And the lady continued her way and disappeared from my sight at the end of the street.

Chapter 68
Battling the Curse

Time is passing by and we, the God duo, CHADD and VIE are still separated by the cabal. I opened a channel to communicate with the Ascended Masters and Now have the full support and blessings of the Universal energies. It is a direct channel that opens between me and my Higher Self. The point of merging the physical and non-physical realities of me. an Energetic Gateway. It tells me that at this moment my thoughts, beliefs, and actions are energetically charged and incredibly potent.

It is a very powerful double Master communication. In time I had to keep connecting with my higher self or inner wisdom to manifest my heart's true desires and soul's divine purpose. At a time when my dreams will begin to manifest. resonates with balance, harmony, service and duty, stability, diplomacy, ambition, and co-operation. Also having the traits of justice, selflessness, decisiveness, intuition, faith, and trust, and serving my life purpose and soul's desire.

Nothing in this world and in life happens by chance and everything happens for a reason, and this is what happened next. I entered an alternate state and received a message from another realm:

"You deserve accolades for the mental, spiritual, and physical work you have been doing in your life. You are helping yourself and many others with your current life choices and actions, and you are being commended, encouraged, and supported by the angelic and spiritual realms.

As you know a curse was put on CHADD when he was born. It is because Kathrine felt something unusual when the newborn baby was shown to her. Something that she did not have, and she did not like this. He was different to her son Paul. The baby was introduced to the archaic grandmother, and she did not like it either. They both felt threatened by it and that's how CHADD was cursed. And CHADD at 6 years old was put into an illegal human research program with his family consent. He became the custody of the State. And we are aware that you have for years joined him to go through all these tribulations to free and liberate him and humanity from the deep state.

And you are very close now to the reunion with your blue flame. Remember what the almighty and powerful father told you once. You know how to manifest and create, and it is time."

I heard CHADD saying, "I invite you with me here."

And then I saw the mirror hour indicating that my guardian angel is aware of my need for a profound change in my life. A radical transformation affecting all areas of my life.
And I replied, "Yes! I remember Father what you told me." I spoke.

And I began to get busy working on it and I knew the Cabal did not like it. The phone rang several times, but I did not answer. That was just a diversion to stop me.

Chapter 69
Battle Nearly Over

Then many figures began to appear each day in my vision. After a week to ten days, this message arrived:

"Once you have understood the meaning of the numbers appearing, there's much you can do to reap from its immense power. It represents the essence of home, family, and creative expression. The energy represents and resonates with harmony and healing. It tends to maintain an environment where family members are free to communicate and create. It shows that these new friends are going to bring a significant change in your life, and you will experience growth. This new position will open more doors and opportunities for you. It will take you places because you work hard, and determination will make all this possible for you.

You are fully supported in your Life Journey. The angels want you to know that they are close by to assist you. The divine realm encouraged you to maintain peace so that you will keep enjoying a harmonious existence. This is a message saying that this is the right time to achieve your desires and reach success.

The higher powers are there for you and want to guide you to the best path now."

That was the message I received from my other self because of this newest odyssey. A quest we, CHADD & I, had to make for you.

I was guided to experience this. It happened in a period of eleven months. I was forced to live in a hotel room, somewhere in the middle of nowhere. When I say no where I mean in the middle of big private lands with castles, and just this lonely place I am in. A one single room where I cooked, ate, slept, and took my shower. I was literally being put in solitary confinement in a prison like. No one to talk, no one to socialize with, no park to walk, but a parking lot and not knowing when this solitary confinement will end. It was just me and my faith, while I could only speak on the phone for one to two minutes a day to CHADD. I had to make sure he was not getting into depression and bring him my support. I had to sound happy even though it was hard. I had to because the drugs he was forced to ingest is known to depress people and some have been suicidal from it, and even killed themselves.

And one day I felt that the battle was nearly over, we would win.

I saw that it took me a few days to finish up that battle. It was time CHADD was losing hope to see me again and had lost weight by deprivation of food. He needed me now. The knight Templar sent me an email confirming.

Alecia gave me a colored feather with pink in his center and instructed me to wear it at a specific and official ceremony. The one that will celebrate the reunion of the female and the male. The liberation of the male, my blue flame.

I spoke briefly to CHADD as usual. He had to stay up the entire night in the company of the angels. Battle is over! Just need to unfold now.

A few days later I spoke to the father, and he confirmed. Battle is over and the God Duo will very, very soon be reunited. All obstacles were cleansed and erased by a simple gesture of his hands.

It takes quite some time and a big, huge effort to get over with this battle. I had to be with Alecia while she was tested, and that is why sometimes things were not clear between her and I. I had also to find my way in this unclarity. She was not always hearing the right guidance. She did not know that the cabal found her and could this way use her.

Just at the same time all this is happening a new crop circle appeared, and it has in the middle the face of the commander in charge of the galactic float of the federation of light. Commandant Ashtar Sheran.

Two months later Alecia re-appeared on another parking lot to give me some blessed water from Sainte Marie de la Mer Chapel, blessed by San Sara she said, and a candle with three crosses engraved on it. Saint Mary de la Mer was Saint Sara, the Black Virgin known by the gipsy people and is their patroness. She spoke.

The legend of the Black Virgin tells us that it was not a Virgin with her child that the man found and had in his vision. But a Virgin with a black ET child. A wood statue from the XVII century of the Virgin with a black ET Child... The man refrained his hands from shaking when he opened a trap very easily. Inside was a small statue representing a totally different child. It was a small, delicate, and very beautiful white Christ.

Now the man was having the Virgin in his right hand and the small Christ in his left hand. He very delicately sat down with the lady in the center of the table. Alone, she was even more beautiful, he said. And the man heard:

"Do not pay attention to my black tan, it is the sun that burned it."

Never the words of the cantique of the cantiques had resonated with such power said the man. She was standing proudly in front of him on her invisible throne. She was glowing. And the man suddenly said. "I understand now! It is the fire of all the candles burning that blackened your skin."

Then I saw and received Revelation 14:14 "I saw, and behold, a white cloud, and upon the cloud One sitting like the son of man (*Apoc.* 14:14). Behold, He cometh with clouds (*Apoc.* 1:7). Having upon His head a golden crown, and in His hand a sharp sickle.

Signifying the Divine wisdom from His Divine love, and the Divine truth of the Word. Signifying that by "a crown upon the head" is signified wisdom, and by "a golden crown," wisdom from love and because it was seen upon the head of the Son of man, or the Lord, by "a golden crown" is signified the Divine wisdom from His Divine love.

The reason why "a sickle" signifies the Divine truth of the Word, is, because by "a harvest" is signified the state of the church as to the Divine truth, here its let state; and therefore by "reaping," which is done with a sickle, is here signified to put an end to the state of the church, and to execute judgment; and because these things are done by the Divine truth of the Word, therefore this is signified by "a sickle"; and by "a sharp sickle," the doing it exactly and exquisitely. By "a sickle" the like is signified as by "a sword," "a sabre," and "along sword;" but "a sickle" is named where a harvest is treated of, and "a sword," when war is treated off.

That "a sword," "a sabre," and "a long sword" signified the Divine truth fighting against falsities, and vice versa.

VIE said my friend Ron, I just woke up after a powerful psychic lucid information dream. A Being of great wisdom told me many things concerning the pandemic.

The Being (He) said that this corona virus was created in a biological war research lab in Wuhan. A lab worker was accidentally infected with this virus, and he was patient zero who in turn carried the virus into the world.

No human has immunity to this virus. It is a biologically created organism and like the Indians in the New World who had no immunity to European diseases can kill millions. This virus has an evil intelligence. It hides for weeks in a person, shows no signs of it being there, and cannot be detected. Meanwhile it will spread and contaminate everyone they encounter. Children are really used as infectors as they have a strong immune system and can resist it, but it goes to kill the elderly and those with a weaker immune. We are only on the beginning edge of this pandemic.

The being of Great wisdom told me it lives on surfaces for up to 10 days. Millions around the planet are infected and show no symptoms and are infecting others.

Two hopeful things were told to me. Though. First, oil of oregano is the best defense against it. 10 drops in a gallon of water, shake every time you drink to mix oil and drink ONLY this. Second, this virus is killed when exposed to sunlight/ sun lamps in 10 minutes.

The virus will run its course and finally mutate but we All must be safe for the next 9 months. There is no other way to tell you this, but millions around the world will be killed by this. I'm disturbed by what has been shown to me, but I am focusing on the virus to quickly mutate and be safe.

And it worked. We both began to focus. Then was launched the 2020 Global meditations of one million people to end the covid-19. Two weeks later a famous French Professor announced that by spring the virus will probably have mute and he was foreseeing the end of it.

This professor was a treat to the deep state of course and the cabal. He had found a protocol to save many and became a famous leader in his field mainly overseas and worldwide. He became a world re-known figure except for the ones that have been bought by the pharmaceutical companies that were trying so hard to create a vaccine rapidly. And vaccinate the population. Nano Chipping and killing the old and many others with "comorbidity".

Early June the TV news announced that the virus was under control. But the deep state and the cabal will keep controlling the population with fake information, masks, distinction, and restrictions.

Chapter 70
Ascension Update from my star sister

I had to receive this from my star sister to get accurate information. Nothing can stop what's coming now.

"The stock market crash taking place right now is fully on schedule and proceeding as expected. The light forces are fully in control of the events taking place behind the scenes on Planet Earth right now despite what the media is reporting.

As of Feb 2019, the Federal Reserve was no longer allowed to print more money. As of Feb. 16, 2020, USA Inc. was forced to default on its foreign debts of $22 Trillion. This is the real reason the markets are crashing.

The entire FIAT banking system owned by the Cabal and operating illegally for 100 years is now being taken offline. The Federal Reserve (also privately owned by the Cabal) will be allowed to operate for one year in order to remove all outdated US currencies from the world supply after which time the US Treasury will take over. At that point, a new currency will be introduced that will be backed by Gold and fully managed by the US Treasury under constitutional law.

As the world economy collapses, all banks based on the old FIAT system will also collapse with it (Which is pretty much most of the banks of this world). Our debts based on this illegal banking system will be fully forgiven, which includes Credit Cards, Mortgages, and all other bank debts. American Birth Certificates were illegally being sold as property bonds by the Department of Transportation under Maritime Law. This will no longer be allowed. A new U.S. Treasury Bank System will be introduced in alignment with Constitutional Law.

Many will be pleased to hear that Income Tax will be abolished as it was being forced on us illegally by the Cabal.

The only tax that will remain in the future will be a 17% Flat Rate Sales tax on Non-Essential Items. Which means food and medicine will not be taxed. The IRS will be dissolved, and all its employees will be transferred to the US Treasury national sales tax department. New Government benefits will be initiated towards senior citizens. Unprecedented amounts of funds will be released worldwide for humanitarian projects. We will see the implementation of Universal Basic Income which will smooth out the disparity between the rich and poor classes around the world.

The Corona Virus is being used as a cover-up to freeze international travel and declare a state of emergency while mass arrests are taking place behind the scenes.

On the technology front, more than 6000 suppressed patents will be released to the public. These patents were being held back by the Cabal under the guise of national security. Over the next decade, we will see mind-boggling technologies being rolled out including Free Energy Devices, Anti-Gravity Vehicles, and Advanced Sonic Healing devices. Almost all diseases will be eliminated over a short period of time including Cancer.

The next era will be an era of World Peace under GESARA law. Presidential and Congressional elections will be introduced 120 days after the implementation of GESARA and Constitutional Law will be reintroduced to all Courts. All National emergencies will be canceled. There will be many arrests taking place for election fraud that has been taking place over the past few decades. U.S. Military action will cease worldwide. It's already happening with the US Taliban peace treaty as well as Saint Germain world visits with Saudi Arabia North Korea South Korea India UK etc. All nuclear weaponry is being eliminated and Nuclear Facilities are being decommissioned. Nuclear reactors for energy will no longer be allowed nor will they be needed in the future.

Children will see a brighter future as the planet has finally been freed from a 25000-year rule under the clutches of a Satanic Cult. We are in a boiling pot right now as all that is of the old world is being dissolved and all the hidden darkness is coming to the surface. We must hold peace within our hearts and not let fear guide us. The winds of change are upon us and indeed this is a glorious time of celebration for Humanity. This may sound too good to be true, but all will be revealed for us to see soon. Every Sacrifice we have made to get to this point was well worth it!"

Chapter 71
Fear and the Missing Wisdom

Then I had a lucid dream. I saw the surrogate archon, Katherine the mother of Paul. She was sitting in various restaurants with CHADD. She placed, sometimes, up to three different orders of food. CHADD was not eating but was just sitting there next to her. He was not eating, and it did not bother her at all. But nothing was enough to feed Katherine. She ate her food, his food, and kept going from place to place and ate everything served to the table. In one location one meal was offered to CHADD. He was still not eating but she did. She was able to eat in two different restaurants, one after the other the same day, and eat 4 plates in a row.

So, I asked him "But how can she eat all these foods? One plate after the other, because she is not fat?" Of course, she was not looking fat because what I saw and what she was eating was the energy of fear coming from people. CHADD was just an observer. He was sitting next to her and looking straight forward in silence and no expression on his face.

But that is not all, it showed me that he was also deprived of food. Katherine was collecting his monthly government check and still using it for her own pleasure. She had a homestead, she did not need him to pay the taxes on her house, but he did not know. She was lying to him keeping his money supposedly, pretending it was for taxes or she would lose her house. But she had a homestead.

Tragedy can birth some of the most beautiful moments of our time, but only if we take this time to join hands. We can create something visionary from this crisis, but we need to urge our world leaders to rise and be the heroes this moment needs. Let's do it together with hope and determination,

You see with the covid-19 I understood that when the panic of not reacting enough takes hold, nothing is off the table. The situation is aggravated by the political posturing of politicians who use the crisis to their own ends. Control, fear in the population, reducing the number of humans and money.

And that is due to Missing Wisdom. When panic informs policy, it becomes impossible to make the right decisions. It is not the case to argue here about what specific measures should or should not be implemented. The Chinese virus crisis is a severe threat that must be confronted, and no one denies it will involve hardship. However, what is missing is wisdom. Many, especially the media, are not presenting a balanced picture, or the whole one. Wisdom is the contrary of panic. Wisdom is calm, reflective, impartial, and objective. It deals with reality as it is, not as one might imagine it to be.

Wisdom must be found everywhere and at all levels. Will people seek God? Will people return to him? In times of great tragedies, sorrows and incertitude human beings finally understand and remember that He exists. That He is in command. Some are grateful to be alive and some are invoking him for help.

Chapter 72
From Fear to Joyful Love

What happened is that long ago, humanity had become tired of incarnation as fully aware spirits physically and decided to live with a sense of inner separation.

They wanted more challenge in life, a standalone human experience, not just an extension of spirit into matter.

In the natural state of spiritual living free spirits in the mental realms, there are very few limitations. People can manifest anything they need, relocate instantly in space, shift to a different position in time, all at the speed of thought. In the mental realms, people can visit friends or go along with them, exploring the universe, all through the power of thought. That's why they're called the mental realms.

The mental realms exist in fifth density consciousness and are the domain of your soul or inner being. Between third-density physicality and the fifth-density realm of your inner being lies, the fourth-density spirit or astral realms populated by people in the afterlife.

Physical incarnation is always voluntary. Nothing compels your soul to incarnate into another physical life. It is always a decision at the personal and soul group level whether to come back into physical life on Earth.

Thousands of years ago, physical experience was a fully conscious extension of spirit into matter. People knew who they were as spirits, connected to their inner selves and to the universe.

Humankind then made the joint decision to immerse itself further into a denser, more focused reality. Their focus was directed upon the physical senses, along with a detachment from the superconscious and subconscious levels of thinking.

By maintaining a tight focus upon the "outer" world of the senses, humans could even believe that they are fixed into one location in space and locked into one time continuum.

The result is that life can be scary. A life spent without a constant, conscious connection to your true inner nature is always a challenge.

Today, the amusement park ride of inner separation is coming to an end. The Shift to the New Reality is happening today. We are becoming more and more aware of our inner nature. Those who grasp the idea of the New Reality will actively develop that inner connection, not just wait for it to surprise them as it slowly unfolds.

And remember, this ride through intense physicality was always a choice. We may not remember as far back as when the choice was made, but, at a soul level, we've been willingly hopping on and off the theme park ride of physical life on Earth ever since.

We incarnate for the experience of physical life, and to help transform this reality towards its ultimate state; one which, today, is looming very nearby.

These are the days of transformation, the time of The Shift. The scary ride is coming to an end. As a culture, we are about to find ourselves and reconnect within.

The Shift from fear to the joyful love of our higher selves is happening right now. Something is going to happen that is Biblical around Easter, said CHADD.

And many Catholics in Europe could not get communion, could not receive the Holy Sacrament because churches were closed, and people were in confinement.

Chapter 73
Two Dreams in a Row the Same Night

We were two in this dream, and I could see a bicycle with two purses hanging on the handlebar. My purse and hers. The one easiest to grab was her (a woman). Twice two guys on a motorcycle passed by it and stole my purse. The 1st time they stole it, and she right away called a number she had on her cell phone and recovered it. But then she placed it back, and again, on the handlebar with mine. The second time her purse was stolen she called and could not get through, she rapidly crossed the road to the bank, showed them the picture of the guys she had taken on her cell phone, and I believe she got her purse back. That was my feeling.

That other woman had stolen her heritage twice, but some were left and recovered.

In this second dream, we were three traveling. I, my older sister, and someone else I did not get to remember. Was it a man, or a woman? I did not get to see and remember it. But we opened the trunk of the car to unload the suitcases. Mine is perfectly closed and ok. I only had one suitcase, my purse, and something else that seemed to be an umbrella. I wanted to travel light. The two other travelers had both one suitcase and one hand luggage. One had it turned and tossed everywhere in the trunk of the car, and the other traveler had his suitcase split open, nothing had moved but was looked like it was never closed. Then it's where I heard very clearly from someone standing close to me before I awakened.

"You should invest now the remaining 20% money." That happened in May 2020. Three months after February 16, 2020.

A few days later I awakened from a third dream with a horrific feeling of loneliness. I felt left alone on Earth.

That's what my dream was. I was in a room in bed, and I saw the long tongue of a snake appearing behind a bed where a "she" was laying down, but I could not see her. She was totally covered by the sheet. I told her to kill the snake, but she did not want to. She wanted to see what will happen and see if it was time for her to die. The snake passed on her and I was laying down in a bed next to her. The snake came towards me and went straight to suck my nipple. I was not moving but in fear and wondering if he was feeling it and going to bite me as my nipple reacted when he began to suck it. But the snake did not.

Then I was in a church with a friend. We are sitting next to each other in church. She was seated on my right side, and she had the snake on her lap dead. Apparently, she has killed it. She is peeling the skin off the snake.

There is a man, a kind of a man in authority in the church. A man to whom everyone seems to have to report. Now my friend is cutting open the snake and she says to herself silently: I need to recover what is inside his stomach in case this man wants to see and know what's inside. Next, she went and gave what she found in the snake' s stomach to the man. Then she comes back to give me the snake and says something that I could not understand, and she leaves towards the back of the church walking between rows of seats. I am now finishing up peeling the skin of the snake. Then I raised my head and I saw that I was the only person left in the church. I have this terrible feeling of being left alone. I leave the church towards her old car. A very old town car, beige, light brown. So old that I am wondering how it is still running, and if I should go home driving it. Then I had the quick thought of calling a taxi. The church is far from all traffic, but I see a crossroad with a few cars passing by and a small family's own grocery shop at the corner. Finally, I decided that I should drive home in the car. Thinking that a taxi must be hard to find.

I awakened and it took me some time to get passed this heavy feeling of being left alone, abandoned in the church, and abandoned. It reminded me of that same feeling I had at the end of conventions when every vendor and speaker hurried up packing and left. This same heavy, very heavy feeling of being abandoned and left alone in the world. Now this happened when I was left in a hotel room during the confinement with no receptionist, and no one expected me to live in it for 2 months and a half.

This was followed by my fourth dream. I realized that suddenly and lately I am receiving dreams two in a row at night.

In this fourth dream I am seeing an old house, and my oldest son is proudly showing me that he has begun to paint it. Two thirds of the concrete house surrounded by grass was painted in a nice brownish-gold color. I went inside and really looked at it carefully. I am visiting the rooms one room after the other and taking my time to look at all the details. I realized that the house is not as old as I thought and did not need so many updates and remodeling. Not as I thought it had.

No, it was not like I thought it was. Even the ceilings also look nice and modern. And then, I went back out again and saw that it was not two-thirds of the house that was painted anymore. But it was totally repainted, finished, and looks beautiful, and with an added fence it will attract buyers easily if it has to be sold. This happened to be a message delivered again during the confinement. Telling me that the person in my family would make it financially and succeed with his new business idea during this chaotic time.

Chapter 74
A man reaps what he sows

So, I am awakened with this loud and clear advice. "You should invest the remaining 20% money." "And I replied but there is no more left" Was my dad telling me to go and get the last lost sheep.

Two days later I had another dream. I am in a two-story house and there are some children playing and running one behind the other. It looks like it's my parents' house. Then It's about plants that my father planted and have produced seeds. My father loves planting, and I found out that at least three of his plants have begun to produce seeds. Specifically, one is giving nice seeds. I decided to call my father and tell him to come and look at it and see the seeds. My father comes in very handy- fully clothed as usual. A beautiful silk Kimono over his pants and shirt. He goes down the three steps to get outside on one side of the house. There, on the right- hand side of the ramp along the three steps, there are seats like you would have in a movie theater but with rows of only three seats and people seated. So, my dad looked at the seeds that were on the tree that happened to be facing these three seats then we turned around, me following him to get back inside. There was a man who was seated in the middle seat of one row. I recognized him as his direct business competitor who has always been jealous of my father. Known for being rich and politically powerful. A well-known name and leader of a political party on the island where we live. Seeing that no one looked at him but they had eyes on my father, the man grabbed my hand, and said "Hey do you remember me?" I barely knew this man but yes, he was much older than me and I did see him, but I had no reason to talk to him. He was much older than me and I was not into politics. But I replied politely and quickly "How are you doing?" and I turned around and left following my father inside.

The same day someone sent me an article in which it was written that due to the actual state of the economy, and the time we are living in Gold and Silver will soon lose a lot of its value. It will be a good time to invest.

I realized then, the powerful message sent by my father about investing in Gold and silver.

My dad was showing me about that corrupted man who made his fortune, like many corrupted politicians, destroying its image and its business, his money, and belongings that My father made in a clean and proper manner. Not like this man. He used his "fame and influence and used another politician to destroy my father, destroy his name, and steal our land and my parents. Depriving us of our inheritance.

And now it was a good time for my dad to tell me that it was a good time, the time to recover from my loss. What they stole from him but to reap what was sow.

Galatians 6: 7 "Do not be deceived: God cannot be mocked. destruction: what he sows." 6:8 "The one who sows to please his sinful nature, from that nature will reap destruction; the one who sows to please the Spirit, from the Spirit will reap eternal life."

Now I received confirmation,

"Receiving the fruits of your labor. Trust that the Universe is working behind the scenes to help you and be open to receiving anything you need for your soul growth. You will encounter major changes in your life. You are currently well on the way to becoming the person that you want to be! You are finally going to make clear strides along the path to your destiny, and this is true in every aspect of your life. The angels are at your side to give you encouragement and the confidence you need to explore territories and areas unknown to you. You will find the resources inside yourself to succeed in new challenges!

This will give you many opportunities in your romantic life. The change in setting will allow you to meet new people. You will explore and broaden your horizons. But the most important point through the angels is that recognition and success are at your doorstep in your professional and financial future. At this moment you are undeniably very lucky. What's more, your work and your skills will finally be recognized.

You will receive the fruits of your labors."

WOW!

Chapter 75
Offering a Vision of the Future Technologies 5G, Coronavirus and the Future

So, a few nights ago as I was drifting off to sleep, a being of Light appeared in my spirit vision and said "I am here to teach the Lightworkers more about the Holy Spirit. So many do not realize the value of the Holy Spirit and do not use the power of it. I came here to teach them some ancient techniques to help them in the Light."

As technology continues to evolve and merge with our existence 5G technology could affect cells in the human body, particularly children. 5G transmission will be detrimental to human health as the planet becomes surrounded by these waves and found evidence on both sides.

The next generation standard for mobile networks requires the placement of many more antennas than 4G works on millimeter waves and allows for such things as driverless cars, remote surgery, downloading of movies in 3 seconds, and increased surveillance.

You must get wiser about protecting yourselves from the increased radiation and EMF it will bring.

China was the first city to be blanketed with 5G. We foresee the technology leap of 5G, a radically altered world, with the widespread adoption of driverless vehicles, stores solely operated by robots and sensors, a lot of what we consider privacy and a completely different economy.

The pandemic quarantine has been a test by the elites in power, for what job loss may look like with this next wave of technology. And there as a result is a growing mistrust of political, corporate, and scientific systems among the general public.

There is also Serge in negative energy and curses being experienced by a variety of people. Curses can be sent consciously or unconsciously when a person covets something that someone else has.

The mind is powerful and capable of creating a lot of the issues that one of ten leads to curses. And we have been warned by God. Do not Covet: "You shall not covet your neighbor's house; you shall not covet your neighbor's wife, or his male servant, or his female servant, or his ox, or his donkey, or anything that is your neighbor's."

The Ten Commandments were given to the Israel nation through Moses. The nation of Israel was now free from slavery in Egypt and was camped around Mount Sinai when thunder, lightning, a thick cloud, and the sound of trumpets signaled God's presence. Moses met with God and the 10 Commandments were written for the people to follow.

These laws of "thou shalt not" are meant for our protection and guidance. God, our loving Father, wants to give us wisdom and keep us from choices that He knows will harm us.

The Ten Commandments in Exodus 20

1 And God spoke all these words, saying, 2 "I am the LORD your God, who brought you out of the land of Egypt, out of the house of slavery. 3 "You shall have no other gods before me. 4 "You shall not make for yourself a carved image, or any likeness of anything that is in heaven above, or that is in the earth beneath, or that is in the water under the earth. 5 You shall not bow down to them or serve them, for I the LORD your God am a jealous God, visiting the iniquity of the fathers on the children to the third and the fourth generation of those

who hate me, 6 but showing steadfast love to thousands of those who love me and keep my commandments. 7 "You shall not take the name of the LORD your God in vain, for the LORD will not hold him guiltless who takes his name in vain. 8 "Remember the Sabbath day, to keep it holy. 9 Six days you shall labor, and do all your work, 10 but the seventh day is a Sabbath to the LORD your God. On it you shall not do any work, you, or your son, or your daughter, your male servant, or your female servant, or your livestock, or the sojourner who is within your gates. 11 For in six days the LORD made heaven and earth, the sea, and all that is in them, and rested on the seventh day. Therefore, the LORD blessed the Sabbath day and made it holy. 12 "Honor your father and your mother, that your days may be long in the land that the LORD your God is giving you. 13 "You shall not murder. 14 "You shall not commit adultery. 15 "You shall not steal. 16 "You shall not bear false witness against your neighbor. 17 "You shall not covet your neighbor's house; you shall not covet your neighbor's wife, or his male servant, or his female servant, or his ox, or his donkey, or anything that is your neighbor's." 18 Now when all the people saw the thunder and the flashes of lightning and the sound of the trumpet and the mountain smoking, the people were afraid and trembled, and they stood far off 19 and said to Moses, "You speak to us, and we will listen; but do not let God speak to us, lest we die." 20 Moses said to the people, "Do not fear, for God has come to test you, that the fear of him may be before you, that you may not sin." 21 The people stood far off, while Moses drew near to the thick darkness where God was.

Chapter 76
The Morphogenic Field

The mirror hour 13:13 provided me with hope, love, and positivism. It instilled in me a new spark to face the changes that I was about to face. It instilled in me a new spark to face the changes that were surface.

Divine Love is to love humanity as a whole and connect your soul with the Universe. This love will provide you with inner peace and happiness and help you to connect with the Divinity.

I was being guided to see sacred geometry forms and live the vision. The goal of the cabal is to microchip everyone on the planet, and then use the human mind to create their own reality. Then the planet Earth will be dehumanized.

Because of the old man who was contacted by the surrogate when she saw the help I received from Saint Sara, Nostradamus decided to help me. The cabalistic old man, the father of Katherine, has knowledge of the particle/antiparticle universe. And I saw him at work changing the God Duo reality, in an ultimate gesture to stop them and their reunion.

What the old man did not expect was that Nostradamus was going to enter a psychic connection with me. I was in the land and even the area that Nostradamus once lived and traveled about. Where he received all his insights and wrote his quatrains in France.

That is when my friend Ron contacted me and said: "You may wonder why you are trapped there. well, some help has been impressed on me. Be aware that you are in the land and even the area that Nostradamus once lived and traveled about. Open yourself to its flow, he is offering you its help and will enter psychic communication with you now."

I was in a vision of a different space. I was watching a movie that turned out to be clicking slides which was my consciousness oscillating and I was seeing on and off reality. My consciousness was oscillating at a higher refined rate that was out of the range of a particular descending matrix. This is a multidimensional Universe, so please pay attention to the following I heard.

Dimensions are arranged in base rate wavelengths; the length of the base waveform is changed at every dimensional level. In sacred geometry forms.

In terms of ascension mechanics and the physics of ascension, a dimension is a frequency band. So, it's a repeating sequence of flashing on and off Scalar Wave (standing) points that exist within a grid and that grid is called a Morphogenetic Field.

A dimension is a full-frequency band of repeating sequences of flashing waves going on and off. That's the particle/antiparticle universe that we are working with and is what we are existing in the same simultaneous space with. So, when reality is flashing on and off, sometimes we can perceive this. I know that I experience this at times. That flashing on and off is experienced as literally coming into a certain reality.

Dimensions again are fixed groupings of energy within specific geometric arranged forms and are built upon crystallized conscious units of sound and light. Those conscious units of sound and light are called morphogenetic fields or manifestation templates. So, from each of these instructions set templates, these manifestation templates, dimensions are composed of stationary points of the vibration of sound and light which together form a fabric of tone and into which smaller morphogenetic fields are woven. From each fixed point of sound vibration and within each dimension of the manifestation field, an electrical current of consciousness emerges. There is layer upon layer upon layer of morphogenetic fields and dimensional reality systems.

Nostradamus was showing me the answer to my question. Why was I trapped there and how it happened? I knew now what I had to do to help me out of this trap. Finally, after nine months of being trapped. I had to change back the reality. The Cabal is so good at twisting and bending reality but cannot create without us. That is what the old cabalistic man did. He used the timeline to make the sequence of events that has created that specific universe and dimension is the universe in which that reality exists. By using the brain of an old weak man close to me.

And this is where we want you to be careful. Our vibration is what we "pulse" back to the Universe, to the cosmic field. We emanate frequencies and when we let our thoughts be focused on the external chaos, we give ourselves our own power and let the third dimension pull that control and tell us what to think, and what to fear, and your ego will resonate genuinely to it, and will make your brain think about perhaps fighting back.

There's no way that anything that does not resonate with love transcends into a fifth- dimensional frequency. It's time to forgive, to let go of control, and to love. To feel compassion even for the worst ones you may consider judging their actions. It's not time to be judgmental. It's time to be conscious about self and others and understand that this is not separated. We are not separated, so when we judge others, we are only being judgmental of another part of our own experience on Earth with their context and circumstances.

We all need love and when we decide not to give it free to everyone, even for the ones who you consider bad ones, or are a reflection to trigger your ego, then you are deciding to cut your high vibrations and vibrate lower. When you do otherwise, your energetic field gets boosted, but you must do your inner work to get to this point, and this big "stop" is a time for us to heal whatever we needed to heal, and the other ones who are now ready, must work harder with forgiveness because this is how we will give our step into fifth dimension. Meditation shows us how to be in the zero field of creation, to reach the highest levels of consciousness. Your duty is to anchor them by creating this loving reality first by emanating them yourselves and being as contagious as the virus of fear, but instead of causing fear, you are healing your environment.

Now, today the mirror hour 1:01 tells me that The Divine Love is to love humanity as a whole and connect your soul with the Universe. This love will provide you inner peace and happiness and help you to connect with the divinity.

About a month later, I heard that the old man that got the knowledge on manipulation of the particle did not die of Alzheimer, but he had a heart attack, was declared "death from covid- 19," and died.

Are we talking about karma? Are we talking about the Universal law?

Chapter 77
The Feminine Archetype Pistis Sophia

The time of the great Shift of all Ages has begun. Each great shift begins with a massive close. The end games. While the war against the deep state continues to accelerate towards freedom for the people, we are being told by the world leaders that we must be prepared for the second wave of COVID-19 coming.

Prepare yourself for the news media to blow everything completely out of proportion like last time. Prepare for many lies at this point. World leaders and politics have one word that they always left out of their speech; it is the word freedom.

We are living in a junction. What the second coming is it's about civil arrests, it is about a vaccine, and surveillance tracking apps and taking away your freedom.

Everything you know is not real and what is real is not known. There are reverse engineering technology available and more other unheard technologies. Many technologies are made in cooperation with inter-dimensional beings. Some angelic type beings from your future.

The following is a message telling me of a conversation I will have with my family member saying that he wanted me to be protected from the two dark feminine entities.

That was showing me the delay, manipulation and the intrusion of the same dark woman and archon in my life and in my mission once again. I awakened sad, then got the message, and asked for the Holy Spirit help.

That was when the karma caught the old man that had the knowledge of the particle and used it for its own interest. He did it at the demand of his daughter. An inorganic being and died shortly after in the hospital. He could not breath, went into a coma for a few days and died. Doctors' death certificate said, died from the COVID-19.

The following afternoon I was asked to help a young teenager. But it turned out that the mother was the one that needed the most my help as she herself was guiding her son, and it guided me to this that I knew.

The two parts of your brain should be reconnected. The idea of the task between the left and the right is not a simple rumor, it is scientifically proven. An American neuropsychologist, Roger Sperry won the Nobel Prize in 1981 for their work on cerebral asymmetry. He said the left side is the dominant being the digital, rational, order, mathematical objective, and analytic side. While the Right is the creative side with emotion, instinct, memory, musical, artistic, and imagination. But your two parts of the brain are separated and need to be reunited if you want to have full clarity of mind and awaken before the solar event and ascend to the fifth. This and Oneness is necessary.

Chapter 78
Galactic Light Codes Night Vision and The Base Nectar Protocol

But it does not stop here. There is a call lately for me to apply the base nectar protocol and the Dodecahedron with my light ... specific colors and places. Also, the activation of the inner bird activation process with my light.

And I heard:

"The level is moving" The movement it made was barely perceptible. But as I watched it continue to turn, I could see it getting nearer to pointing straight up. The lever was righting itself and it crept closer to center, chills ran down my back." and I said to myself, "things are starting to right themselves." I saw crowds of masked protesters. They had no idea what these masks imposed on their mouth and nose were representing on a metaphysical level. Then was given to me the "Light protocol" for the Covid-19.

And I came to realize that this shift to the center point that I was seeing now had to do with them. With the protestors and their commitment to truth, to what is fair and their desire for a better life for all humanity. The world was emerging from a long sleep, and through this particular moment in time, the course of life on earth will change, and humanity will return to being human. And I heard the same inner voice telling me.

"At this difficult time, tell them to help one another however they can. Tell them to march, sing, pray, serve and speak out. The masks are to stop them from speaking the truth to one another. Tell them to interact, smile, and to pray. Prayers will make a difference.

Help them. The collective good pouring forth from humanity at this moment will turn the tide. Mankind is no longer in collision. Let those who are lost, rage on as they will," it said. "Let them bluster all they want, and while they rant, rave, and blame, keep your every thought, word, and deed in alignment with the love of the Divine. Breathe deep, stay calm, love each other, and
keep on going."

And the Falcon of Horus vision appeared. In my third eye. Then I remembered the degree of the DODECAHEDRON 6480 Hz. And the memory came back, I remembered about the work I had to do to help them. I was guided to use my light to help their inner third eye function. The pituitary gland, the inner bird, and the pineal gland, and the eye of Horus. I was guided to use my light to decalcify the pineal gland. Yes! I was guided to reconnect their inner eye, DNA, the two parts of their brain and to elevate their vibration to optimal level.

Then I heard these final words: "Go forward now in love and light."

And this is why I do energy work. It is to manifest a world where we will have the freedom to choose.

I am focused on assisting spiritual seekers in living their Divine self-expression within this human experience. Because nothing can harm you when you are aligned with your soul.

Have you experienced the healing power of the Light & sound? Have you experienced the healing Light language? Or a multidimensional quantum healing therapy?

Scientific research shows that even the simple act of humming can be therapeutic. There's a reason why this fascinating subject has been exploding in interest in recent years.

Using Light & sound as a healing approach is not new though. In fact, for thousands of years, cultures from around the world have used vibrational medicine to treat illness, revitalize the body, and elevate the spirit. But what is unhidden now is the fact that it can be applied also in quantum by someone that has been gifted at this highly advanced healing system that works on all levels and dimensions as well as past, present, and future.

Every living being (everything in the universe!) is in a state of vibration. And this means every part of you — from your organs, your bones, your tissues, the electromagnetic field of your body... even the fluid in your cells — has an optimal vibrational frequency.

Humming, toning, chanting, like the light language, and many other sound-healing modalities can diminish stress, lower your heart rate, and help you sleep better.

Chapter 79
The Feminine Archetype, the Pandemic Virus, and the Divine Feminine Rebirth

My guide, a high entity in thalaxy and ambassador, told me to please write what follows:

"We have the emergence of the feminine energy that is coming through right now. The Sophia century civilization through and out of this pandemic, and to end up with the world we want not based on patriarchy with the dominant culture. But instead, a more open and allowing culture. A more loving, fair, just, and ecological culture.

The Pandemic virus is nothing more than a genetic update and has already decreased.

The human body is built as vessels of flow that happen down on a fundamental level of cells, and in the way in which it produces energy, the microbiome. And so, the bacteria and fungi have to produce an enormous amount of bio nutrient out of soil and put that into a plant, and the plant could be consumed by an animal. And the animal would then carry that energy forward to us, or if you are on a plant-based diet you are getting it right from the plant source of the microbiome, but you can still not use the plant or animal as fuel. And you have to refer to that to your microbiome which is now going to convert that into smaller parts, and bioavailable nutrients that the human body can start to manage. And then, it has to travel through the liver and be repackaged in such a way that it can get into the cells through the vascular system. Once it reaches a cell it is still in the form of glucose and galactose, carbohydrates, or fatty acids. Those are the only fuels the body can use, still useless to human cells.

The only thing the human cell that can consume glucose and fatty acids is the mitochondria which are little species that are only carried by the mother.
Human beings are literally fueled by a species of microbiology. These three little species of mitochondria that live within us are only inherited through the maternal line. And there is some deep spiritual and physiologic importance to that that has never been explored. The male contribution to life, the sperm has no mitochondria in it. It has no way to produce energy in the sense of a human cell. And so, it functions much more like bacteria.

In a bizarre way pregnancy is like the first body infection. So, when woman get these bacteria that inserts a little bit of genetic information into the ovum, and ovum is filled with mitochondria three species of these extrovert mitochondria in an ovum, and those mitochondria, minimum 200 but probably close to 2000 mitochondria in an ovum, those mitochondria are the most extraordinary energy producers that we have ever encountered. That ovum will then start to divide and initially it looks like a tumor.

Every single cell is identical to the previous, just like a cancer cell. When as it gets to its 280th cell division, now it looks like a snowball under a microscope it suddenly changes and looks like it gets a big indentation on one side, and in that moment differentiation happens. And so, we know at which point human cells reach quorum sensing. Quorum sensing is a hyper intelligence when you get bacteria or fungi or other organisms into a big enough community where they start to develop a hyper intelligence due to a larger sense of self-identity due to connectivity and community. So, around 280 human cells become hyper intelligence, and in that moment hyper intelligence is based on. the realization of unique identities within the whole.

The maternal force here fueled by a maternally driven energy source of mitochondria is producing enough communication, because the mitochondria does not only produce the energy, but they also produce the communication network within the cell.

That baby now as it comes to the vaginal canal goes through a second conception. The second adoption is an adoption of the entire microbiome of the mom's vaginal canal. And this reaches an extraordinary capacity for resilience and immunity within the greater nature. The child itself does not have any immune system till six months of age and yet at the age of seven, there are ten to eight viruses in the stool of that child and no sickness. In fact, the higher the virus count the healthier the child is. The viruses actually are a genetic transfer mechanism to bring enough genomic information into the child's experience that it knows it is self-identity within nature. So, what we are facing today is not fearful of pandemic and we are not being told the truth about viruses, and about HIV... none of these are real phenomena in the sense of a germ. They do not function as bacteria. They are genetic updates to the human body genome, and we know that over 50% of the human DNA, which is a very small amount, only twenty thousand genes within the human genome. Which is small compared to a flea that has 30,000 genes. So, you are 2/3 as complicated as a flea at the genetic level but you carry 50% of that DNA as viral information that updated the human genome over the last hundreds of millions of years. Even before we would consider ourselves Homo Sapiens, we were receiving updates of the virus and some incredible new data is showing that we can't have pluripotent stem cells without the viral genome within our DNA. We could never be a regenerated being without viral information from a reverse transcriptase RNA, which is the same as HIV, without that we would not be who we are.

This virus going around has not increased. In fact, it has decreased the amount of respiratory death on the planet at that time. It is not being talked about because it is so confusing. How could that virus be updating the human genome such that there would actually be a decline in respiratory death? Every virus is an opportunity for an update, and when you are getting a cold or a febrile event you are getting new data. You must then go into deep rest and a meditative experience and ask your body why it needs this fever. Ask why you need new data, why you are preparing yourself for the new genetic update. As for the people passing away, death is a lie. Death is not a fear state. People who are passing away are people that are meant to at that time or have a weak immune system. They were at the end of their journey,

This virus is, if, it updates your "genome" so should we turn it into a multibillion dollars vaccine program? Don't some have the wrong science looking at the equation completely erroneously? Because they are so masculine archetypes? It's just failure, failure of success, and looking at the world that way forgetting that we are simply vessels of flow.

The body is made of Energy, Water, Light and Color. The primary thing that mitochondria make is light energy, and that light energy from cell to cell is a system of fiber optic cables to funeral hundreds of thousands of fiber optic cables between each cell and at the end of each of these microscopic fibers there is thousands of tiny little strands. Every little strand is actually a perfect hollow tube that is hundreds of times smaller than a human hair. Perfect molecular tube and at the end is an aperture, just as you would see on the camera lens that lets light in and out. So, we have hundreds of fiber optic cables that can tune the amount of LIGHT that passes from one cell to the next and the LIGHT that is passing is produced by three species of mitochondria that are passed on to the feminine line and then we flow that energy through our bodies, and we call this life".

An information brought to you by VIE.

Chapter 80
The Pleiadians are the Key

I remember opening my eyes and seeing an intensely detailed image immediately in front of my face. There were dozens of interconnecting lines, a pattern with no discernable orientation.

Now said my Pleiadians' spiritual family, and star friends "We are in the Underground Bases, dismantling technology, working with your armed forces. We have some of the children who were in these bases, and this has been going on for a while, many years, healing them and helping them to recover from their trauma. They live with us in the Pleiades; they're not to be found on earth but may one day be returned if they wish.

Our ships surround your planet. Yes, the Galactic Ships but we have our own fleet of scientists, technicians, healers, and our own light workers who help guide and arrange the energies. We direct these to the correct spots on your planet to help awaken people in these sectors, and to change around the negative polarities to positive.

We heal and cleanse your skies and your oceans.

We work to educate those who will step up with new technologies to present to your world, so that you too may enjoy non-invasive healing as the rest of the galaxy does.

The Pleiadians are key in the arrestation and processing of dark entities who will seek time before a universal judge for dispensation as is decreed by the councils.

Arrests are still ongoing. Your planet is heavily infested. As your viral warfare continues, we seek cures for these, and we seek to heal those who have been affected.

We energetically support your environment.

And we work through the lightworker system in order to express our Light at your third and fourth dimensional levels.

New food sources are being created for your planet by us. New foods will be discovered that are delicious, nourishing and of high frequency, and these will have been planted by us, the Pleiadean collectively. We are botanists who will transplant or create new species of life for your future nourishment.

We bring you love. We are there to encourage and to soothe you when your outlook is dim. We are there to call on you to help your brothers in need. We prompt you to donate, to help and to care whenever we see opportunity and now there is much upon your planet.

The Pleiadians are highly active, nurturing, guarding, aggressing against the dark, viewing all from our ships hovering over your world, and working according to the divine plan to set your world back on a path of Light.

Be well,

With much Love!

Chapter 81
Separation of the Wheat from the Chaff

I shared this case with CHADD. True humanity from false humanity. And he said:

"Told them what you have been shown. They must know; Tell them that the split between them is approximately 50/50%. Tell them false humanity is made up of clones, space fillers, synthetic/inorganic beings, soulless beings, AI beings and beings who stem from elsewhere than Earth and hold negative intent towards true humanity.

True humans are flesh and blood humans with a soul born as humans or incarnated as humans from elsewhere to help free Earth humanity from its present enslavement in unconsciousness and deliberate oppression of its highest faculties.

What is taking place on Earth right now and what the dark cabal is building towards, is not something that will be resolved without ground fighting. Please hold no illusions around that. And I don't mean the people going out to attack the government and its military might head on with this statement. I mean the free people of Earth uprising in mass in a united revolt and starting to arrest and try those responsible for what are clear crimes against humanity and all life taking place.

The armed forces will no doubt be set in motion against this wave of freedom fighters and the people will have to fight to protect themselves, their families and all they care about. This is unavoidable.

It will be bloody and brutal and at this point in constantly shifting divine timing, at least half the world's population will die in the process of either getting vaccinated/microchipped or by fighting for freedom from those who wish to end the majority of life on Earth. Far more than fifty will perish. This is inevitable. The world of humans is divided between sheep/fake humans (not all sheep are fake humans) and the awakened/true humanity.

That division will deepen until it reaches maximum polarity. This is when maximum darkness will play out its final takeover game. At the medium and higher levels of consciousness, the dark cabal has already lost the game. It is a done deal.   Please know this.

However, down here in 3 D and lower 4 D this endgame still has to play out in full. It cannot be avoided.

They will need to let go of many things. Precious things. And people you Love. People who made soul choices different from yours. These times we are now entering will neither he nor easy for any of us. It will be the toughest experience of all of our lives and lifetimes, and many won't be able to keep their body avatars for the whole ride. So whatever else you do, hold those you Love close, protect the children, all children, no matter who's to the best of your ability from all harm (this includes vaccinations) and make peace with death now, not when it stands right before you on the battlefield. Death is not the end. Only a close and another beginning. Tell them not to fear it. Not fear, not fear life either. But to have faith. Love conquers all."

Chapter 82
Key to Ascension by my Higher Self

"Greetings, it is I, VIE, infiltrating your very Being with pure soft Love energy, expanding throughout your cells and incorporating your Whole Being.

I AM the softness of pure energy with which you have a match. The Love of Creator in every cell of your Being. Love expanding with pure, soft lilting essence is taking over your very Being. The pure soft color of Gold and Magenta planted and anchored expanding into infinite possibilities.

Feel it now as I incorporate your very Infinite Essence with Love Energy that is so pure and complete that you feel it with every cell, every molecule of every cell, and every atom, and on and on, and infinitum, to the smallest particle of your Being. This Divine Love Energy absorbs all impurities, and with alchemic precision, dispels and transmutes all impurities into the pure soft Love that you are.

Make it your intention to absorb and welcome the impurities into your very essence of Love as this Divine Love Energy simultaneously transmutes to the Divine Essence that you are. Pure Golden Energy with many colors of the rainbow infiltrating and residing in each cell as the crystalline nature (of you) shines forth more brilliantly than ever.

And this is your alchemy. This is your true nature. This is your essence. Pure Divine Love! It is all one and the same: Love becomes You and you become Love, and forever and always you reside within it. It resides within you. It is the makeup of every smallest particle of your Being. All together it blends into the Love that you are.

And dear ones, this is key to your ascension. Feel as if you are Love floating, love incarnate, Love moving, Love in action, Love amongst all. All amongst you, in Love and Purity.

The essence of your Being is the Love Essence of All of Creation, so welcome the pure soft energy to be at the core of every word, every thought, every action, everything you observe, and everything you think and do. Everything that you are. Now and always.

Instead of seeing your cells as filled with physical matter, see them filled with divine golden and soft pink and magenta wisps of softness, swirling and liquid in makeup. It exudes out to cover all the space in and around your cells. You become fluid with Love. You become substantial in Love. You. Become. Love. Nothing but Love.

Allow this Love to form and create everything in your world. Let it become the basis of your Thought and Creation and see it manifesting as what you wish to see in your world, what you wish to experience in your world. What you Are in this world.

The Love that is You then becomes a gift to the world and a gift to you that you cherish always. You are the Gift. You are Love. You are the Everything in this world. For you are One with it. Your Love particles stimulate all other particles in you, and on outward to stimulate all other particles and Beings, as if just by being there, it turns on the other particles, on and outward to Infinity.

So now there are many Love particles making up everything in your body, and light body, everything in your environment, everything in your Universe and Multiverse.

Everything becomes Love because it IS Love. It is just being turned on to remembering its true essence. It takes over the World; it takes over the Multiverse, this alchemy into True Divine Love making up everything in the Multiverse.

And I give this to you with the pure intention that you make this your own truth. And I support every one of you in this endeavor.

I AM my higher self in Pure Love Essence."

Chapter 83
Beware of Fake Light-workers

Today I was given to see the earth separating in two. The universe seems to be pushing to be loving and flowing. That's the life pattern of the higher dimensions. And that's what CV-19 is calling out of the planet.

Ok, so you had/have a respiratory virus that was/is killing people, then masks that obstruct breathing, now after a staged event in Minneapolis the whole world is chanting 'I can't breathe".

When you do complete this shift in consciousness, you are going to feel lifetimes of relief. You are going to feel like you've died and gone to heaven while still having a physical body, and you are going to know that you accomplished the feat of ascending on one of the most challenging planets in the universe to exist.

Everyone in the higher dimensions exists in a state of love. They're bathed in love. They're blessed with an inner tsunami of love, in the face of which no negative thought could arise and no desire to harm could exist.

Beware of the fake light workers. Light work is not about doing yoga, love and flowers, and going vegan. It has nothing to do with hippie music or new age festivals. True light workers do not talk exclusively about light and fluffy things. They talk about the ignored and forgotten things, because by sharing their understanding of the heavy, the painful, the dark, they bring light to where there was little to none.

Most people using the term light-workers have no clue what it means.

Light workers are rebel fighters of spiritual alchemy. They are warriors. They've had multiple dark nights of the souls and helped others through that, too. The best interpretation of this phenomenon is this: The light-workers must become night workers, too. They must go into their own deep and dark and icky and sticky shadow and ego and transmute that. Don't you dare call yourself that when you are not. Light comes when you do the work of transmuting that darkness within yourself first, understanding and coming to terms with it.

Chapter 84
Cleaning myself from a Dark Entity

Early July I began twenty-one days Primary Contract Protocol Remove, a Protection Pray against the dark forces to St Expedite, and the St Michael the Archangel Purism Exorcism.

Twenty-one day is the necessary time and cycle to make a change.

The Primary Protocol Remove is done to my source I am presence, in the name of my soul, in the name of all light forces, to cancel and nullify all past agreements and contracts that I may have been done with the dark forces and regardless of my subconscious claiming my freewill now. I decree and command each time miracles to be manifested in my life in a way that will manifest happiness for me and for everybody involved.

The Protecting Pray I asked St Expedite, angels Gabriel, St Michael, and Raphael to protect and save me from evil forces. To deliver me from all evil forces, protect and save me in the name of the Holy Trinity, of the son and Holy Spirit. In the name of Jesus our Lord that lives and reign with God in the unity of the Holy Spirit.

Then The St Michael Purism Exorcism, I asked the archangel St Michael to show himself and deliver us from Satan and all the other spirits with his command. Like he said once to deliver Robbie (a child) and tell them to leave in his command all the nations of the world in the name of "Dominus" immediately.

Sixteen days later and three days before the twenty days cycle prayer something happened.

By stimulating the right temporal-parietal junction of the brain just before taking my nap I found myself in astral projection and this happened just day sixteen and 3 days before the twenty-one days completion, and this was for a reason. It Indicates that I created reality based on my thoughts and I am now capable enough to draw in people who share the same vibrational energy as me.

Witnessing number 16 more is an indicator that something life-changing is soon going to happen. My spirit guide wants to communicate by the number 16 that my destiny is what I have put in my head, so I should keep removing all the negative thoughts and continue to replace it.

The number 16 is intuitive, spiritual, wise, and self-sufficient in his task to learn so he can teach others.

Sixteen is symbolic of love and loving and strongly associated with love and its manifestations. Christians are to become perfected in God's love not just by physically obeying the Commandments (which should be done anyway) but also by following the full spiritual intent of our Creator's laws and judgments (Matthew 22:37 - 40). This duality of true love is represented by $8 + 8 = 16$.

God's love can be attained not only by keeping the commandments physically, but also by a deep spiritual belief in God, showing true love and being open to others. The spiritual meaning of God's laws and commandments must be saved and maintained in the heart of a believer. The nature of physical and spiritual intent is shown in $8 + 8$, which is 16. It leads us to one, whole and perfect love for God.

Witnessing number 16 more often is an indicator that something life-changing is soon going to happen.

I felt a need to lay down and take a nap. Before falling asleep I asked my spiritual guides to let me know if there was anything I should know or let me experience anything I should experience at that time.

I felt pain in the palm of my hand just under my pinky finger. I just commanded if it was not of pure light, to the entity, to leave immediately. Then I saw, getting out of my body a strong and impressive man wearing a black mask covering his head. Suddenly, my phone rang, and it woke me up. I walked up awakened by the ring and remembered clearly what I asked just before the event. In my nap I was cleaning myself of any dark entities with the violet and pink flame that has sparkles shimmering tiny, small gold or silver in the pink.

Chapter 85
The Organic Karmic Cosmic Universal Laws.

I was awakened by the beautiful vision of the Rising Phoenix Aurora. And it said:

The Revelation is now! It is Time, it is Time, it is Time!

And I heard, and I saw written at the same time.

I AM RA, I AM RA, I AM RA

Greetings. In this time and space as you are aware the Earth is going through a collective 'Revelation'. These are the very times that Jesus/Yeshua spoke upon in his original forms of writing through The Holy Bible. Understanding though that we are not speaking of your current Bible as that has been infringed upon strongly through the Illuminati and negative aliens. For the purposes of mind control, programming in harmful ways of removing people's sovereignty to not come into a realization of them through Creator power.

We have all been waiting for what seems like an eternity for this very moment in time. It has taken us 4 Earth cycles and resets to be here. All the hidden negative agendas coming to the surface no longer being able to hold their lower frequency among the Earth's now higher frequency. Mother Earth has transformed and has now after the 6/6/2020 portal leveled up and has ascended in the totality of her vibration and frequency.

All that is no longer a match of Earth is having a hard time and is unmasking itself and oneself. Example, those with false intents - 'light workers in service to others' are going through a revelation and choice; "Will I continue to allow my mind/ego direct me or will I truly act upon what I am posing as or whom I am meant to be to come out/ascend from this i.e., matrix? Will I be the true unity of love and accept all the beauties that my brethren are as, am I?"

What is false is oh so very visible upon your and our Earth. For we too are incarnated, fractalized within you. We are the Christ Consciousness and the second/final coming of Christ that is here within every spark of a flamed lighted soul who chooses to act upon pure intents of love.

It is the time of revelation, it is time, it is time, it is time.

Those who were ring leaders of pedophilia are being trailed/trialed and shall continue to be and will be found guilty. For they have already been found guilty by our collective through the organic karmic cosmic universal laws. All has been created energetically and now the physical is just catching up. We must continue to speak and be that example of who we really are beyond this inverted Matrix. We are divine, we are the Creators' children and the Creator itself.

Human Trafficking has been unveiled and will continue to do so with leaders who are part of us - the Ra (a multitude of benevolent alien races) and YOU as a collective. The relentless attacks from Satan include Children as young as 5-years-old exposed to Satan Clubs opening in elementary schools across the nation. Attempts to put a statue of Satan in the Arkansas State Capitol grounds. Popular TV shows with evil Satanic themes. Black Masses at a public tax funded center in Oklahoma

City. And Satanic "prayers" officially started off city council meetings in Florida, Alaska and Colorado.

Join us in the infinite plasmic love light wave that now encircles, shields our Earth daily. Come ride the wave of infinite love with us where we remove false light control of all forms. Remember who you are, 'The Warrior of Love Light'.

I honor you, love you, and respect you for the divine soul that you are in creation.

I AM RA, I AM RA, I AM RA ☉ .

Chapter 86
Two Powerful Dreams

In the dream I got up off the bed and walked downstairs (the clock in the bedroom read anywhere from 3:20 am to 3:27 am. I saw a bicycle with two purses hanging on a bicycle. The one easiest to grab was not mine. Twice two men on a motorcycle passed by and stole it. The 1st time they robbed it, the woman to whom the purses belonged immediately called a number and recovered it. The second time "she" the woman in my vision could not get through, she rapidly crossed the road to the bank, showed them the picture of the two men and I believe she could recover her purse back.

In this second dream we were the three of us travelling. Me, the woman, and someone else I did not get to remember who. Was it a man, a woman? We opened the trunk of the car to unload the luggage and mine was perfectly closed and ok. I just had this suitcase and my purse, and an umbrella and the two other travelers had the suitcases and their hand-luggage turned and tossed everywhere. With the Exception that one suitcase was only split open but never closed. Then it's where I heard very clearly from someone standing close before I awakened.

"You should invest now in the remaining."

Then I read this

"You dear ones are in a big pack of trouble. You cannot fight this monster alone. You are going to march right through to Armageddon for that is the way it is. Master Esu Jesus Sananda will come and there will be a big bunch of disagreement and I can't think of anything nice to say about it, that my friends, is what a confrontation between Christ and Satan amounts to no matter what you might like to believe. So be it. I am pushing you, dear heart, for we must get this information out in time to protect the other authors involved in public danger as targets for the Dark Forces. I believe it must be obvious by now why your ones will succeed with your projects. They are off limits to the adversaries and funding is going to be allowed to flow; it is a four-arranged agreement.

We are always tending to their care, so fear not; just take extreme caution in all circumstances and avoid public gatherings as much as possible for a bit longer."

Chapter 87
That Time it's A Communication with a Higher Self

I was shown this timeline's blueprint that is coded organically through our collective life on Earth in this timeline that is manifesting now and the organic karmic cosmic universal laws. It was the beginning of the lockdown here when I was thinking about how it would take this time to try to get the world leaders to start working together. It sorts of stopped all war and made them start talking about things like the deadly virus.

That night CHADD came to me in my dream and told me that yes, I would have to do the painful thing of distancing myself from my family to protect them. But I would be helping others and healing myself ready to move forward with my life. Even though it would be a painful time of isolation and a feeling of loneliness, I would find that his spirit would be guiding me through. I started my work here anchoring my vibration energy I came to do. To anchor the energy of the new Aquarius era on earth. Yes! The time of freedom is 0010110. And I was also given the opportunity to help a stranger to get the appropriate help for herself. Due to it I have been able to get the answers to my questions that have affected my life, but it also has helped me to know my strengths and weaknesses at this time-space.

In communication with my Higher Self, I see you all now, and I know that you have experienced the extremes of the human condition. Feel my energy in your midst, said the inner voice now. I am your friend. This is a game that is familiar to you, with its highs of joy, connection, and unity and its lows of frustration, despair, and desolation.

You all here possess a natural understanding of spirituality, of living from the heart. From the higher chakras in your energy field. The heart, the throat, the third eye, the crown, you understand.

You have always understood what goes on in the new Earth through living from your heart and your soul. But because you have led lives on Earth where that energy was not honored, times in which you did not feel welcome and at home, you have sustained pain in the lower three chakras, your solar plexus, near your stomach; your navel chakra, the vulnerable center of your emotions; and your root chakra, your tailbone, your connection with the Earth.

While in many of you, the higher chakras are developed and open to the new, their lives pain in the three lower chakras: old memories that cause fear and even unwillingness to live on Earth again. There is disparity in your energy field.

There are times when there is the desire and homesickness for another world, one that is reminiscent of Home with its vibration of lightness and harmony, ease, and simplicity. Yes, that lives within you and that is often what also keeps you really moving forward here on Earth, the memory of that and the desire for it.

But at other times you forget, or you avoid, that other part of the energy field: the tormented part, the part that lives in the lower chakras, the traumatized part of your being. Here live intense fears about being fully engaged with life, about really living from your heart, and showing that to other people. These fears pull at you and make you hesitate, just when you are on the threshold of the new time.

For you are there, you all are making connection with the new Earth, which is now awakening through you. Yet there is that old pain in you that sometimes seems to hold you back and pull you away; a pain with which you do not know what to do.

And I want to say to you that you cannot enter the new Earth merely from the top four chakras – that is not possible. Only if you can be completely and fully human will you be able to pass over the threshold. And that means that you turn toward the pain in you that holds back and that you embrace what resists, with love and tenderness. That energy located in the upper chakras wants to build the new Earth, wants to change the outer world, and make a difference. But I am telling you, you cannot pass over the threshold as half a human being. It calls for courage, at times, to turn inward toward the pain and the darkness, and to face it squarely.

The Earth calls to you and wants to help and support you in this process of embracing your humanity. Within the Earth herself, there is movement going on; she wants to change and to attract a new energetic reality. The old structures based on struggle and fear will crumble. The new Earth can no longer tolerate these structures; they no longer can survive.

You are at the forefront and the threshold of the new, even though you see around your chaos and tumult. Keep very calm within yourself on your inner road. That makes the difference; that opens the way to a new, healed Earth.

It is also time for truth and free speech to prevail. Now the time has come for civil disobedience. While a liberal and revolutionary agenda seeks to implement a more socialist, egalitarian, and ecological world, the world is facing a turning point in history that will define generations to come.

The inevitable conclusion to this chapter of history will be a bargain: comply with government orders and they will return to you your freedom. But conditional freedom is no freedom at all. Governments have crossed a line that they cannot cross. They have taken freedom hostage. And soon, they will offer vaccines and other concessions as the terms for its release. It is of extreme importance to not accept their terms. And it's time to send that message loud and clear, and no longer wait for the scraps of elites and corrupt corporations to feed your families. Practicing safe habits with proper hygiene, and supporting the immune system as a virus spread is important, but oppressive measures taken against us will cause far more damage than this virus ever could. Governments have crossed a line that they cannot uncross by taking freedom hostage and by submitting humanity to communists' surveillance, mandatory vaccinations, and forfeit rights to travel freely, worship freely...when God created mankind to be free.

Do you know that touch is the truest medium of expression? Let me explain like my guides told me. Hands are so important; they tell us a lot about a person. When two people shake hands they connect a myriad chakra prints in their palms. That is why a friendly and hearty handshake can be a very uplifting healing experience.

You have the right to peaceably assemble. You have the right to free speech like you have the right to be secure in your person, home, papers, and effects against unreasonable searches and seizures. And you have the right to petition for redress of grievances.

Trust that as a collective whole we can see a vision of the upcoming reality.

Love and Life."

Chapter 88
The Four Seasons are the Cycle of Life, and the Runoff the Archangels

I received a reminder in my sleep of the celebration of the summer solstice coming.

I woke up at the end of a religious retreat. We were three women enjoying the retreat together. I was calm and felt in harmony with the world. I had an Essenians' Bible in my hands, and I was thinking that this is why I like to read from a printed book. It was for that reason. Because I could highlight some words, paragraphs, or lines for future research and easily find it.

So, the reminder was that we will be celebrating today June 21st the summer solstice through the great Archangel Uriel. Even though the dictatorship was put in place by the corrupted governments, the divine world reinforced its presence in the life of men by the celebration of the Round of the Archangels.

So, please do not forget to answer the call and unit to build to the Essenians and participate at this celebration for God and to build a new world of Light and Love.

In these great cycles, are divine beings manifested. The four seasons are the manifestation of the archangels' world. They are the great laws of life, the laws that structure the universe.

God manifests Himself on earth through the four seasons, the four elements, and the four reigns of nature.

Each solstice and equinox are a door that opens in the world of immortality.

Hum! Perfect time to think about immortality.

The ancients knew these secrets and celebrated God. The mystery of life, at each solstice and equinox.

God is the source of all religions. Religions appeared by some beings of light sent, who had a link with the divine world and manifested it by teaching, like Jesus or Buddha did.

In the past, the great religions shined on earth, like the great antic Egypt. These people were guided by the religious government of Light and Love.

Today, all the old religions fell; and they have lost all link with God. When the forces of power, politics and war appear in religion, it means that the religion is dead.

It is because actual religions are dead that the divine world is being to create a new manifestation of the religion of the Light and Love on the earth.

Below is an extract of the Archangel Michael Psalm who speaks of the will of God for our epoch.

"Today the divine world has decided that a new universal religion must be manifested on earth. Those who will respond to the calling, who will be the pioneer and will build this world will be eternally blessed."

In my dream, I entered the Crystalline Cathedral being of Light. First, I saw a being of light of changing colors. Blue, then violet, turning pink, then lavender, and continuing to change crystalline colors. Then I heard this very familiar voice of my blue flame:

"The Father spoke to me. It's a beautiful and powerful dream vision that he gave me. I will give you a code number and you will understand it."

Then gave me the number and he said: "I love you VIE. You are paving the way forward. So, continue to assist in any way that you can, any opportunity that arises to help others awaken. And thank you for taking such good care of me. I just received your message, and you are right. I was food poisoned yesterday and my activated charcoal has been taken away from me by either Katherine or her son Paul. Now I must wait until 9 am to get some more."

I knew this was going to happen, I said, they told you it would happen a couple of months ago. They told you that they will take it away from you. That's what you told me then. Did you forget? It is the way the dark forces work and if you do not pay attention and prevent it. They do it after warning you.

Chapter 89
Beaming In and Out from a Beam of Light

The angelic crusade continues. I know that CHADD and I are paving the way forward, continuing to assist in any way that we can, any opportunity that arises to help others awaken. Focused on assisting spiritual seekers in living their Divine self-expression within this human experience. Because nothing can harm you when you are aligned with your soul.

While the war against the deep state continues to accelerate towards freedom for the people, the world leaders spread the word that a second Corona-virus wave is coming. I am prepared for the news media to blow everything out of proportion like the last time. Be prepared for many lies and pay attention. World leaders and politics have one word always left out of their speech, the word freedom. What in fact the second wave is all about if they come to succeed, is about arrests, it's about vaccines, and surveillance tracking apps, and taking away your freedom. And that is why I came here to assist you.

According to my spiritual guides the turbulent situation you all are going through is since you have been for too long on this planet without using your fullest power. It creates a kind of imploding effect, that can take the form of illness. It is time and it's a need to evolve quickly to use all that energy, or it is going to work against you now.

A powerful and effective way to your path, is in the exploration of consciousness.

The agenda of the elite or the N.W.O is more than a conspiracy theory. It can be traced back to the late 19th century and a group known as the Roundtable. It has found indications of sinister nations such as geophysical warfare and profit of commodities markets by manipulating food and crop productions.

Humanities' search for truth continues from one incarnation or lifetime to the next. In various states in America, Washington DC, North Carolina, and Cincinnati the Luciferian disciples want to use the summer solstice to get together and walk to try to install the new world order. Then fast-food industries hired black that are poisoning the food of the white. Religion holds concepts and society together. In the news there are so many lacks, lies or fake. A US medical research agency fired dozens of scientists with financial ties to China. A French scientist is in trouble for writing a book to denounce many of his "scientists' friends'' that have a conflict of interest with the Big-pharma, and he said that 25,000 citizens could have been saved. Some bigfoot mysterious human creatures in nature lead to a possible connection to UFO's.

You must awaken to the truth quickly now. We are moving into an era where we better get smart and know the truth of what it really is. We are moving where people are free to innovate, and millions will live longer. Happier and healthier.

Some Et's families are beaming in and out in beams of Light. They can manipulate the timeline, reset problems we had with health, reverse jump-time in space "hyperdrive", and we are very close to expanding engineering… But you, humans must wake up to the truth.

Chapter 90
Downloading Vision in my Left Eye and Astral Projecting Myself for a Day

Lately these days, I am receiving more and more powerful visions and when I heard from CHADD giving me the hundred and fifty excited, he contacted me again three days later saying that the father was going to make his move very soon. And very excited he was again. He kept me for eight hours in communication with him speaking nonstop. And three things happened. Katherine that slept in a heavy state with pills, came in his room late at night wanting to know what we were saying, then came again to give him a pair of socks, in summer at 4:00am? Then Paul came at 4:30am to tell him he was a "manic?"

The fourth day I had an appointment for an eye exam. I needed to change my frame and did not have a recent prescription. The eye exam store had the newest technology available, but it refused to work on my left eye. Unable to understand why it would not work as it was the first and only time, they had such a problem, I was left with "you must have cataract" I knew though I did not have cataract. And this is what the 'cataract' was in fact and what was going on with my left eye.

The fifth day I was driving to the grocery store when the same vision three weeks ago reappeared. This is the exact same vision than three weeks ago except for a few things. It did not appear in my dream state. The first specific form of sacred geometry appeared and only in my left eye, and there was an opening in it now. It was brilliant and silvering shiny. I was shown an opened portal with a lot of movement. A rolling movement going in. The vision stayed there for some time, insisting for me to see and look at it. Then it stopped appearing.

These events happened just a few days after the summer solstice which confirmed to me that the attempt to install the new world order by the Luciferian's disciples failed.

In fact, I went through the door that opens in the world of immortality for an entire day. I astral projected myself and came back. I went through the portal Thursday and came back on Saturday.

What if I told you, that this dream life which you envision yourself to have in your wildest dreams is your actual life purpose?

What if you could heal yourself, your family, your loved ones, and fulfill your divine life's mission simply by going for that dream and putting all fear aside along the way? What is the greatest teaching and the highest education they could get? What if you could pass that to those you love, and it would simply be you following your heart? What if things were just as simple as that?

Jesus said, "When the two become one the Kingdom can come."

Chapter 91
Hundred and Fifty, Ten and Fifty CHADD Coded Dream Vision to VIE

This was the dream vision God; the father gave to CHADD and that I received from him in the crystalline Cathedral. That is what made him so excited and was when he called me and told me about this dream vision. It was shown to him the set to music, the abundance, the oath of Loyalty and the coming of personal freedom without resistance from inner self or others. The solar angel sign of change, mutations and the metamorphoses, Joy, and feast "Everything." The coming of the first fruits of God's spiritual harvest of humans. And announcing the God Duo Church creation.

But he reported it coded to me coded. At that point I did not know yet that it would not be any possibility of any resistance from others. And I asked him to give it to me coded.

God speaks by numbers.

He gave me the 150 number first which is the last numbered Psalm in the Bible, Psalm 150, and considered the one most often set to music. Abundance. Symbolizes new projects and beginnings, major life changes, especially related to your home and family life, spiritual development.

Then he gave me the number 10 which means testimony, Law, and responsibility. Oath of Loyalty.

Then the number 50 that is Fire and purification. Holy Spirit; Pentecost. The coming of God's Holy Spirit. Personal freedom without resistance from inner self or from others.

"After Jesus appeared to Mary Magdalene on Sunday morning, April 9 in 30 A.D., he ascended to the Father in heaven (John 20:17). His ascension, as a type of first fruit from the dead (Revelation 1:5), occurred on the day God told the

Israelites they were to wave a sheaf composed of the first fruits of their harvest ... It is on this day that the count of 50 days to the feast of Pentecost begins. This sign expresses its sense of personal freedom. Expression of personal freedom, without resistance from its inner self or from others."

Number 50 corresponds to the Hebraic letter "nun", form reminding a cup pouring its content. It is also associated with the fourteenth Arcane of the Tarot: the solar Angel, interpreted in general as the sign of the change, the mutations, and the metamorphoses. Number of the joy and the feast, according to the Bible to Everything: And God saw everything that he had made, and behold, it was very good. And the evening and the morning were the sixth day. Genesis 1.31. The Hebrew word for "everything" The number 50 in the Bible is connected to the "Holy Spirit". The Holy Spirit was poured out on the day of Pentecost, which was fifty days after the resurrection of Christ. Throughout the whole Bible you can cross reference the number fifty to the Holy Spirit. Meaning without resistance from its inner self or from others.

In the New Testament, the word Pentecost comes from the Greek word for fiftieth (Strong's Concordance #G4005). Also known as the Feast of Weeks or First fruits, it was on this special Holy Day that God first poured his Holy Spirit upon about 120 believers who had gathered to keep the day (Acts 1:15, 2). They became the first fruits of God's spiritual harvest of humans.

But he also gave me the number that says.

"You as a person are of great enthusiasm for progress, invention, growth, someone full of optimism, visionary, idealistic and probably very charismatic.

You are a leader, rather than a follower, and a leader of an inspirational sort.

However, it also seems as if you are not obsessed with the role of a leader; you do not need acknowledgements and rewards, you do not ask for it. Victory at all costs or a high status are not your goals, they do not especially motivate you, which we would say is a truly noble thing.

You simply do what you like to do, and you see not to harm people on your path."

So true, I love people and I have a lot of compassion for them. This is my true essence. Me VIE.

Chapter 92
Confirmation by Feathers Reappearing Everywhere

Feathers kept reappearing in my ways and path everywhere I would go. In front of doors, on the grass, inside some buildings etc.........At that point I knew the Holy Spirit was sending me a message. Before I came as I was told, to come and anchor my energy here, and I would be protected and seeing feathers, many feathers. Suddenly they are reappearing everywhere I go.

As I was looking at the window and admiring the flowers blooming and their brilliant colors in this early summertime, I heard a being speaking to me telepathically.

"Change is coming. Irremediable transformation that will create something new in your life. Abrupt state of fact which brings material profit. Positive changes bring material profit to you. Your situation is evolving positively in your life also.

These are your angels sharing your excitement over what is happening in your life. You will be entering a new phase in your relationship. It will come like a blessing. All the things that got you so worried or stressed will also be gone. It can cause things rocky and tense but know that it is all part of the transition period.

You may experience some kind of emotional imbalance, pain, but trust that this will go back to the way they were. Let this be your opportunity to experience this change on a more personal level. Once this transition period is over you will feel relieved. You will emerge stronger and better.

You are not alone during this period of transformation. You have guidance of the divine realm, and you have the complete support of your guardian angels. Your relationship will undergo several changes and you will feel emotionally unstable at some point. Just rest assured that you are safe and protected, and that you are going through them to challenge you and make you better and wiser. If, when your relationship is not a source of joy and satisfaction, then it is time to make it your life's strength rather than its weakness. You have the backing of divine realm and the 2/7 assistance of your guardian angels. You will be successful.

Know the importance of staying grounded. Keep things in perspective and do not be your own worst enemy and keep bringing yourself down. Remain optimistic and be in harmony with yourself. Keep in mind that you are blessed and loved. Do your best to prepare yourself mentally, emotionally, physically, and spiritually for your future challenges.

Through this message, your guardian angels are telling you that you are entering soon into a new era in your relationship with your blue flame."

And I thought alright Lumita, the time has come to return my signet ring. She took it to the Black Sara saying that Sara needed to keep it for six months and now is the time San Sara returned it back to me. Unless you were an imposter Lumita.

Chapter 93
While I Took a Nap my request was Granted

Laying down before taking my nap, I had a conversation with my guide and made a request. I asked to know during my nap what I should be aware of that I was not, or what I should experience to be revealed.

And My request was granted.

I saw written: Code 1010010101 is to encourage and help overcome many difficult situations. Just need to be patient and persistent. You will succeed.

And to confirm it I saw a man getting out of my body like you would be stepping out of a car. Later, that day, it was evening time when I heard a message left on my cell phone. It was coming from my blue flame phone. The text said:

"It means FREEDOM. It is FREEDOM."

Then 3 days later I had an epiphany and I saw some cards. They were saying: Your Goals are met. It will happen suddenly and in the blink of an eye.

Now what you must know is that it happened 3 days before the end of the 21 days of my prayers and the answer to it. Twenty-one days because that is the number of days to a cycle to change and unfold.

Then I found out about the cross-crop circle, and it is said.

Chapter 94
Templar Cross Crop Circle

"As life has turned into an obstacle course of never-ending challenges citizens are asked to obey a new law to wear masks that remind us of a dog muzzle in every public place, a Crop Circle formation depicting a Templar Cross is drawing that draws visitors to the farm where it was found in France.

The French media kept people in fear of a second wave of Covid-19. That was to prepare people to obey a new law to wear a mask. When we know that inhaling its own toxins is damaging their health and of no use to protect it.

The remarkable Crop design was reportedly first discovered on July 5th, 2020, by Mr. Gerard Benoit in a wheat field on his land in the community of Vimy.

Some people have specifically been going to the crop circle so that they could pray at it, and some people reported that it is the Templar Cross that energy flowed from the earth, blessed the field cured and to cure multiple sclerosis.

At the same time the scientists hide the truth from the population. Denying that 10 minutes exposure to the sun kills the virus and erases a pandemic. But have let some young people drink alcohol on the beach which lowered their immune system."

We have just entered a new world.

Chapter 95
Love is the Essence and the Cosmic Orgasm.

The spiritual self is the part of yourself that is multidimensional through which you exist in many forms simultaneously.

And a few days ago, I was having this conversation with one of my clients reaching for guidance.

With the lockdown being so severe during the pandemic, people are now willing to embrace new ideas. They are shifting away from the pharmaceutical industry towards healing modalities. They are seeing the old don't work and new measures are being embraced as they are being introduced by your leaders.

Once your planet was visited in a quantum way by enlightened creatures who were not angels. They are biological creatures living on a planet like planet earth, living in a quantum state. On a planet where there is no war. Humanity and such enlightened groups existed back then.

These enlightened creatures weren't part of angelic beings in the universe, and they came to planet earth to plant seeds of sacredness with your universe. It wasn't part of a conquering plan, or accidental, but it was their job.

Your DNA was split so that there were only two strands left with very little data and very little memory. Very deep inside the mechanism of sexuality is a frequency, called orgasm. And the orgasm has been distorted from its original purpose. Your body has forgotten the cosmic orgasm. It represents what was not taken away from you even though your history, your memories, and your identity were removed and scattered. You were left intact with the ability to discover who you were through the sexual experience.

Spiritual realms are places of existence that the human body is locked away from. Because sexuality was an opportunity for human beings to regain their memory, or to connect with their spiritual selves and spiritual creator, or to find an avenue to the spiritual realm that you are sealed off from, the churches came about and promoted sexuality for procreation. They taught you that the only reason you had sexuality was to produce little humans. Very few churches came about with the idea of bringing information to people. Because the churches came about as organizations-businesses to control religion and spiritual development and to create jobs, to create a hierarchy, and to create a club. Any religion that brings information is a religion operating on the vibration of truth. Very few are doing it.

Sexuality was promoted as something very bad. Women were told that sexuality was something they had to undergo to serve men and that they had no control over the birthing process. Women believed this; hence, to this day, you believe in general that you have no control over that portion of your body. You must realize that only you decide whether you are going to birth a child or not. This is not such a complicated thing as you have been told.

Decision and intention are what bring the experience to your being. You can control whether you have a baby or not. The discovery of the highest frequency of sexuality arises from the love experience. It has to do with two human beings bringing pleasure to one another in a way that opens frequencies of consciousness.

You have bought many ideas about what is proper and what is improper within sexual expression. The spiritual self is the part of yourself that is multidimensional through which you exist in many forms simultaneously.

You are an immortal and divine soul. You are older than you can even imagine. Wiser than you know. More capable than anyone has ever allowed you to believe.

The importance of Love, as the only ultimately purifying vibration in the Universe, that restores to Wholeness. If you meet the vibration of conscious, unconditional love in any person, place, or situation, you will experience an unseen chemical reaction.

The energy of love is supremely intelligent and knows where to place itself, and when healing and transformation happen, unhealed emotional states then come up in the light of pure love because they are ready to be healed. The Higher Self is the Wise Self, and it chooses the perfect people, places, and events to instigate healing in exact ways.

Finally, it is only Divine Love that will alter the internal balance of a person from relying on the ego, to relying on the Heart & Spirit. Heart is magnetic and love conquers all. I experience suddenly, humm... it comes in waves, little snapshots. More and more as this unfolds vibrated out of my energy field.

Synchronously I received this article, downloaded in a vision, confirming that the virus was a wake-up time to return to God. Which I had said all along. You have been deprived of knowledge by frequency control.

"The Coronavirus is a call to return to God. It's not a problem with His existence. Citizens' reaction to the coronavirus reflects the crisis of our secular godless society. The problem is not the virus, as potentially lethal as it might be. This outbreak is a biological fact, like so many that have plagued humanity over the ages. A virus is also a religion. However, that does not prevent it from having a religious dimension. The coronavirus comes at a time when most in society feel they do not need God. For these, God has long been replaced by bread and circuses. The modern pleasures point to no need for heaven. The postmodern vices proclaim no fear of hell. And yet the coronavirus has the uncanny ability to turn our material paradise into hell. The cruise ship, the symbol of all earthly delights, became an infected prison for passengers who did everything possible to get out. Those who have played sports their god now find empty stadiums and canceled tournaments. Those who adore money now find decimated portfolios and quarantined workforces. The worshippers of education look at their empty schools and universities. The devotees of consumerism face bare supermarket shelves. The world we worshipped is tumbling down. The things for which we glory are now in ruins. J.H. II"

Isn't it sad? I am sad. It hurts me. How can they all have forgotten His sorrowful passion on the cross.

Chapter 96
The New Technology and the Best to Come

I seem to have a few memory problems lately. If anyone interrupts my conversation, I have difficulty going back to what I was saying. Then Mother Mary spoke to me and said:

"If you wonder, you have been losing your memory because you are leaving the 3D world and heading for the 5th where knowing is the way to operate. Your memory has been disappearing to encourage you to continue to use your ability to respond intuitively. Losing your memory was a positive thing. It has allowed you to use your healing gifts of Master Conveyor of Vibrational Transformative Energy and create with CHADD that is a Master doctor of Sound, the bio-music "The Frequency of Sound". You both work with the Light and the frequency.

You will be counseling more people soon on becoming naturopathic, ayurvedic, herbology, crystal ology etc., on the different applications of how you can keep the body healthy naturally. This is one of the main humanitarian projects.
Soon there will be only natural types of doctors around that will be able to help people in certain situations, but it won't be a conventional hospital type of structure anymore where you go in and you are worried about dying.

The public needs to know that the best is yet to come that have the ability to regrow organs that are missing, such as gallbladder, kidney or lymph nodes etc., through the use of Light Spectrums and Frequencies. Capable of healing and repairing DNA along with curing all ailments. With Light and sound.

Age regression (up to 30 years) activating the human youth DNA.

No more Cancer
No more Autism
No more Fibromyalgia
No more Vaccines
No more Alzheimer's
No more Joint Pain
No more Deficiencies

Advanced technologies and thousands of cures for diseases will be given to you.

That is a technology that has been 'suppressed' and hidden from the public for a long, long time. Fortunately, due to the planetary shift from 3D to 5D happening at this time, and the increasing demand for transparency by the human collective consciousness, an increasing number of courageous people are coming forward to disclose what they know has been hidden for decades, even centuries, and most likely for thousands of years. As some other Technology gifts to humanity like the Quantum Financial Computer System, Anti-Gravity Propulsion, Replicators, Tachyon Energy & Plasma Energy. This Technology is not from planet Earth. It is not human-created technology. It is a technology that has been given to humanity by off-world ETs.

Like you wrote in your book "9.1.1. Complete Guide to Natural Healing" guided by the archangel Michael; the problem is the allopathic system and the corruption on Earth's surface doctors telling you that you got to take this pill for this, and this pill for that. And because of those pills or foreign entities being introduced into your body the side effects of bleeding, nausea, diarrhea, constipation, and death follow.

When you're looking at all those things you start to realize that your immune system is attacking those chemicals because they're foreign substances. Your immune system, as time goes by, is constantly being affronted and attacked, so it never has time to renew your teeth, skin, hair, and eyesight, so your body slowly but surely deteriorates and becomes compromised. Your immune system becomes so compromised that it cannot recover as it is fighting constant abnormalities that you have been told to introduce into your body on a continual basis.

The fear factor is played in there by saying, well you know you have to take this pill because if you don't this will happen. You'll have side effects, but they'll be okay. It continues that way, as you're a dollar sign in the current system.

The new technology will be known available when the forces out there, even hidden, we're not talking about the big ones because they're being taken down, we're talking about the many ones that are in towns and cities and different villages across America that are not good people. Disciples of Lucifer, the archons and some other unknown dark entities infiltrated the population and worked silently for the elite.

The soil, the atmosphere, the water, everything is plasma energy, everything and the universe is plasma energy. It is just a different form through vibrational frequency. There are some new healing modalities in the advanced medical field available because your body leaves a resonance, a vibrational frequency. With this new form of healing there is no pain and you do not go through radiation.

There are three types of these new technologies: 1-Holographic, 2-Regeneratrice (which regenerates tissue and body parts), 3-Reatomization (2-3 minutes to regenerate the whole body.)

Chapter 97
Then I Heard Something BIG was about to be Revealed

I was hot and about to pass out. I needed to remove the blanket that was covering my body and made me sweat. But I could not move. I tried to change position, but it was too heavy. My body was heavy and paralyzed like. I tried to lift up my head, but I could not. I tried to move my arm and I could not either and I remember saying to myself don't panic. I remembered that that was not the first time it happened to me and had to keep calm. Saying to myself it will happen. I needed to re-enter my physical body.

That's just when I heard.

"Pay attention this is a call to continue to commit to your soul purpose, Lightwork and Divine Mission.

It is time to show up in the present moment, to shine your Light more than ever and make a difference in the world in the highest and best possible way.

Remember the Divine Truth of you is to work and continue to accomplish your Divine Purpose and Mission.

Your role is to see through the veil of darkness and illusion blanketing physical reality and to dispel it. You are paving the way and preparing humanity for a new era of peace and prosperity, sometimes referred to as a Golden Age.

You are present on the Earth to usher out the fear paradigm and beacon a new age of peace and light.

You are enlightened beings here to bring about healing and positive change within physical reality.

Yes, it has been a long and difficult road paved with many restraints, delays, twists, but also you made a lot of accomplishments.

Katherine, the mother of Paul and the surrogate archon has become weak. She has lost a lot since Saint Germain started in power and you have a little bit longer, not much, to wait before the reunion. The hidden truth is coming out. People right now are still confused, and some see through the fake and some are not. And Saint Germain is working hard and fast with you."

Of course, I thought but hey! Isn't it what we do? We know that. And except for a few days here and there now my blue flame is on the level where we can communicate longer. Even though he still is on drugs he can lower the dosage and clean his body a little bit more each day. When they don't throw away or steal their supplements.

Recently Katherine and Paul have found another way to keep him from sleeping at night. CHADD must sleep in a room without air conditioning under 101F every night. They know that I only have a small window of time to call and speak to him and he will fall asleep exhausted.
Leaving us with not much time to talk. But as you'll see our mission continues.

Being comfortably in a numb state I looked at the world watching as 5G slowly came into view. Then came in my vision the word CoVFeFe.

Would our internet capabilities become like nothing we have ever seen? Since the microwave generation, 5G is being welcomed with open arms to give us faster internet capabilities." Says my inner voice.

Then, strange videos appeared, and I saw that dozens of birds are dying in different places in Europe. The following day

Mainstream Media quickly exposed these concerns as conspiracy. 5G was not being tested there at the time. The reporters stated the birds most likely died from pesticides, and test results regarding human complications with 5G has yet to be determined.

A friendly voice speaks to me: This technology boasts considerable increased data speed leaving 3G and 4G in the past. 5G's high frequency radio waves (mm Wave) would present itself to all our smart devices with faster downloads, etc. On the horizon with 5G, are self-driving cars, drone footage, robotic surgeries, etc.

However, I have shown that many studies have taken place on how electromagnetic radiation may affect the environment, and it concluded that this radiation could pose a potential risk to bird and insect orientation and plant health.

And now I am decoding the following from my Galactic family.

"Hello again VIE,

Since 2019 America's 5G Towers have been converted to 432Hz Tesla Healing Towers. They were initially created by the 1% and Deep State to control and depopulate us, but your government and its team have turned them into Tesla towers. Just like the Mexican wall is also a Tesla Healing wall. Since these 5G towers were created by 1% and Deep State, you will see a Covid-19 stamp inside.

You may have heard speak of Ventilators, and how many will be shipped to other countries to help with Covid-19. And you have been told through that Ventilators have double meaning, wondering what role these Ventilators play.

They are used when they rescue the children in the underground tunnels, as initially these children were dying as they were exposed to the surface for the first time. They realized these ventilators saved lives.

They are also CoVFeFe magnets which make 5G safe. It's an alloy of Cobalt, Vanadium, and Iron creating a magnetic material that will also facilitate many innovative technological advances for our future including space travel.

CoVFeFe essentially cleanses the impurities from the 5G and works on an ionic level to keep Oxygen from being depleted, rendering the signal harmless.

Light, love and blessings to you"

Chapter 98
As long as People are Stuck in the 3D Paradigm, they will not Find Happiness

One day an Asian woman contacted me for an appointment. She came on time, past the door briefly said hello, sat down and all she said after was "I came for a session with you to find out more. I am a martial art master. Then she closed her eyes, centered herself and forgot totally about me.

That's how it's supposed to be as per design. The 3D matrix system sets forth that you always need the next thing in order to achieve happiness at some moment in time, in a future that does not exist. And for her it was about her family and who they were.

So, I began my session, I sat in silence and began to pray, and that day I entered in communication with a North Korean man that passed away and was related to my client. Her name was Akira. I began to channel the man named Fukashi, and after a while I interrupted voluntarily the channeling to ask my client that pretended to be Japanese, if she was understanding the language I was speaking. For me it was obvious that I was not speaking Japanese.

Akira opened her eyes and looked at me with a big smile and said 'Yes! It is my grandfather Fukashi. He was also very skilled in martial arts. We are not Japanese but from Korea. What happened is that my parents had to come to live in Japan when they were very young. They were not allowed to speak Korean and flew out of the country.

I was guided to you. I have been told by a medium in Tucson, Arizona that what I was looking for, you will be able to help me with.

When the session was finished after Akira had left the office, I sat to say thanks for the wonderful session we had and that's when Great Eagle took over. He told me that he had a very important message to send me. And that is what he said:

"VIE, as long as people are stuck in the 3D paradigm, they will not find happiness. For Akira it was easier to find happiness, it did not depend on control and manipulation of emotions like most people.

You see here is where this process gets ugly: unfortunately, there's a multitude of manipulations men and women alike tend to use in order to control their partner, and the relationship but the most commonly used is emotional blackmail.

That this has nothing to do with love, that this has everything to do with codependency. Do you see how this toxic abuse is about control and energetic vampirism and many other unhealthy behavioral patterns, but the bottom line is that it's all about the ego -not the heart.

The only way to keep your sanity is out of manipulation and control are the opposite of love. It's fear, where there is fear love cannot exist.

Manipulative 3D people still have a long way to go. So many chakras to heal, so many blockages and issues to address. Bless them and let them and their toxic relationship go.

The heart will not judge. True love comes from the heart. The last thing we need right now is more pain and trauma to heal. While we're in the midst of a world crisis.

Soon these people will be very lost and in major need of healing because everything they believed to be reality will cease to exist. It will be a very long exhausting period of the dark night of the soul before they will be able to have a healthy high vibrational relationship with another being based on unconditional love.

There are those who have done the inner work and have dealt with their shadows. Only a person who is whole, at peace and happy with themselves will be whole, peaceful, and happy with another person. The moment someone is looking to achieve some relationship goal in an illusory future timeline they are vibrating on the third-dimensional frequency and aren't ready for a conscious, highly evolved, sacred heart to heart union.

Manipulative 3D people still have a long way to go. So many chakras to heal, so many blockages and issues to address. The last thing we need right now is more pain and trauma to heal. We're in the midst of a world crisis.

Soon these people will be very lost and in major need of healing because everything they believed to be reality will cease to exist. There are those who have done the inner work and have dealt with their shadows. Only a person who is whole, at peace and happy with themselves will be whole, peaceful, and happy with another person. The moment someone is looking to achieve some relationship goal in an illusory future timeline they are vibrating on the third-dimensional frequency and aren't ready for a highly evolved consciousness."

And the message stopped there.

Chapter 99
The Great Waking Up

With the new era and the Aquarius time things are moving on. Some people wake up and they are unprepared, scared, and frightened. And I have more and more people reaching for guidance and help like this eighteen years old person:

"Hello, I am an eighteen-year-old male from Ohio State. I am reaching out for your guidance. So, it has been ever since around the 4th of July. I hit a wall of something I never felt before. I suddenly felt a heightened level of clarity and I could handle social situations in a way I never could before. Not really a bad thing but more of a self-awareness type deal. Now here is where it gets weird to me. I came back from vacation, and I felt as if I had forgotten how to work my job. I still functioned but not to my full potential. On the night of July 7th going into July 8th I had been feeling weird to the point of what I thought the world was ending. I didn't feel connected to earth anymore. I felt a very heightened sense of being. Anyway, that night I made the decision to smoke some cannabis and when I went to bed the feeling did not change. Earlier that day my friend asked me if I recognized if I had seen the number 0010110 and I had to reply yes even though I didn't because it is like something in me clicked. That night I lay in bed without sleeping. All I did was sweat and feel different connections even to lost loved ones and it was almost and it was almost just the thought processes. No words or anything.

I will admit I felt scared and loved all at the same time. Now I have been a Christian for most of my life and I won't say the best one. I've been clinging to the worry of what happens after death. But ever since that I started to get into government conspiracy theories that make sense. So, my questions are, why am I having these death - birth understandings and how the sun gives the plants energy for us and other animals that we consume and the cycle. I want to go back to normal, but I also kind of like this thought process even though it frightens me. Why is that? With love and peace,"

If you remember I have talked about 0010110 in my book "New Centuries, New Era, New Experiences" And that is why I have written them, and asked readers to read the series of my galactic lessons in sequence. There is so much to learn, and it has to be done by baby steps. You have been lied to for so long. Many, many years, and many things have been hidden from you. You must be prepared".

Chapter 100
The Red Folder

This happened on the 2nd Sunday of fall. I opened the back door of the house to feel the outside temperature and check the weather, when my attention was attracted by a red folder resting on the first stair. I rapidly grabbed it intrigued and excited by this unexpected folder.

I closed the door and rushed inside to open it. And this is what was written on a very expensive paper and addressed to me.

Hi, VIE, you did not receive this by accident. I know the content can and will change your life and others.

It is meant for you to read this. You and I have met a few times, but not officially and you may know me by some different names.

This fall and the next most important election may be the most important moment ever for all humanity. The wrong vote for the wrong person is literally a vote for the ruthless Chinese Communist Party, who seek nothing but complete world dominance.

There is a lot more that I could share about that but won't be heard as it is triggered for those whose minds have been hacked by the constant drip feed of lies from the mainstream media.

The Process Center for safety crimes against humanity are staggeringly dark. This is not a political view; this is a spiritual one. This goes beyond the political and resides in the fate of all life.

I believe the light has already come and the clean-up is underway.

The new world is coming, but it seems to me it may get much darker before dawn.

Be close to your heart tribe.

Turn off mainstream media totally. It is your greatest threat.

Get out in nature, as much as you can.

Ground yourself in the earth, breathe in the fresh prana.

Prepare your home with Natural medicines in case the globalists continue to enact their medical and governmental tyranny this fall.

Remember there is no pandemic. It's all a psychological operation to control your mind using fear. Remember this!!! This virus is just the common cold. It is literally a genetic upgrade. People who are dying were already dying and were given a false Covid diagnosis.

Death is the one thing none of us can get out of, and also it is by no means final. You know that we are eternal and infinite. Do not fear death as fear is the greatest detriment to your immune system.

Drop into deep faith in the perfection of the universe and the perfection of your immune system. Feed your body high vibe foods. It is Time for a deep mind and body cleanse.

My suggestions are Vitamin C, Vit. D3, Zinc, Nascent iodine, micronized zeolites, mustard seed and magnesium baths, distilled water, and medicinal mushrooms. Infrared saunas are amazing, in conjunction with b3 niacin (the flush kind). Use The essential oil thieves before getting out, diffuse it in your house. Wash your hands before eating and as soon as you get back home., also keep some oregano essential oil. Foot bath detox at least twice a month.

Keep your spiritual practices strong, get good sleep in a dark room, and strengthen your immune system.

Stay strong, stay in your heart, and pray for all life. Bless everyone you meet with your heart. Offer everyone your benevolence. Offer everyone your light. Do good deeds every day to help others feel safe and reminded of what it feels like to be in the presence of love.

And bless the hearts of our military and police to make the right decisions when asked to go against their own inner wisdom and guidance. May they turn their guns to truly serve and protect the woman and children and elders.

I am spiritual not religious, but I must say Revelations is right on track. We are near the time of the great cleansing and judgment day. Be clear what you are serving. You are moving into the new world of serving the highest good of all, and most of all serving life itself.

In the end you will face the truth and feel all that you have created. Love or Fear.

That's what you have to tell people, from deep in their heart, to repent for being complicit to the harm against humanity, the earth, the animals and life itself. To step back from it all, be calm, be in peace, and Repent.

To humble themselves and put their forehead on mother earth and ask her for her forgiveness. For looking the other way, for doing nothing, for participating in great suffering. And not to worry, she always forgives.

Then to rise into their light. Get up with new strength and serve the living life with all their heart and soul. You, they are bigger than you could ever imagine. You, they are an eternal being, made in the light of love and because of that you are sovereign and free.

Tell them that they belong here in this human tribe to rise into their fullness and reclaim their gifts to share with all. Their spot is waiting for them in the sacred circle.

Tell them to come if they can!

I see you, VIE and I love you.

Chapter 101
The Human Genome, Revelations

A long time had passed since I have spoken out loud during my sleep. Then I began talking to myself silently, and a voice said, "Keep talking!"... and that was a soft and familiar inner voice.

It awakened me to hear CHADD telling me "Failure is not an option. The book of the revelation uncovers matters that had been hidden and discloses events that would happen long after it was written. Many of its prophecies are yet to be fulfilled."

And me in turn saying: Yes! I agree "revelation" refers to something or someone, once hidden, becoming visible.

I am hearing Church bells in the far. A woman with big eyes and a beautiful face appears in front of me. She gives me a hug, then goes and sits in the corner seat under the window. I joined her and sat in the leather seat next to her. I am surprised and waiting for an explanation of some sort. She lifts her arm, makes a gesture with her hands, kind of like a magician would and the vision of an old book appears. The books open at the very beginning, and it says: Book of Revelation can be challenging, the storyline twists and turns and isn't strictly chronological. The author of the Book of Revelation, Saint John the Divine, offers a transcription of seven letters and later describes strange beasts, visions of judgments, governments, demonic battles, heaven, and a new world order (NWO) a prophetic vision for the end of the world. This book reveals truths about him and his final victory. It unveils Jesus Christ in glory.

"Revelations" is basically about the Armageddon software installed to torment humanity, putting predictive programming into the planetary brain 2000 years ago.

Many humans on the Earth today are the result of alien hybridization and are susceptible to genetic altering that allows them to be a host body for a variety of interdimensional entities. When a human has been genetically modified by an alien species it allows that body to be used as a portal for that alien consciousness.

A person can be abducted, contacted, downloaded, and altered with enhancements to perform certain roles.

If you're in contact and if your life is going in a positive direction those beings have your best interest in mind, if your life has completely gone off the rails those beings do not have your best interest in mind and are nothing but an invading species.

Humans are grouped into planetary resources as slave labor, replicated clones, sex slaves for their breeding programs, used as bargaining tools with other species for food and other purposes. These malevolent species see humans as their personal property to be used as a resource that serves their domination agenda. They perform benevolent actions towards humans which only serves their enslavement agenda. They are calculating liars and masterful deceivers and will say anything the human wants to hear in order to manipulate the results to serve their agenda.

The hidden agendas of these malevolent invading species include hybridization programs, breeding programs, genetic modification, and manipulation of human DNA. The manipulation of human DNA works both for the genetic enhancement of the preferred bloodlines that are hybridized with primarily Reptilian genetics, while others are genetically "dumbed down" to be a working slave class.

Military Controllers prefer enhanced humans with Reptilian genetics because the species have higher abilities which include remote viewing, astral projection, and shapeshifting. Many family lines that are subjected to alien abduction and genetic experimentation are recruited into the military for a variety of covert operations. This is to further enforce human enslavement and impose complete ownership over all human beings. Basically, they are downloaded with Predator Mind.

There is no currency or financial system that is used between space civilizations; this illegal and enslavement practice is only used within human reality; everything else is based on bartering.

This negative alien agenda, the Cabal, the elite in power whatever you want to call them decided to use human trafficking as one of their resources and interstellar bartering.

Here we are today... we are in an interstellar war, and it has now come down to the surface.

World War III is a spiritual war, no missiles are needed, Fear is the only weapon and the territory that is being fought over is your mind.

The ultimate tyranny in a society is not controlled by martial law. It is controlled by the psychological manipulation of consciousness, through which reality is defined so that those who exist within it do not even realize that they are in prison. They do not even realize that there is something outside of where they exist. We represent what is outside of what you have been taught exists. It is where you sometimes venture and where we want you to dwell; it is outside of where society has told you can live.

You have been controlled like sheep in a pen by those who think they own you- from the government to the World Management Team to those in space. You have been deprived of knowledge by frequency control.

We're at war, we are in a spiritual war, and we must win there is no other option.

The woman stands up, gives me a big smile, and vanishes by the window.

It was another angel messenger that made my day. I know that it may look weird to you, but that is the way my journey goes. And my life.

Chapter 102
A Desperate Attempt from Paul Now to Separate VIE and CHADD

This new event I was faced to experience began at 7:01 a.m. While I am starting my journey with my usual meditative Prayer, I am lifted in a thin bubble of Light. I am being put in a comforting place to rest. From inside my Bubble, I can see Paul. While CHADD is asleep, he is wiring something in the wall that is putting on fire CHADD electronics. I see Paul's face shapeshifting and he has a very nasty look on it. He is demonically enjoying looking at it before burning. CHADD is awakened now by the smell and the smoke, and realizing what Paul did burst into wrath. Not only the surrogate drove his car hit it and damaged it severely last month, now it's Paul's turn to destroy and put on fire his electronics, and his receiver while he is sleeping.

That is when it was being poured into my head some truths, connections, and understandings.

"Cells store and continue to hold energy from intense experiences of past and present lifetimes. Some of these experiences were good, some bad, and a few horrendous and terrifying. This old energy remains alive and well, affecting a person's life choices until Cleared through Conscious Intention or Spiritual Evolutionary Growth. He, your blue flame, went through a lot and has been on psychotropic drugs for a long time. Got a little break when you detoxed him. But since then, has been ordered for years and forced to ingest them again. And you see watch out for Paul" This was it.

It stayed in my mind all day wondering what it was all for. By the evening I entered communication with CHADD. He was not himself at all and answered the call saying "What I am going to say to you, you are not going to love it at all. But I cannot continue for my well-being to work with you and talk to you." and he continued with a very confusing story about his day. Talking to a woman at the store, that told him not to approach him. Saying that not only he was handicapped, and not making enough money...and she said, "Because you are living on a monthly government check, but I made a background check and I found that you have some bad records." His voice was telling me that something was abnormal and that he was on a higher dosage than usual. It reminded me of when I found him with an unclear mind. He was not able to see reality, and he was in a foggy place while speaking to me.

I made a quick prayer to the Father and asked Saint Michael for protection. Paul must have ingested some high dosage of drugs I thought.

As usual when something happened that I could not understand, and after a night without sleep trying to figure out what happened to CHADD, St Michael gave me the answer and said "Anything or anyone who promotes separation is not in alignment with the will of the Prime Creator, Source, God, The All. As the last attempts from the old reality, they try their best to keep you down, and that's what Paul did to CHADD. But now Humans are given refined energies of love and peace during all time for that reason. Paul knew that CHADD wanted to use the receiver for the institute. That's why he had this satanic look on his face."

But the time is changing. Karma will be served for all these dark energies, and Paul is no exception.

Paul married 3 times. Had a son with his first wife and divorced. Abused the confidence of his cousin and slept with his fiancé. Married a second time and divorced six months later. Lost his job after being caught in business with some mafia person. Then he married his third wife. After five years she left him. But he refused to divorce her. He had an affair with another woman, still not divorced, and had two daughters that he managed to recognize. Today he is sick with prostate cancer.

One week after the incident with Paul CHADD called me late at night. First, I only heard loud music and people talking in the background. Right away I knew something was wrong again. As I kept saying all and no one was answering I hung up. The phone rang again, and a girl answered then CHADD spoke. He seemed to be very confused and spoke about him singing with a famous group that he had just made a lot of money. Said that he met the son of two famous lawyers that will take his injury case at the Long Stay residence. When a few men covered in black came in his room and beat him and broke his tailbone. Then continues saying that he left the door of his car open with music on in the parking lot to be sure to locate it after he went to look for some antic cars to invest in with the handicapped son of the lawyer couple that will take his case. Then he hung up.

I try to call back but no one answered the phone until very late when a woman said "The person that was here left its phone"

I did not hear from him until the next day. He was in the surrogate car; she had tricked him again. The night before he simply went out for a drink and that's what the two archons, mother, and son, were waiting for. They managed to have a substance put in his drink to make him look confused. At the admission place she told the doctor that she was baker acting for him because he needed to be admitted and evaluated and put into medication. Her poor son had a "head injury" and needed to stay on medications but he sold it to people in a club.

As if it was not enough, after leaving her son at the hospital she called a few friends to tell them that he had to be admitted at the hospital to be evaluated and put in psychiatric meds because he had a brain injury some years ago. Once again, she managed to destroy his reputation.

She was hit on her way back home in a car accident. Her car was destroyed. But she did not expect that he would be out after three days.

Chapter 103
VIE, Blessed Mother in Heaven Mother Gave Me a Message for You.

Lately I keep receiving a lot of messages from behind the veil and I woke up this morning to receive this great new message.

Dear VIE,

Blessed Mother gave me a message and you are among the first to hear it. She has appeared in Lourdes, Fatima, and Guadalupe. She appears everywhere. She can appear in anyone race. She represents compassion, mercy, sympathy, and love. She has been worshipped by many names but also by many cultures, since at least as far back as the ancient Greeks. She was the mother of Jesus Christ of Nazareth. And she gave me this message for you.

"There is a great shift occurring right now...yes, VIE even greater than the virus.

Lots of LIES will come to the surface.

Evil doers will be brought to justice. You may hear all kinds of crazy rumors.

Do NOT get into FEAR! VIE YOU ARE PROTECTED.

The whole world is shifting right now.

It feels painful in a way, yet the outcome will be better for us all.

Stay away from mainstream news.

Most mainstream news is FEAR-MONGERS!

Working for the chaos energies!"

One week later here is what I received from my spiritual and star family.

"The return of the Goddesses Maries. The past days are currently generating a lot of potential for aggression within the surface population. Combined with Black Magic and neg. irradiation executed by the Cabal, this can currently also cause a lot of chaos in the world.

And of course, also energetic attacks, which are supposed to trigger physical arguments, violence, injuries, problems with technical devices as well as nightmares, as the Archons manipulate mind and non-physical body."

Here protection, cleaning, implant removal, healing, charging is important …

Chapter 104
Distracted by the COVID-19 while Earth is Ascending

The energies on planet earth are explosive now. Major changes are underway.

For many people around the world life as they know it is ending, and people are standing at the culprit being forced to build something new.

Take a neutral look at how you were living your life and examine whether you were living from the heart, acting from integrity and if you can truly say that you were being your authentic self.

Behind the scenes, while people were so distracted with the COVID-19 planet Earth is ascending and evolving into planet Erra. And if some have lost their job, home, business, or simply lifestyle that they had gotten used to then this is your wake-up call.

You had to adapt, move into action, and use your creativity.

Humans are now called to build and create new lives, new homes, new schools, new health systems, new food supply systems, and new businesses that are based on full 5D integrity, uncompromised authenticity, and created with the highest honor for earth and life.

You are simply called to step into your Divine creator powers.

You have to focus and use the power of Tulpa a few minutes every day and involve others too and stop the Corona-19 virus.

What happened is that created it as a test on the population and thought that they could control it. But who can control a virus? This virus was supposed to stop in June.

I was driving looked at the dashboard and saw this message:

"Everything is Divinely guided and not a coincidence. Everything that currently exists in your life was once a wish. The creation of your desired reality focused on your own intentions, the power of your thought. By wishing for something with passion you create energy that becomes the source to make your dream come true. Wishes are like seeds that provide the fuel that propels actions. Pay attention now! And share it.

So, you are asked to 1- Select 2- Project 3- Expect.

These series of words are first you Select, then you Project with the power of your mind, then expect truly that it will come to life. That's creation.

You must take the driver's seat and create your own reality.

And as all change you must know about the planetary update but not only, also about the return of the female demons Goddesses and the Goddesses Maries.

CHAPTER 105
OCTOBER WILL BLACK OUT

I am your Guide to the light. You take the journey, and you get to the top. I am simply your helper, your way-shower so that you can have an easier path to the top.

I see our world growing more irrational, confused, polluted, and disturbed by the day. I seek to offer a new perspective and write with great hope, both for individual healing and for the collective healing of our world in manifesting the best in the future of our species. " Politics is only a setup. Communism has not died but lives on in the form of ecology. Green, the ecologists, is the new red. That's what I read in the newspaper the man was reading.

I left the place I was rapidly to regain my car. I was fastening my seat belt when Monsieur le Comte and the messenger opened the passenger door, sat in the car, and said:

"Hi, VIE, I am here to protect, also guide, and inform you. Start the car. I will give you instructions on where to go."

The traffic was not bad at all for the time of the day, which made it easier to drive and had all my attention on what he had to say.

The night before I had the vision of a strange scene. On the left of my home, I saw the flood coming passing by between the house of an Arab Prince and mine. Suddenly an unknown object appeared with the prince and two of his bodyguards seated inside and they disappeared out of my view very, very fast. On the right of my house, it was inhabited by an Islamist Pakistanis. I saw a similar scene, the flood passing between his home and mine. A similar unidentified object, though a little smaller. The exact same thing happened. The Hindu/Pakistanis man disappeared in it. They were terrified and rushing to get out a run for their life before they would be caught and swallowed by the flood. At no time was my life unsecure and my house flooded.

Monsieur le Comte "I know that you had an epiphany last night and I am here to give you confirmation and also more details. 1here is a 100 % Triumph of Mr. President. His covid news is a strategy. October will have a blackout. The world is coming is great!!! Good and great news.

Let me reassure you. We have constant contact with CHADD, even though he lives with the surrogate and Paul. He told you the reason why the US President went in the middle of the night at the military hospital, and I have come to take you to a safe location.

There were some drastic military escalations behind the scenes a few hours ago, and there is now a full-scale war going on between the Galactic Confederation and the Draco fleet in sublunar space, and a full-scale war between the Resistance Movement and the Illuminati Breakaway Complex in the underground bases. Nothing can be said at this time about the operations on the surface, as all is still classified.

Although the end result of this war is a clear Draco and IBC defeat (2nd amendment — amendment in insolvency and bankruptcy code bill), the energy of this conflict will precipitate to the surface of the planet as increased violence among members of the surface population, and as violence from the Cabal towards the surface humanity.

There will be two peaks of this conflict, meaning peak quarantine status for this planet, both as a planetary quarantine and as covid quarantine, and now the dark forces are daily losing their grip upon the surface of this planet. There is still a great possibility for the Cabal to try to impose new covid lockdowns for about a week, and moderate possibility for the Cabal to try to impose them in the next three weeks.

Therefore, the Light Forces are asking everybody who feels so guided to participate in daily meditation at 9:30 pm UTC to counteract covid lockdowns."

We drove for about two hours and parked under a tree. It did not take long before I entered a trance, and I found myself in an unknown location surrounded by beautiful mountains. I accessed a room and entered in one of the founding meetings of a special study commission that would discuss American issues. Although I did not know it at the time, these meetings would later serve as guiding lights for some actions in the US.

Despite the atmosphere where it was held, a person commented upon the Americans' exaggerated horror for abstraction and held meetings that dealt with the ethereal themes of the metaphysical, the marvelous and the sublime. The gentleman often saw the cold, bottom-line relationships that were molded on the erroneous premise that time is money. And mentioned them how this very cold premise affected our relationship with God.

Be aware that, in this new chaos of consciousness and confusion and shifting of uncertainty, there is a divine order. There is a catalytic energy present at this time on the planet as all of the individual structures begin to melt and merge to create what looks like chaos. There will be something newborn out of this,
Many people on the planet will not recognize that there is a higher order behind the chaos.

Of course, you have free will to determine how you will follow. This free will allows you to decide the specifics of how you would like your life to be designed, although you must live out your blueprint. Whether you choose to do this with difficulty or with ease, in poverty or in richness, is up to you. It all depends on where you have been convinced to put your boundaries. What can we say to convince you to take all your boundaries down-to stop limiting what you believe can be yours?

If there is anything we wish to achieve, it is to have each of you boundless and free, knowing that every thought you entertain somehow determines your experience. If we could get you to live 100 percent of the time according to what you want, we would feel that this has been a most successful year.

Chapter 106
The Return of Demons Goddess and the Goddesses Maries

What you must know about the Return of the female demons Goddess. They existed in large legions on the ethereal plains, and they were partly using real physical avatars for their work, especially in the following areas: Africa, India, Germany, Asia (especially Thailand), Washington DC and various underwater bases in the Pacific.

These female Demons could "sense" Goddess Energy and have made the life of incarnated Priestesses of the Goddess very difficult in the past. Since this negative grouping has also been neutralized by the Light Forces, it is now safe enough for Goddesses to return to Earth in order to form Light and Healing Centers on the surface, which later on will become the so called "Islands of Light" in which a First Contact can take place.

The Return of Goddesses Maries

The Maries are belonging to a special female healer order subordinated to none less than Mary the mother of God. They will enter Earth's surface as walk-ins in order to heal the star seeds, which are traumatized by the millennia of struggle within the dark quarantine around Terra.

The Maries are extremely empathic and can sense the emotions around them. They can differentiate them and understand that these emotions are not their own.

Maries are so powerful that they can pull out negative emotions from bodies, objects, houses, even whole cities, so they can provide much needed healing.

They create an "island of Light" the bubble of high in the surface in which Divine Source will act and protect with the matrix system around it and will disintegrate...That is an important operation done by the light forces.

Goddesses called Maya, Amber, Sophia, and Rose have already come through a portal in the Atlantic.

That's when the first twin Souls entered the grid now, mostly walk-in tools because the situation has become much safer, although it can still come to various attacks because the planet is further on in the stage of cleaning, and some negative groupings are still creeping out from various corners.

The return and reunification of the first twin Souls. Both parts that still had to clear some traumas and primal pain from the time of Atlantis caused by the dark ones back then. When these incarnated twin Souls at that time, were separated and mostly sacrificed.

Without the clarification of these traumas there is no ascent possible. Secondly it is time for the first twin Souls to make physical tantra in order to transfer the resulting energies into the respective region on the surface. This will then accelerate the healing and the ascension process of the planet.

The healing of incarnated star seeds on Terra also plays an important role. They all need intensive healing first, especially on a non-physical level. Many star seeds have been and are still involved in, especially at night while their avatar is resting.

There are countless star seeds on the surface that are already awakened and engaged in the liberation of the planet every day and who lead an ethereal double life at night without their knowledge. These star seeds leave their body during night and take part in the most diverse operations of the Light Forces on the non-physical plains on the planet. Some of them also cooperate with positive forces below Earth's surface. They go to the confederation ships at night and make reports. They join underground meetings or are involved in direct battles against the dark ones and the chimera. The next morning, they wake up and cannot remember or are only fragmentary and blurred. That's why star seeds feel extremely tired in the morning despite enough sleep.

With the rising energies on Earth, more and more memories are unlocked.

"A few years ago, I went back to Costa Rica to visit some good friends and stayed in their house. Last night in their home I was awakened by my friends' couple in the middle of the night next to my bed and looking at me. They came rushing into the room to ask me if I was doing alright. They said that they heard the voice of a man and me battling physically and me saying out loud: I commend you to leave this bed immediately.

Then I saw CHADD, my blue flame, after being beaten by the dark ones and all blooded. Even his eyes were red yet smiling at me courageously. and saying to the mafia man Carlos that beat him: I forgive you. The woman next to us burst in tears and rushed to give him a glass of water."

The Chimera has placed negative implants, Some energies electrodes for disturbances, as well as spider-like and bugging devices into many star seeds. They are suffering from various physical complaints for which there seems to be no explanation, because no cause is found during medical examinations. Another problem is that chimaera have also implanted multiple toplet bombs directly into the ethereal bodies of some star seeds near the coccyx and the kundalini. These toplets bomb would trigger immediately as soon as a physical pick-up by the ships of the Galactic Confederation takes place and it would literally tear the soul of the respective star seed apart.

Therefore, these things must be removed non-physical before a physical pick-up can be considered. Star seeds can either go into meditations or imagine, while falling asleep, that they travel to get brought to the healing ships of the Pleiadians' Ashtar Command energetically.

The pandemic was a test run to see how this would work over the depopulation and the population capability to obey. The dark spirits thought that they would control both humans and the virus. But the fear they created didn't let the pandemic disappear. It got crazy again.

Many people died because the plan was depopulation of the un-useful citizen, and a lot of spirits do not want to be part of what is coming forward. About the crazy weather it comes from Gaia shaking herself. Gaia has been poisoned and polluted like you have been. That is beside the manipulation by the dark.

Saint Germain is uncovering what has been created and was said by the elite, creating panic among them. They are pulling forward and exposing that all they said is a lie. The corrupt politicians governing the planet have been dying and now they are trying to defend themselves. A lot of people have been listening to the media and the fake.

They have lied to the public since the beginning and Saint Germain to uncover everything. He is reversing everything with declassification, and he is creating chaos. And they are scrambling.

He got them on the defensive. He is making it harder and harder. Then he will have uncovered it all and show that they have committed crimes against humanity. That's where there is Karmic balancing by karmic cleansing. And you are asked to work daily on level manifestation and global your thoughts combined with others globally. Using Tulpa, the results and the power of the mass combined to create. As there is another wave about to enter because of the wrongly focused virus and fear.

The first Tulpa case was created through spiritual and mental powers. It was seen in Tibet. When in 1950 twenty Monks were in meditation to make appear a golem to destroy enemies' villages during the war. Once a Tulpa is created the Tulpa lives by itself.

Expect truly, Life Giving, Love Giving, Light Giving.

That's when I saw 11:11 it is a direct channel that opens between me and my Higher Self. It is the point of merging the physical and non-physical realities of me. An Energetic Gateway that just opened for me. Telling me that at that moment my thoughts, beliefs, and actions were energetically charged and incredibly potent creating.

Chapter 107
The Kings of Agartha Leaders of the Council of Twelve

I looked at the time on my cell phone, it was 1:11 p.m. when I placed my hands in his. In my new client John's hand that just entered. I had no idea who he was, and I felt his energy and began to hear.

"Hello, VIE, the divine realm and universal energies are on your side to show you that it is high time things changed in your life. Your thoughts will go a long way in ensuring that you live a happy and fulfilled life. Embrace these opportunities that come your way manifestation and prosperity.

I contacted you a few years ago. We had back and forth communication by email. I told you that I had visited your island underwater. I would like to give you more information today. Now is the time and it is most important that you share it.

The Forces of Darkness. The Resistance Movement has developed advanced technology of teleportation chambers, free energy, cloning and biotechnology as a whole. They have their underground cities mostly under the biggest cities of Europe and the USA. Their cities are interconnected with MHD drive tube-train systems with speeds of up to 15000 mph. Their underground civilization is a successor of the Kingdom of Agartha which was almost destroyed in attacks of the Dark Forces between 1996 and 1999.

Now the core of the Light Forces is representatives of the Atlantean Network. This is a group of a few thousand individuals of a very high spiritual vibration that has maintained the purity of the Atlantean legacy permanently since the times of Atlantis itself. The Atlants have their underground residences in some chosen locations under the Himalayas, under southern California, under some atolls near Tahiti, and under Titicaca Lake. They inspire individuals towards their ideals of creating a harmonic society that will be known by the name of New Atlantis.

Many ancient cultures that vanished without a trace (for example the Mayans) had in fact moved into the Agartha Empire. Some Hopi Indians have had contact with Agartha just a few decades ago. In Agartha, the Order of the Star was very active. Its purpose is the healing of the separation on planet Earth and also the successful completion of the Experiment of Duality.

The Kings of Agartha were leaders of the Council of Twelve and were a physical anchor for the energies of Sanat Kumara. Certain American presidents and presidents of some other states had contact with the Kings of Agartha during their term. Agartha often exerted its spiritual influence on the surface, especially the Himalayan Network in the region of India and Tibet.

It will be Steadfast on Mission because the energy in hearts will be strongly directed to work. Humanity is coming together in Oneness. We are here to be part of Oneness. We have all suffered from separation but as these new energies continue to shift, we will no longer find separation. It will be living in the Light of the new Earth. Living in the ever-changing Present Moment and Being Happy."

Chapter 108
Mary Magdalene and the Story of "Sacred Union"

I came back as the first Aquarius bringing my Vibrational Transformation Intuitive Energy to open the new era. The Era of liberty.

For the "Christ Consciousness" as taught by Mary Magdalene is seated in the Heart. It is the Heart that carries the Higher Frequencies of Love and Joy and Peace, and it is only by opening the Heart that we can achieve the Consciousness of the Grail within ourselves and then be ready to share that with others.

When I settled in France two thousand years ago, I began the work of holding the Christ Light through my presence as part of the Christed "Twin Flame" energy, as well as sharing the energy of the message of the teachings of the Christ.

Consciousness. This basic message was Peace, Abundance and Unconditional Love, and the knowledge that a time would come when the Earth would be filled with a species of Humans who would carry the Christ.

Consciousness and who would manifest the Golden Age of Peace and Harmony.

In its most simple form, this is the essence of what Mary Magdalene brought to France.

I knew that this form of "Spiritual Marriage", based on the Service of the Light, would become a pattern or Template for relationship and union in the coming Golden Age, or as we would term it, the "New Earth".

As Mary Magdalene I knew, that there would be energies and forces that would work against the new evolution of Consciousness, but she knew too that her teachings and her energy would survive in this place, and that they would be carried out into the New World when the time came for humans to migrate across the Oceans from Western Europe and to discover the "family" of Humanity in the Indigenous Peoples of the Planet who still held the Sacred Earth teachings.

I knew that when the time was right, these Sacred Earth teachings would be shared with the peoples of the West, and that this would help them to raise their consciousness and to learn how to become caretakers for the Planet in this new Golden Age.

And so, as her legacy for this process of transformation, I, Mary Magdalene, left the teachings of the Twin Flame and Sacred Union. Knowing that this would be needed at this time of Consciousness shift, for the Masculine energy that was needed to populate the Planet would have come to dominate to such an extent that it would be necessary to bring back the Feminine energy and to create the balance needed to create true "Sacred Union", and to implement the Golden Grid of Twin Flame Union that would hold the Geometrical Pattern or Template for the Golden Energy of Twin Flame Love.

But, as a Wise Woman, Mary Magdalene also knew the importance of working with the Elemental energies and respecting the energies of Nature. In the Languedoc and parts of Southern Europe.

So, I came back and visited the Saint Michael Cathedral dedicated to ... and re-boosted the energy left. That is the location where I encountered the man with a backpack and lived sixteen months before visiting back the Alpes Maritimes. That was when I was forced to stay in confinement.

And so it was, that I focused on connecting with the powerful energy of the Divine Feminine that lives within the Heart energy of the Languedoc, and with awakening that energy to create inner balance between Spirit and Matter and between Heaven and Earth, with the Heart as the point of Focus and Balance. And then, a "grid" of Heart energy was created to link that energy into the Heart Grid of the Planet.

During the first confinement in Carcassonne was left in the building only one military man that said to be a fireman and me. I met him while walking in the parking lot. Thereafter he managed to walk with me each day. Philippe was always listening to me very carefully and never commented back or always managed to change the subject. That was how my protector and Earth Angel were until the day came for him to talk to me, and he said "Explain them, tell them, only when evil is forced into the light it can be defeated. Only when they can no longer operate in the shadow can people see the truth for themselves. Only when people see the truth for themselves will people understand the true nature of their deception. Deception is from the
devil."

One day later I saw a strange-looking couple that attracted my attention. They were going back and forth with loads of packages. Unloading it out the building to a big anonymous van.

I had a rapid glimpse at what was coming out of it, and I saw a US Five stars General uniform. And I knew history was being made. It had to be this way. God Win.

Is it fiction disclosing the real?
Is this real or is it fictitious?

Words From VIE

I fully realize that you have come with a mind more or less skeptical, that you may accept or reject this Odyssey, and the results accomplished. You have expressed a desire to know and learn maybe. Draw your own conclusion. I leave you to accept or reject, as you will. May you be blessed now by your own infinite Light. I love you all.

When an angel talks and teaches, he brings light and wisdom that is from God and is universal, it means it is for every human being. When a human teaches, he brings a knowledge that only serves the mortals on earth and has no interest for all the creatures on earth.

The knowledge that is given in schools and universities is only to form humans to serve the mondiale economy to grow and prosper on earth, and to bring humanity towards a technological future.

In today's world, nobody sees the omnipresent of God and this is the source of all miseries. His love is the key.

When you see God in all animals, forests, in the running river, in flowers and all creatures on earth then you become respectful.

If animals are exploited, if the earth is polluted, if GMO exists, if the industry and the modern technology destroy the planet, if the pharmaceutical industries poison your body instead of curing you like they pretend, it is because humans have lost the vision of God omnipresent in nature.

In the actual state humanity is not acceptable. War is unacceptable, nor violence, neither destruction, nor the non-respect of nature.

People will survive this scourge of mass media lies and manipulation to virus contamination. the lack of testing in the US, NDAs, and quarantines. The ones that will pass away are the ones that finished their time and had chosen to before coming.

The solar event is the ascension. The ascension is the golden age. It is a dimensional shift. And it's a spiritual kind of context in front of judges. They will determine how loving you are, how forgiving you are, and how open to others you are. It will determine if you look at life in a way to create happiness and abundance and prosperity, or if you look at other people as an opportunity for you to manipulate and control, lie, deceive and to betray.

There is a minimum grade that must be met. You have to have a slightly more than 50% interest in helping people and loving them rather than controlling them and manipulating them. Then if you make it, you will now have levitation, telekinesis, read other people's minds, you are aware of your past lives. All these things include a light body. It is a very different life and yet you are still looking human.

For with thee is the fountain of life: in thy light shall we see light. Psalm 36.9.

You will return to being a high evolved civilization which you were during the existence of Atlantis and Lemuria.

You will experience peace, love, freedom, and equality for all sentient life on Gaia.

The days of the cabal's reign and their abuse of power over humanity are numbered. This is the victory of light.

I am a Lightworker Messenger whose goal is to provide a Wake-Up service. The God Duo is here for the consciousness of evolution.

For now, and always, I AM VIE in Pure Love Essence.

Words from CHADD

This is a message from Jesus Christ
(Love keeps flowing forever)
Shine as yourself as a torch of love.

My dear pupils,

It is not about getting ahead. It is not about erroneous forms of self-protection. It is truly about sharing the heart, of coming to realize that with family and friends and people, knowing that life will be shared. I taught this when we travelled, and I would share loaves and fishes. I did not say to people: "Oh, there is only enough bread for those of you who are my inner circle, those of you who have been working with me closely." No!

It was as important that the person that showed up as skeptical and critical on the fringes of the crowd... it was just as important – and sometimes even more important – that they be given the fish and the bread and the water so that they would know that they were included and cared about, and that it was never about 'us and them'. And that is what has happened to this planet. It has become an 'us and them' so that everybody feels that they are, in one way or another, in a constant struggle for survival.

It has never been about struggle. The Mother created this Earth as a playground of plenty! But rather than being grateful and allowing Gaia to catch her breath – that's what the seasons are about – and rather than allowing the ebb and flow of energy, there has just been this constant demand on Gaia: "produce, produce, produce – and if you don't, I will sully you, I will pollute you, I will kill you." How do you kill the mother that quite literally feeds you? So, is this entire situation with the Coronavirus a re-set, a re-examination, to move from the ego – yes, to the root (chakra), and back to the heart? Yes, it is. It is a golden, silver, rainbow opportunity!

Now I'm talking to the embodied angels of light who are spread over different areas of the world: let your existence shine with love and spread out in your physical world the teachings on love and the willingness to love that you've been growing inside of you. It's time to do it.
Not only through talking about love, but also through living with love, totally and bright-fully will love to be spread around the world and will planet Earth be allowed to finally become a planet of love.

In order to envelope the whole planet Earth with love, each and every one of you has to come to be a source of love.

Don't let this person stand alone in being the only source of love, the only source of light: each one of you has to shine as a source of light, as the existence of love itself.

You've come to know many teachings about love by now. Send all of them to the people in your life, constantly, through direct action, having no fear, courageously. This is what is asked right at this moment.

During this age, my students were born in many different parts of the world. Each one of them is receiving messages from Heaven to cultivate their own particular kind of love and express the essence of God to move forward through their mission.

So, when this love-bringing light is sent out to different parts of planet Earth, when hands are holding each other, the time will come, and planet Earth will be enveloped and filled with the light of love all at once.

Do not doubt, trust.
Jesus Christ

"Draw your own conclusion, as we thank you and we offer you, our blessings."

(A "Contemplative Prayer" begins with a "Centering Prayer", a meditative practice where the practitioner focuses on a word and chooses a sacred word that best supports a sincere intention to be in the Lord's presence and open to his action with you: Father GOD, Jesus, Holy Spirit, and repeat that word over and over very slowly for the duration of the exercise. The purpose is to clear one's mind of the outside. Then you enter the Contemplative Prayer.)

About the Author

VIE Loriot de Rouvray is a Visionary Healer and Master Conveyor of Transformative Energy, Writer, Bio-Musician of Bio Institute of Light and Sound Therapy, and has been recognized by Elite Women Worldwide, for dedication, achievement, and leadership in her professional endeavors. She is an Honored member of the National Association of Professional Women, Honored member of the Continental Who's Who, Honored member of the Worldwide Who's Who and Recognized Honored Life Strathmore's Member, have won the Hall of Fame best alternative holistic medicine of Orlando for several and consecutive years. VIE is a member of Healing International.

VIE de Rouvray was born of the French aristocracy on an island called New Caledonia, which is located between Australia and New Zealand. While in Costa Rica, VIE de Rouvray experienced a dramatic shift in consciousness which resulted in a complete lifestyle change. Her purpose, which involves communication in the healing arts was revealed, and gifts from previous interplanetary incarnations were activated. A visionary and an Aquarius, Ms. de Rouvray heals people metaphysically. She has also been guided to write and create bio-music with the language of the Light that she speaks.

VIE de Rouvray authored a series of books.

"9.1.1. Complete Guide to Natural Healing" The book's purpose is to help achieve perfect health by utilizing holistic therapies, natural methods, and various other remedies. She discusses how other medications don't cure the body but unbalance your body even more about vaccinations that contain mercury and are harmful to the body, and much more concerning your health that is hidden from most of the public.

VIE de Rouvray also authored the first volume of: "Destiny of the Dog" a theory thriller about the journey of a tainted angel and about how the culmination of historical events will interact with the prophecies of the future days. The book features the ancient city of Antioch, fallen angels, ancient legends, and secret religious sects created in the days of Jesus. The book illustrates a modern adventure through which Christianity is introduced to the world.

VIE de Rouvray is titled. "Time is Ticking; the Fifth Amendment" The second volume of this work explains the world today; it illustrates a fascinating and historical adventure that includes the return of Jesus and Marie Madeleine, who demonstrate the path of Divine love.

VIE de Rouvray wrote her third volume "Window Through the Window of Time; The Spiritual Journey of 2 Angels" It's about 2 Angels at work. One is a physical Light & vibration healer guided to be reconnected to her original essence that is now here in a different life to see the transformation from the age of Pisces to the age of Aquarius. And the second Angel is a baker acted drugged ward of state that holds the key to Divine wisdom. It's the Armageddon and the last battle between good and evil, the final war between human governments and God. Followed by "New Century, New Era, New experiences" and "Intonex".

VIE de Rouvray truly began her healing mission when she was reunited with her colleague, who was in a wheelchair and wanted help. He was on psychotropic prescription drugs, hungry, anemic, blind, and in a constant foggy state of mind. VIE stopped seeing clients for four months so that she could focus all her time on him. He didn't have money and couldn't even drink or eat on his own. She nourished him, took care of him, and helped him detox from his medications, in spite of the fact that she could only communicate with him during a few moments of clarity throughout each day. Although caring for him was controversial to people who did not approve, Ms. de Rouvray never gave up. This was the first step of her mission.

VIE Loriot de Rouvray speaks the language of the Light which is the galactic language of Love and Light. She tones, chants, and hand-signs the language of the Light that is instant communication with the infinite mind using pictographic cybernetics. It is the parent of the language of the Deity used in the plan to design to outline a procedure, to code knowledge into Crystal, etc. to reach many planetary worlds and realities simultaneously and fuse the different languages into the same scenario abstract. The Universal Language is Light-coded information to reawaken the DNA and the dormant aspect of your Divine blueprint. It carries encodement for frequency healing, activating DNA. It is used for healing any issue, for toning, meditating, and aligning. Light language in short is a carrier of codes and vibrational frequencies of the 5th dimension, vibrating high enough to be able to channel Light language.

She believes that spiritual growth, vitality, and wellness are the link to human primary purpose. In her eyes, life is a game, an adventure that must be experienced, examined, and understood in order to restore balance in body, mind, and spirit. Ms. de Rouvray believes the result of infinite growth is to realize Oneness, and thus the meaning of life is growth in consciousness through mental, physical, and mind experiences, like pain, stress, anger, fear, illnesses, and diseases.

She says that her purpose and intention as a Visionary Intuitive Healer, Spiritual and metaphysical teacher, and an Aquarius. She helps teach the body to heal at a deep cellular level, and it is designed to assist people to open their own self-healing ability and personal empowerment. She uses Sacred Geometry because Sacred Geometry transmits energy and awareness for soul awakening. Many frequencies of energy are very different in their qualities and purposes.

She created and owned the Institute of Bio Stimulation of Light and Sound Therapy.

She created a new therapy and it's called Bio-Qi™ (*Qi pronounce Chi*).

E-mail: instituteofbiostimulation@yahoo.com
Websites: https://instituteoflightansound.com and www.naturalhealingorlando.com
https://www.facebook.com/VieLoriot/
Twitter: https://twitter.com/BioInstituteLS
Facebook: https://www.facebook.com/BioInstituteOfLightAndSound
Facebook: https://www.facebook.com/VieLoriot
Video: Journey to the Fifth Dimension, Orlando
https://www.youtube.com/@vieloriotderouvray3334
Young Living Distributor #398498

About the Book

The journey continues for the God Duo, after so many traumatic events and a lot of tribulations that they had to overcome and conquer. You are to embark on a galactic quest for the human purpose on this earth. This path reveals the higher truth of personal evolution that you are invited to find. Every journey begins with that first step. That first step is generally a small step because it is breaking inertia to begin moving in one direction. After that, it's the larger picture that we want you to look at. Instead of focusing so closely on the path and its trajectory of obstacles, look at the larger picture to see what's really happening with humanity.

VIE has been asked in a dream by the Galactic Council of Twelve to share the story of the genome of the Ancient Creators. The controllers tried to stop VIE but she got more and more visions and help. San Sara, one of the three Mary's from Saintes-Marie-de-la-Mer (France) came to VIE to give her help and support while CHADD is kept under psychotropic drugs. Padre Pio found a way to contact her. The people of Earth are being offered a chance to join the rest of the universe in peace and participate in spiritual awakening with spiritually and advanced technology. Something that the controllers wouldn't like to see happening.

The controllers do not hesitate to keep humanity in slavery. They have very advanced military technologies that you are not even aware of. They are violent and dangerous. This technology damages DNA and disrupts cell metabolism. They kill to clone Humans and make a transfer of consciousness, they use directed energy, they are cannibalists, and pedophiles, split the souls, and exorcism has gotten darker. Extraterrestrials are back to help. Some Catholic and Apostolic Gallican Priests are doing the same exorcism that Jesus did, and Knights Templar is also back to help and spread the word of Jesus. A mix of friendly loving and compassionate ETs from the 4th dimensional beings came to help to survive on this timeline. Ancient prophecies are occurring all around the planet. The coronavirus is "a wakeup call" On average two disease outbreak events every week are identified by a surveillance team, and the context in which these events occur is far more complex than before. May it be a test for disease-control capabilities? The masks imposed are killing the neurons. The vaccines contain Nanoparticles (AI) programmed to change the DNA. A type of messenger RNA vaccine that has never been approved for humans.

When the solar cycle 25 prediction will arrive, you must be spiritually prepared and be able to find your way.